More Praise for

8

"Every word counts in Edgar-winner Hamilton's masterful ninth novel featuring ex-cop Alex McKnight. . . . A sensitive exploration of tragedy and redemption."
—*Publishers Weekly* (starred review)

"In the latest of the Alex McKnight series, Steve Hamilton again demonstrates why he is one of the better authors at giving a sense of depth to the stage where his characters reside."
—*San Diego Union-Tribune*

"Hamilton does an excellent job creating strong, believable characters that are frequently put in violent, deadly situations. Deftly structuring his novel, the author slowly increases the tension while providing useful background information and offering societal insights into life on the reservation." —*Lansing State Journal*

"Steve Hamilton keeps getting better and better, and in this latest Alex McKnight novel, he seems to have hit a fast-paced groove. This book is so spare and so elegantly assembled, it seems effortless. . . . This book has enough twists, emotional and otherwise, for me not to want to give away too much other than to say this is a powerful, and powerfully told, story by a writer who is at the peak of his narrative powers." —*AnnArbor.com*

"*Die a Stranger* is marvelously atmospheric with characters and locales so realistic, they jump off the pages. Alex is a flawed but totally captivating man whose principles are put to the test time and again. A great series!" —*Fresh Fiction*

"A master wordsmith . . . His prose is not flowery, but is loaded with a quiet descriptive power that is easy to take for granted, so effortlessly does narrative slip across printed page. Hamilton makes it look easy, but I doubt it is." —*Bookreporter.com*

"*Die a Stranger* is an excellent book in every way."

—*Reviewing the Evidence*

"Hamilton's plot is swift and dialogue driven, his observations skillfully linking setting and character."

—*Milwaukee Journal Sentinel*

"McKnight is tough as nails and inordinately lovable, with an unerring, offbeat moral compass and a dark, ironic funnybone."

—*Chronogram*

"Hamilton keeps us on edge to the very end. His writing is sharp, his characters have dimension, and his settings are richly authentic. *Die a Stranger* is, quite simply, a terrific yarn."

—*Open Letters Monthly*

Praise for Steve Hamilton

"I really like his main character, Alex McKnight, and I'm ready to revisit Paradise, Michigan." —James Patterson

"This is crime writing at its very best." —George Pelecanos

"Hamilton's compelling, vigorous prose doesn't allow the option of taking a break." —*Los Angeles Times*

"Steve Hamilton writes the kind of stories that manly men and tough-minded women can't resist." —*The New York Times*

"Hamilton . . . paints a rich and vivid portrait of a world where the chill in the air is often matched by that of the soul."

—*Providence Journal*

"Hamilton gives us mysteries within mysteries as well as a hero who simply won't be beaten down." —*The Miami Herald*

Also by Steve Hamilton

DIE A STRANGER

STEVE HAMILTON

MINOTAUR BOOKS

A Thomas Dunne Book
NEW YORK

A THOMAS DUNNE BOOK FOR MINOTAUR BOOKS.
An imprint of St. Martin's Publishing Group.

DIE A STRANGER. Copyright © 2012 by Steve Hamilton. All rights reserved. Printed in the United States of America. For information, address St. Martin's Press, 175 Fifth Avenue, New York, N.Y. 10010.

www.thomasdunnebooks.com
www.minotaurbooks.com

The Library of Congress has cataloged the hardcover edition as follows:

Hamilton, Steve.
    Die a stranger : an Alex McKnight novel / Steve Hamilton.
        p. cm.
    ISBN 978-0-312-64021-7 (hardcover)
    ISBN 978-1-250-01319-4 (e-book)
    1. McKnight, Alex (Fictitious character)—Fiction.   2. Private investigators—Michigan—Upper Peninsula—Fiction.   3. Missing persons—Fiction.
4. Upper Peninsula (Mich.)—Fiction.   I. Title.
    PS3558.A44363D54 2012
    813'.54—dc23

                                                                    2012010695

ISBN 978-1-250-00010-1 (trade paperback)

Minotaur books may be purchased for educational, business, or promotional use. For information on bulk purchases, please contact Macmillan Corporate and Premium Sales Department at 1-800-221-7945 extension 5442 or write specialmarkets@macmillan.com.

D   10 9   8   7   6

To Dave

ACKNOWLEDGMENTS

Thanks as always to the "usual suspects," new and old—Bill Keller and Frank Hayes, Peter Joseph and everyone at Minotaur Books, Bill Massey and everyone at Orion, Jane Chelius, Euan Thorneycroft, Maggie Griffin, Mary Alice Kier and Anna Cottle, MWA, Bob Randisi and PWA, Bob Kozak and everyone at IBM, Nick Childs, David White, Elizabeth Cosin, Jeff Allen, Rob Brenner, Jan Long, Phil and Dennise Hoffman, Taylor and Liz Brugman, Larry Queipo, former chief of police, Town of Kingston, New York, and Dr. Glenn Hamilton from the Department of Emergency Medicine, Wright State University.

Also, to the memory of Ruth Cavin.

And as always, to Julia, my best friend more than ever; to Nicholas, who has the biggest heart of anyone I know; and to Antonia, who amazes me every single day.

CHAPTER ONE

On a clear, warm night in June, a small airplane is flying low over Lake Huron. It's a Cessna, a single-engine four-seater. The pilot is flying alone. The back of the plane is filled with the cargo, all wrapped up tight in plastic bags.

The plane's transponder is turned off. The pilot is flying by sight only. At such a low altitude he is undetectable by radar. As he approaches the airstrip in Sandusky, Michigan, he can barely make out the dark runway. It's a tiny airport, after all, and it's been closed for hours. But he does the one simple thing that all pilots know how to do. He keys the microphone five times in a row on the ARCAL frequency. That sends the automatic signal to the beacon on the ground, which then turns on the approach lights, the runway edge lights, and the taxiways. These lights will remain on for exactly fifteen minutes. More than enough time to land and then to take off again. It's one part of a simple, perfect plan.

A truck is waiting next to the runway, with its lights off. The two men in the truck will transfer the bags to the back of the truck.

Working quickly, they can do this in under three minutes. This is also part of the plan. Just as simple and just as perfect.

Except that the two men in the truck are not the two men the pilot is expecting. That's where the simple, perfect plan begins to break down.

You can only imagine the pilot's surprise when he lands and finds two strangers waiting for him.

The two men who were originally waiting with the truck, they'll be found handcuffed to the fence at the end of the runway. When the two newcomers have emptied the plane of its cargo, the pilot will be allowed to leave, with a very simple and very clear message he'll carry back to Canada, to the people who sent him across the border in the first place.

The deliveries will not stop. Two men handcuffed to a fence, with guns pressed against their heads . . . Everything that happened on this night will be merely an inconvenience. It will not interrupt the transport of high-grade marijuana into the United States from Canada. Not when there's so much money to be made.

That's how this business works, no matter what the product, no matter which border. New business arrangements are made. New partners replace the old partners, if they're muscled out of the deal. But the planes keep flying.

It may have been a warm night at that little airport in Sandusky, Michigan. But I was three hundred miles away, due north, sitting in front of the fireplace in Paradise, Michigan, where it was a good twenty degrees cooler. We don't rush into summer up here. Of course, I had no knowledge of anything happening on that airport's runway. Or any airport's runway, for that matter. I found out about it two days later, the same way most other people did. I read the story in the newspaper.

I still pick up the *Detroit News* most days, even though it's a world away and it feels to me like a million years ago when I actually lived and worked in the Motor City. But old habits die hard and I need my daily news fix. What the current mayor was up to, how the Tigers were doing and whether they had a chance to go all the way again. Like 1968. Like 1984. The story about the hijacking on the runway caught my eye and I read the whole story, complete with local reaction, how futile it would be to try to stop these small airplanes from landing late at night. How you can't turn off the automatic runway lights because God forbid an airplane would need to land in a legitimate emergency. How you can't station somebody at every tiny backwoods airstrip twenty-four hours a day. How long and porous the border was between the States and Canada, and how this kind of smuggling has been going on in one form or another, dating all the way back to Prohibition.

That part was easy to understand. When you had a boat full of liquor coming across the lake, you took your chances that hijackers might be waiting for you. Now it was indoor-grown hydroponic marijuana, at which apparently the Canadians are just as handy as they were for producing those bottles of Old Cabin Whiskey back in the day. Now it was an airplane instead of a wooden motorboat. But the basic idea was the same.

It was the kind of story that made me think back to my own days as a police officer, how it sometimes felt like I was the little Dutch boy trying to plug the hole in the dike. That's really as much as I thought about it. It was an interesting story, but I forgot about it five minutes after I folded up the paper and had my second cold Molson. How it could have any effect on me or on anybody I knew, that was something I wouldn't have been able to imagine, even if I had known enough to try.

I had no idea that this incident on a lonely runway three hundred miles away would mark the beginning of that strange roller coaster of a summer for me. But looking back on it now, that was Event Number One.

Event Number Two? That was an Ojibwa funeral.

CHAPTER TWO

A funeral shouldn't take place on a perfect day. I've had a strong feeling about that for most of my life. No, funerals should happen only when it's raining. Or when it's freezing cold. Or preferably both. It should hurt to be there, is what I mean. It should hurt right down to your bones when you're standing there on the edge of a grave site, as you're looking down at the box being lowered into the ground. You should have to hold your coat tight around your neck as you stand there taking the physical punishment for still being alive, for still being able to feel anything at all. While the man says ashes to ashes, dust to dust, the wooden top of the box should be splattered with rain and mud. Instead of tears drying fast on a perfect sunny day.

I haven't attended any more than most men, but there are two in particular I'll never forget, and both of them were on days that were heartbreaking enough without having to be so horribly, wrongly beautiful.

Especially up here in the UP. I mean, for God's sake. You get maybe a dozen picture-perfect days in a year. Maybe twenty if you're lucky, or if you happen to have an extra-loose definition of picture-perfect. Either way, a day like this is too rare a thing up here to spend crowded under a big white wedding tent that's been drafted for the occasion. You shouldn't have to sit there holding a plastic cup of nonalcoholic fruit punch, hot and miserable in your only suit, looking out across the parking lot to where the boats are tied up on the water and feeling like the rope to your own personal anchor has just been cut forever.

Of course, this time it's not my anchor I'm talking about. Not today. It wasn't my friends and family gathered under that tent. No, I was there, according to the little booklet they gave me, to "celebrate the long and happy life" of one Hazel Nika LeBlanc, a woman who had been pretty much royalty around here. Hence the huge turnout. She was a direct descendant of the family most responsible for the existence of this place I was standing on. The Bay Mills Indian Community. She had been the living heart and soul of this place, and her influence went well beyond it. As a counselor and adviser. As an oral historian and a resource to Indian colleges all over North America. The kind of person who could spend one hour on the phone and end up with a hundred different people working on that day's big problem. None of which you'd even suspect just looking at her. So quiet and soft and round and with those big glasses. You wouldn't find out how much power she could generate unless you happened to be on the other end of it. A place you did not want to find yourself, believe me, if she wasn't happy with you.

She had been like a mother to the whole reservation, that much was certain. But she was the literal birth mother to four children. Three of them were still alive to mourn her this day. One of them was Vinnie Red Sky LeBlanc.

Vinnie was my neighbor, the only other person to share the old logging road that wound through the woods to my cabins. He was my friend, maybe my best friend, even though he was half a generation younger than me. Even though he'd disappear for days at a time, and I'd drive right past his place with absolutely no idea where he was. Even though there were gaps in his personal history that I could never fill in. Things he wouldn't talk about, ever.

Even though the friendship had once all but ended, and we'd gone weeks without speaking to each other. He was always there for me, if I really needed him. He'd saved my life more than once. So of course I was here for him today.

I had lost my own mother when I was just a kid, so that much I could relate to. That was the first of those perfect-day funerals. Me standing next to my father, trying to hold it together. I don't remember much else, but I do remember it being a pretty small affair. Twenty, thirty people? Hell, I don't know. But it wasn't like this. It wasn't the whole town showing up to say goodbye. Or to celebrate a long and happy life, whatever kind of face you want to put on it. It didn't feel anything remotely like a happy occasion when it was my turn to be the grieving son, and I was sure it didn't feel any better to Vinnie.

Of course, the whole thing had started days before. On the night Hazel Nika LeBlanc died, the neighbors gathered in her yard to build the fire. They watched over it and kept it burning every single minute between then and today's official service, which was held in the little Catholic church up the road. There wasn't enough room to hold everybody, so I didn't even try to get in the door. Extended family only, I guess. Although around here that could still mean a hundred people.

After that service, everything moved up to the graveyard on top of Mission Hill, all the cars nosing their way slowly up that steep road. With no guard rails, nothing to stop you from rolling over that steep drop-off. If it had been an icy winter day, they probably would have had to dig a few more grave sites.

Once we were all at the top, filling up that old burial ground, the priest and the medicine man held court together, the Ojibwa burial ceremony taking place now that the Catholic funeral Mass was over. The Catholic part, hell, they've been doing that around here for at least 150 years, and the Ojibwa part, with the four-day journey to the west, the tobacco offered to the spirits, some of the ceremony even done in the original Ojibwa language . . . I guess that part's been around a little bit longer, like say a few thousand years. But somehow it all worked together and we all stood up there in the sunlight, looking out over Spectacle Lake and Monocle Lake just below us, and beyond that, the endless horizon of Lake Superior.

When it was done, we all drove back down the hill, nobody in any kind of hurry. The crowd ended up down the street, at the golf course. That's where the big white wedding tent had been set up, and it was almost blinding in the sunlight. I stood there on the outer edges, trying to catch a glimpse of Vinnie whenever I could. He had two younger sisters, and each of them had a husband, a baby, and another kid just old enough to run around through people's legs but not old enough to understand what was going on. Someone would end up chasing them down and returning them to their parents. They'd stay put for about five minutes and then take off again. There were cousins, too. I can't even guess how many. I knew Buck to say hello to, a few others to nod to and give them a quick smile.

I looked around the place for Vinnie and finally saw him standing across the street, on the edge of the casino's parking lot where it runs close to the shoreline. He was standing there looking out at Waishkey Bay. There were maybe a dozen boats tied up, but the parking lot was almost full. No matter how beautiful it was outside, or how heartbreaking this occasion, how many different good reasons you could come up with for not spending your summer afternoon inside a casino, still there were plenty of people filing in with a burning need to lose their money.

It was a big building, of course. There was something like fifteen thousand square feet of gambling space and a conference center and two restaurants and a hotel with 150 rooms. Vinnie worked here dealing blackjack so I knew what this place meant to him. He led downstaters on hunting trips in the fall, but that was nothing like a full-time job with benefits.

As I crossed the street, I heard some people laughing as they walked through the front door, ready to hit those slot machines.

There were two fountains set in the bay behind the casino. They were both spraying water high into the air, and as I stepped next to Vinnie the white noise drowned out every other sound around us.

"How you holding up?" I said.

He took one quick glance at me and turned back to the water. Dark hair hanging free down his back. Wearing that suit I had seen only once before. At the last funeral, a few days after we brought his brother's dead body back home from Canada. That day had the common decency to be cold and miserable. That's the one thing you can say about that day.

"Place is packed," I said. "Your mother meant a great deal to pretty much everybody."

Vinnie nodded.

"It's a lot to deal with all at once," I said. "I can see why you needed a little break."

He nodded again.

"Just wanted to check on you. I can leave you alone now."

"No," he said, finally speaking. "Stay here for a bit."

I stood with him for a while, looking out at the water. Then I opened up my little booklet and took one more read through it. I felt like I should say something, but I couldn't think of one word.

"Why do we do it?" he finally said to me.

"Why do we do what?"

"Why do we go through life every day without even noticing all the things we're missing?"

"I don't know," I said. "But you're right. We shouldn't take one single day for granted."

This is the kind of insight you have at a funeral, I thought. Two days later, you've already forgotten it—that promise you may have made to yourself, to wake up every day and realize what a gift you've been given.

But no, Vinnie seemed to have something else in mind. Something more specific. More troubling.

"All we have is time," he said. "That's all we're given. You ever think about that?"

"Sometimes. Not often enough."

He turned to face me. His eyes were red. "I'm serious, Alex. This isn't something you put on a greeting card. This is real. You're given a certain amount of time on this earth and absolutely nothing else."

I looked at him. I didn't try to agree with him. Clearly that wasn't what he wanted from me.

"You don't get any back when it's done," he said. "You don't get to do anything over. One shot through and then you're done."

"Vinnie, are you okay?"

"The last time, I saw her . . ." He stopped himself, swallowing hard and looking back out over the water. "She was almost gone. She could barely talk. We were all there, my sisters and me, just standing over her, you know. She looked up at me. You know what she said?"

"What?"

"She said, 'I'm glad you came back. It's been so long. Look at your children. Look at how they turned out. I'm so proud of them. I'm so glad we made them together. No matter what else happened, it couldn't have been all bad.'"

He stopped again, took a deep breath.

"That's what she said, and she was looking right at me. Right in my eyes. She reached up and took my hand."

"You mean she thought . . ."

"That I was my father, yes."

"Well, okay," I said. "She was kinda out of it, right? I mean, with the drugs and everything."

"He's been gone a long time," Vinnie said. "But I guess you never forget, huh? What your old husband looks like?"

"No. I don't imagine."

"He must have looked just like me, right? If she took one look at me and thought I was him?"

There was an edge to his voice now. I didn't say anything back. I just waited for him to work this out, whatever it was that was bothering him.

"That's the thing," he said. "I don't even know if I look like him or not. I haven't seen him since I was like, what, six years old?"

"You've got pictures?"

He looked at me again. We were getting into one of those things he rarely talked about.

"If my mother had them, we didn't see them. She didn't exactly have his portrait over the fireplace."

"He's in prison, right?"

That was as much as I knew, the basic facts of the matter and not much else. I knew it had all happened before I moved up here. Before Vinnie left the reservation and bought the property down the road from my father's cabins.

"Yes," Vinnie said. "He got drunk and ran over four people. Three of them died."

I knew Vinnie had some pretty black-and-white views on drinking. I'm sure this event in his father's life, even if it had happened years after he left, on the other side of the country, was probably a big part of it. Bottom line, you do not want to get drunk in front of him and attempt to get into a motorized vehicle. Especially if you're a tribal member. He'll knock you flat on your back and throw your keys into the bay if he has to.

"He was already long gone by then," Vinnie said. "This all happened way out West somewhere. A thousand miles away from here. My mother didn't tell us about it. We had to hear it from one of my aunts."

These were new details for me. The things he left locked up inside, and probably never would have said at all if not for the sad heart he was carrying around on this one day of his life.

He picked up a rock from the lawn and threw it into the water.

"If he left when you were that young," I said, "that must have been hard on your mother. Raising all four of you on her own."

The more I thought about it, the more it seemed like the understatement of the year. If you do a little more math, you realize that this went all the way back to the years BC. Before Casinos. Before the King's Club opened up just down the street, the first

Indian-operated blackjack casino in the country. Before the much bigger Bay Mills Casino, in whose shadow we happened to be standing. Before the jobs and before all of that money to be shared by every member of the community.

There were shacks here, all up and down this road. Little two- and three-room shacks no bigger than my cabin, but filled with entire families. When the casinos came, they tore down the shacks and they even moved a few of them down by the prison, for families of inmates to sleep in when they came up visiting. You can see the shacks lined up there by the road when you drive to the airport, each a monument to the past.

Now it's all nice split-level ranch houses with vinyl siding and basketball hoops in the driveways. A typical middle-class development, or at least you'd think so if you happened to miss the sign as you drove by it. WELCOME TO THE BAY MILLS INDIAN COMMUNITY.

But going back to the old days, when it was one of those shacks and you were happy to have it, and a minimum-wage job that would last all year long if you were lucky. What a hard life that must have been for an Indian woman on her own, raising four young children.

"How'd she do it?" I said. "I can't imagine."

"You work," he said. "You take care of business. One day at a time. That's what she always said to me."

"Can't argue with that," I said.

"You always watch out for your family."

That's the tricky part, I thought. That's how Vinnie grew up, right here on this reservation, surrounded by his entire extended family, brother and sisters and parents and aunts and uncles and cousins. I've been in a house or two here on the rez, so I've seen small glimpses of how that must have been. Nobody in your family needs to knock on the door. They just come in, they make some coffee, they sit down, they talk, they argue, they fight, they kiss and make up. Every hour of every day, it's an earsplitting pandemonium of family all around you. And it's everybody. That's the thing. You live here on the rez, everybody is family.

To be surrounded twenty-four hours a day by so many people who care about you, who would gladly lay down their lives for you.

I'd last one week. Maybe two. Then I'd lose my mind. I'd have to get the hell out of there, go somewhere far away where I could be by myself for a while. To hear myself think again.

Vinnie had the same impulse, apparently, because that's exactly what he did. He worked and worked and saved his money, and as soon as he could swing it, he moved off the reservation. He bought the one free lot on my father's road and built his own cabin there. I can imagine him on the day he put the roof on, the way he must have sat down on his own chair in his own kitchen and breathed the longest sigh of relief in the history of mankind. Finally, some peace. Some silence.

His family never forgave him.

They still loved him, of course. But he carried a mark now. He was different in a way they couldn't understand. I had a feeling that even Vinnie himself couldn't explain it. Not really. It was just something he had to do.

Even now, with Vinnie standing here on the edge of the water, away from the crowd of family under the big tent, I could feel at least a dozen sets of eyes on our backs. There's Vinnie, the wayward son, who moved a full thirty miles down the road to live in his own little house like a hermit. Along with his good buddy Alex, who's obviously not a good influence. A strange white man who doesn't need any family, either. Who's always dragging Vinnie into one mess of trouble after another.

Yeah, even on a day like this, I could feel it. Fair or unfair. Although I suppose that part about dragging Vinnie into trouble was dead accurate.

"I'm sorry," he said. "This is my mother's day. I don't know why I'm thinking about my father. It's just that, when she thought I was him . . ."

"Give yourself a break," I said. "You're dealing with a lot today."

"Yeah, well, I probably need to go see some more people now." The edge was gone from his voice now, replaced by a vague unease. I knew his batteries would be completely drained by the end of this long, hot day. "But I'm glad you came. I appreciate it."

"I wouldn't miss it," I said. "I'm so sorry."

"There'll be a sweat tonight. You feel like coming?"

I'd done it before, more than once. You go to cousin Buck's backyard and you strip down to your underwear, no matter the weather. He's got the hot rocks piled up in the middle of the hut, with all the old rugs thrown over the top to keep the heat in. He pours the water onto the rocks and the steam rises and fills your lungs. He adds the sage, that old healing medicine, and you feel your whole body releasing like a fist that's been clenched for too long. I could have used it that day, but something told me to leave Vinnie to his family.

"You go ahead," I said. "I'll catch up to you later."

Of course, I knew "later" would probably be a while. An Ojibwa funeral starts a good four days before the burial, and then keeps going. I had a feeling this one would set a new Bay Mills record.

"I should go back," he said. But even as I walked away, I could see him still standing there by the water. Alone and apart, with his family and everyone else in plain view but not close enough to touch him.

It was going to be a long week for Vinnie LeBlanc. That much I knew. And this time I couldn't help him, not one bit.

As I walked back past the tent, I overheard a hundred conversations going on at once. Remembering "Nika." The last time somebody saw her or talked to her. Something she did one day for somebody else, long ago or just last week. A few yards farther and another conversation, about some inconvenience at the border, how long someone had to wait to cross the bridge. It all sort of caught up to me at once, how many unmistakably Canadian accents I'd been hearing all day without really noticing. But it made sense. Of course they'd come from Canada. There were just as many Ojibwa on the other side of that border, and the border was right *there*, out in the middle of that water, so close you could walk to the other side when it was frozen. I could see Ontario from where we were standing, those windmills turning in the far-off hills.

Of course they'd come, I thought. From miles and miles around.

Some of them Vinnie would know. Most of them would be strangers.

Before I got into my truck, I turned one more time and caught my last glimpse of him. He had finally gathered his nerve and was walking back to the tent.

I kept thinking about him as I drove home. Those thirty miles from the rez to Paradise, on that lonely beautiful road that follows the shoreline, all the way around Whitefish Bay. The weather stayed picture-perfect, like a consolation of pure sunlight on such a sad day. There wasn't a hint of trouble on the water.

But of course the trouble was there, just below the surface. That cold, cold water. Just ask the crew of the *Edmund Fitzgerald*, all of them still out there, not twenty miles from the safety of land.

No matter how beautiful the day, before you can do anything about it, without any warning at all.

The storm will come.

CHAPTER THREE

A few days passed, and I still hadn't seen Vinnie again. I figured he was spending time with his family. That seemed totally natural to me, so I didn't think twice about it. I drove up our road, past his empty cabin. No lights were on. His truck was gone. I kept on going all the way to the end, to the last cabin, to finish my work there. I had a few last pieces of trim to install, and then there was painting to be done on the walls of the kitchen and bathroom, where it wasn't just the rough wood of the logs. The whole place was finally coming back together again, and it felt strange not to have Vinnie there helping me with these last details. Every time I spilled a drop of paint on the floor I could almost hear him clucking at me. I'd half turn, forgetting for one moment that I was alone.

Summer's an odd time in the rental business. You get people visiting Tahquamenon Falls and maybe the Shipwreck Museum, but it's not the same people every year. Not like fall, when it's the same groups of hunters, as regular as clockwork, some of them going back so many years they can remember renting from my father. Winter is snowmobiles. Or "sledding," as most people call it up here. Spring has become, believe it or not, birding season. More and more birders coming up every year, to watch the raptors and the shorebirds make their migration north. The birds come across the great expanse of Lake Superior and stop to rest at Whitefish Point. Hawks, owls, harriers, merlins, ospreys. Best of all, eagles. Every single day in the spring, you can see eagles. The ultimate good-luck sign for the Ojibwa. Or so I'm told. In fact, I think it was Vinnie's mother who told me that.

She was gone now, and it felt strange, knowing that she wouldn't be there in that house on the rez, even if I saw her only a few times a year. I could only imagine how Vinnie was feeling. How he was dealing with it. Or what he was doing to find a way past it.

The wind coming off Lake Superior is usually the biggest air conditioner in North America, but on this one strange night the air stayed warm, and I had to drag out some fans and deliver them to the cabins. I stuck around to talk to two of the families for a while. It was dark when I finally headed down to the Glasgow. The sun doesn't even go down until after nine o'clock at this time of year, so it was late. Vinnie's truck was parked in front of his cabin, but I didn't see any lights on inside.

When I walked into the Glasgow, I saw Vinnie sitting in front of the fireplace. He didn't turn when I walked through the door. Jackie was behind the bar, looking a little more agitated than usual. With that weathered old Scottish face of his, that Rudolph's nose and whatever hair he still managed to put a comb through.

"He's in a state," Jackie said, nodding his head toward Vinnie. The slight brogue in his voice still, all these years later. "I'd be careful if I were you."

"What do you expect?" I said. "It's only been a few days."

"No, you don't understand."

I stood there waiting for him to enlighten me. But he didn't.

"Just go see," Jackie said. "Go sit with him a bit, eh?"

I wandered over and took the other seat by the fire. Vinnie still hadn't looked up. I watched him stare into the fire and that's when it finally occurred to me that there shouldn't be a fire going. It was the one and only genuinely warm night of the year, and it probably wouldn't even go below seventy all night long. Up here, that was the kind of heat wave that would have the natives passing out in the parking lot.

"Who needs a sweat lodge?" I said. "You can just sit right here."

He didn't respond. That's when I noticed the second thing that was out of place. This one was a lot more alarming than an unnecessary fire on a warm night, because cupped in Vinnie's hands was a glass filled with amber liquid. It didn't look like ginger ale and there was no ice in it. The glass was half empty.

That's when it hit me. He had left his truck at his cabin, and he had walked down here. A perfectly sensible thing to do if you plan on drinking, but for Vinnie it was the last thing I ever would have expected.

I sat there watching him watching the fire. I wasn't sure what to say. Jackie came over and he had a cold Molson. Force of habit, and on any other night it would have been the most welcome sight in the world. A cold bottle straight from Canada, not the watered-down stuff they bottle in the States and slap a Canadian label on. The real thing from the real home of beer, after a long unseasonably hot day.

I left it on the table. I sat there in silence while the condensation on the bottle made a wet ring.

"Vinnie," I finally said. "What's going on?"

He shook his head.

"What are you drinking?"

He looked down at the glass. "Scotch? Ask Jackie."

I looked over at the man in question. He threw his bar towel up in the air and rolled his eyes.

"Something tells me Jackie didn't force a drink on you," I said. "Come on, what the hell?"

"I asked for a real drink," Vinnie said, finally looking me in the eye. "I'm a grown-up. I'm in a bar. I wanted a drink and he gave me one. Then I paid him some money for it. Then I made a fire even though it's the warmest night in years, because I felt like having a fire. Are we good now?"

"Yeah, we're good. Since when do you drink scotch?"

"What's the problem?" he said. "It's been a hard week and I'm having a drink. You go through a case of Canadians like every night, right?"

"I don't think I drink a case of beer every night, no."

"A case a week then. Whatever. You're way ahead of me, that's all I know. So what's the problem?"

"I'm not the one with a lifelong hatred of alcohol." I could have reminded him of at least a dozen times when he'd left a room because of too much drinking going on. Too much liquor, too much noise, too much goddamned foolishness. I knew Vinnie couldn't stand it.

"Maybe I need to lighten up," he said. "Just let go of it once in a while."

Yeah, that'll be the day, I thought. Let's go to the Cozy and watch a few of your cousins doing shots after their shift at the casino. You so enjoy watching that scene.

He lifted the glass and drained it. When it was empty, I saw a quick grimace on his face, the look of a nondrinker who can't quite believe how bad liquor can taste. Then just as quickly the look was gone and he was on his feet.

"Set me up again," he said as he went to the bar. He didn't waver or stumble. Not yet. There'd be plenty of time for that later.

"Ah, one's enough," Jackie said, "wouldn't you say now?"

"No, I wouldn't say. I'll have another, please."

Jackie looked over at me for help. I didn't know what else to do except give him a shrug. Hell, Vinnie was a thirty-whatever-year-old man and he'd just lost his mother. Now he wanted to have another drink. He wasn't an alcoholic. He had no history with the stuff whatsoever, not that I knew of. What were we supposed to say?

Maybe this is exactly what you need, I thought. Press the Reset button on your life. Get out of your own head. You'll feel like death tomorrow morning, but for tonight, I mean, why the hell not?

He came back to his chair with another glass of scotch. There were ice cubes in it this time. Blasphemy for a true Scot, but I guess Jackie was doing whatever he could to help him keep it slow and easy.

Vinnie tilted the glass back and drained it.

"All right, come on," I said. "If you're gonna drink, do it right. You don't shotgun that stuff."

"I beg your pardon," he said. "I'll try to do better with the next one."

"Seriously, why don't you take a break for a minute, okay?"

He stood up, and this time I saw a little wobble in his step.

"Don't even ask me," Jackie said. "You don't even drink, Vinnie. You're just gonna make yourself sick."

"If I can't drink here," Vinnie said, "I'll go somewhere else."

"Look, I know I'm not your father, but—"

"No, you're not," Vinnie said, reaching into his back pocket. "Here's my father right here."

He threw a photograph onto the bar. Jackie picked it up. I got up from my chair and went around to look over his shoulder. The photograph was half folded from being in Vinnie's pocket, but the faces were unmistakable. One was a younger, thinner version of Vinnie's mother. The other was . . . Well, it was Vinnie. That's the only way to say it. At least at first glance, with the man himself standing right next to you while you looked at the picture, even with the washed-out color from the seventies, you'd have to believe that this was the same man, like somehow he had not aged at all since this photograph had been taken.

"My God," Jackie said. "You're the spitting image."

"Yeah, thanks," Vinnie said. "That's great to hear."

"This can't be a big surprise," I said. "I mean, you knew you looked like him, right?"

I thought back to the day of the funeral, standing next to Vinnie on the shore of Waishkey Bay, what he told me about his mother's last days, how she had looked up at him and in the haze of her painkillers had mistaken him for her long-lost husband. Now that I was seeing this picture, it was a lot easier to believe.

"I found this picture in my mother's house," Vinnie said. "When I was cleaning out some drawers. She didn't exactly have his portrait hanging over the mantel. Not after he ran out on us."

"I understand," I said, "but you must have seen pictures like this before."

"I did. Not for a long time, but yeah. Once in a while. I don't know, there's just something about this picture, though. This picture I've never seen before."

I looked back at the two faces. They were standing outside in the sunlight, the mother in a plain dress, the father in jeans and a white shirt. That dark hair tied up behind him, the way Vinnie does it. An automobile behind them, some big hunk of American metal from the seventies. They were blocking the grille, but I would have guessed a Chevy Impala. It didn't look new, but it was probably new to them and they were standing there on the reservation in front of the car and looking proud and happy. There was no hint on either person's face that he'd soon be gone and she'd be left to raise four kids on her own.

"He's a good-looking man," Jackie said. There was a soft tone in his voice, something we hardly ever heard. "They look like a nice couple here."

Vinnie took the photograph back and looked at it. He closed his eyes and let out a long breath. Then he put the photograph back in his pocket.

"I need that drink now, Jackie."

"I've got a better idea," I said. "Let's go up the road. I finished up the work on the cabin and you need to see it."

He stood there, not saying anything.

"I've got a bottle," I said. "We'll pick it up on the way. I'll show you the cabin and then we'll have another drink."

He thought it over for another moment. Then he nodded his head and followed me to the door.

"Good night, guys," Jackie said. "Vinnie, I hope you feel better."

Vinnie put up one hand without turning around. Then we were outside, in the warm night. He climbed into the passenger's seat of my truck and we were off.

"It was too hot today," he said, laying his head back against the seat. "This place is not supposed to get hot. Ever."

I nodded and drove. The town was empty. I turned and went down our road. We whipped through the trees and kicked up gravel. We passed his cabin, then mine. I saw lights on in my second cabin.

The third, fourth, and fifth were dark. As was the sixth, but I knew it was empty. I pulled up in front and turned off the ignition.

"Let's see this paint job," he said, getting out of the truck. But when he went inside he sat down at the table and seemed to forget all about checking out my painting or anything else about the place. He took the photograph from his back pocket and put it on the table. I sat down across from him and looked at the two smiling young faces again.

"You said you had a bottle."

"Sorry, I forgot. I should have stopped at my cabin."

"What are you doing, Alex? You guys don't have to treat me like a child."

"You're right," I said. "I apologize. We'll go get the bottle. Just tell me why this picture bothers you so much."

"Look at him."

"I know. I get it. You look like him. But he is your father. It's not so surprising."

"I'm the only one who really remembers him. My sisters were like, what, three and four years old. Tommy was only a baby. No, I was the only one who could go out and try to throw a ball to him, or . . ."

He stopped.

"What?" I said.

"I'm supposed to be thinking about my mother this week. She's the one who raised us. She did everything. Now she's gone and I can't stop thinking about my father, and all the things he *didn't* do."

"You're thinking about them both. It's natural."

"You should have heard her, lying there in that bed, the last time I saw her. Thinking I was him. Calling his name like she was so glad to see him, like he finally came back after all these years."

"You know the mind does some funny things at a time like that. Maybe, I don't know, maybe that wasn't even so bad. Maybe it was a good feeling for her to have."

"I wish it was me she was saying goodbye to," he said, looking down at his lap. "Not him."

"She was," I said. "Come on. You know she was saying goodbye to all of you."

"He doesn't deserve to be remembered."

This is getting a little heavy, I thought. I could actually use that drink myself right now. But at least he's talking. That has to be good.

"Tell me again," I said. "Just one more time. So maybe you can leave it right here in this room."

"He left. Just *gone*. Never saw him again."

"He's in prison?"

"Yes. Rotting away in a cell on the other side of the country. He might as well be dead. I kinda wish he was."

"Did you ever try to contact him? Try to find out why he left?"

He shrugged. "No. Why bother? Just like we didn't look at the old photographs. We just . . . we just moved on. What else were we gonna do? He obviously didn't want to be with us. That's all we needed to know."

He folded his hands and put them on the table.

"He'd already done a few short stints," he said, "even before the DWI and the vehicular manslaughter."

"For what else?"

"I don't know exactly. I think it was burglary, receiving stolen goods. A whole bunch of chickenshit crimes like that. Until they had to start locking him up. Like I said, my mother never talked about it, but other people on the rez would find some excuse to mention it to me. There's more gossip on the rez than any sorority, I swear."

"When did he go away for good?"

"It was right around the time I moved off the rez. I think I was just starting work on the cabin."

"So right before I moved up here. You were just about done with your roof then."

He picked up the photograph one more time. Then he closed his eyes and spun it across the room. It hit the wall and fluttered to the floor.

"Vinnie, what is it? Is there something you're not telling me?"

"Don't you see? I'm just like him."

"No, you're not. Just because you look like him—"

"I'm exactly like him, Alex. I'm a carbon copy."

"You didn't leave anybody."

"Yes, I did. Hello, what were we just talking about? I move off the rez and build my own place up here."

"That's not leaving. You're right down the road. You go back all the time."

"Yeah, I go back all the time. Then I leave again. Every time I go, that's how I feel. Like I'm doing a miniature version of my father's routine."

"Oh, come on, that's nonsense."

"Actually, I did him one better."

"How? What do you mean?"

"I'm just talking about my mother and my sisters and my little brother, right? What about *my* family? My wife, and my kids?"

I looked at him. Like what the hell.

"I don't have that, right?"

"Yeah, no kidding."

"Okay then. There you go. I live all by myself and I don't even have a girlfriend right now. I've totally avoided the whole family thing altogether."

"Vinnie . . ."

"My father would be proud. Just don't even have a family in the first place."

"You're not making any sense now."

"Yeah, well, your father didn't run out on you."

I leaned back in my chair. On most days I would have called him on the bullshit, but this wasn't most days. He was still one-quarter drunk and three-quarters grieving, so I figured I could give him a break.

"Okay, I've been a patient man," he said. "Where's that bottle?"

I drove him down to my cabin and produced a bottle of Jim Beam and two glasses. I was about to sit down at my kitchen table, but he grabbed the works and took it outside. When I caught up to him, he was back in the passenger seat of the truck.

"Where are we going?" I said as I got behind the wheel.

"I don't know. I just don't feel like being inside anymore."

"Fair enough."

I turned the key and backed out. When I got to the main road, he had me go north. Which could only mean one destination. We rode in silence, until he opened up his window and let the night air rush into the truck. He took the cap off the bottle and took one long pull, to hell with the glasses. Straight Jim Beam for a man who doesn't drink, that should've rung him good, but he didn't even make a face.

"Take it easy," I said, but he ignored me.

Twenty minutes later, the road ended. We were at Whitefish Point. The Shipwreck Museum was to our left, the old lighthouse rising high above us. To our right was the birding station. The whole point was deserted. One single light burned at the base of the lighthouse but otherwise there was nothing but darkness. He opened his door and got out, taking the bottle with him. The glasses he left behind him on the seat.

I followed him out onto the wooden walkway. He took the stairs down to the beach. The night was still warm. Freakishly warm, here at the edge of the world, the one night all year when it might be warm enough to do this without wearing a jacket. Before I could say another word, he ran down to the water. There were light waves. He went in to his waist, still holding the bottle. He looked up at the stars. Then he took another drink and fell backward into the water.

"For God's sake," I said to nobody.

By the time I got to the water's edge, he was already sitting up, the waves hitting him neck-high. He was doing all he could to keep the bottle dry.

"Vinnie, come back, okay? I'm serious."

"It feels so warm," he said. "I can't believe it."

I was about to take off my work boots, but then he went down again. I didn't see him come up this time, so I went in after him. I just about tripped over him, grabbing him by the back of the neck and pulling his head above the water.

He was right, though. You wouldn't mistake it for bathwater, but it wasn't even close to being deadly cold. For this lake, that's saying something.

"Don't worry," he said, holding up the bottle. Somehow he had replaced the cap.

"Can we get out of here, please? Before one of us drowns?"

"We used to come up here. My whole family. In fact, I think I even remember my father coming up here. Like one time."

"Okay. Good. Can we remember on dry land?"

He shook me away and stayed where he was, sitting there on the rocks and sand and letting the waves hit his chest and spray his face. He uncapped the bottle and took another drink. I took the bottle from him and drank from it. He took it back. That's how we spent the next few minutes, draining the bottle and watching the waves come at us, one after the other.

"Okay," I said when the bottle was empty, "it's time to get out of the lake."

"I want to go see her."

"See who?"

"My mother. I can't go back home without seeing her. Just one more time."

He started to cry, each wave washing the tears from his cheeks. I let him sit there for a while, then I reached down and picked him up by the armpits. I felt the strain in my back and we were both soaking wet now, but it was the warmest night of the year and we had one more place to go.

We walked up the beach to the wooden walkway, then back out to the parking lot. To my truck, and then we were both sitting in the cab, getting the seats wet. I turned the truck around and headed south. Back toward Paradise.

When we hit town, I saw the lights still on inside the Glasgow Inn. We passed by, going through the blinking yellow light at the center of town. Down to Lakeshore Drive and around the rim of Whitefish Bay. Past the abandoned railroad car that sat at the fork of the road, like an eternal marker for something long forgotten.

We drove through the reservation, the quiet houses and the cars and trucks all parked outside. Everything supported by the casinos. Every last thing.

I took the right turn and started climbing Mission Hill. This thin road hugging the side of the hill, with no guard rails and nothing but trees to stop us if we went over. It had been such a busy place just a few days ago, all of the mourners gathered up here. The whole reservation and people from all over North America, all here to celebrate the life of this one remarkable woman. Now the road was dark and empty and as we came to the top we were the only living souls.

I parked the truck and turned the lights off. Vinnie got out, and I left him alone to walk through the graveyard, to find the stone next to the freshly turned earth. I went over to the edge and looked down at the two lakes—Monocle Lake, a single flat oval, and Spectacle Lake, looking more like a pair of lenses. Beyond them both, the part of Lake Superior that narrowed from Whitefish Bay into the St. Marys River. The night was clear enough for me to see all the way across to Canada. I saw a dozen of the great wind turbines, each one with a blinking red light to warn away any aircraft.

When Vinnie was done with his visit, he came up behind me and stood looking out over the edge. His hair was still wet and plastered to the side of his face.

"My sisters want me to move back here," he said. "To the rez. They want me to take my mother's house."

"Are you going to?"

"I was just talking to my mother about it." He nodded back toward the graveyard. "I told her I couldn't. I told her I needed to stay in my cabin."

"You built that place," I said. "With your own hands."

"Yes," he said, pushing my shoulder. "Exactly. Right?"

He started to lose his balance then. I caught him and held him up straight until his head cleared.

"You do realize," I said, "that tomorrow morning's gonna be a little rough."

"My first day back at work, too."

"Ouch. Take the day off, eh?"

He shook his head. "No, I've been away long enough. I'll get through it."

I took him home then. He went to his cabin and I went to mine. I dried off and went to sleep and he tried to do the same.

A few brief hours of rest before Vinnie Red Sky LeBlanc began the longest day of his life.

CHAPTER FOUR

When I got up the next morning and went down to the Glasgow for breakfast, I didn't see Vinnie's truck parked outside his cabin. That was a surprise. I figured he'd be down for at least ten or twelve hours. You're a younger man than I am, I said to him in my mind as I passed by, but you're not *that* much younger. I know you wouldn't lose your job at the casino if you slept in one morning, so you must have some kind of attendance streak going. Either that or you're completely insane.

Jackie gave me two seconds after I walked in the door. Then he was all over me. "So what the hell happened last night?"

"What do you think happened? We drank a bottle of Jim Beam and talked about life."

"An entire bottle?"

"Half a bottle, two-thirds, I don't know. He's the one who drank most of it. Did he stop in on his way to work?"

"He's actually working today?"

"Yes," I said. "It's his first day back. His truck is gone, so I just assumed . . ."

"And you had to go get him wrecked the night before. What's the matter with you?"

"I didn't get him wrecked, Jackie. He got himself wrecked. I just made sure I was the one driving."

"Driving where? I thought you guys went back to your cabin."

"We went up to Whitefish Point. You wouldn't believe how warm the water was."

"I can't believe what I'm hearing," he said, slapping down his bar towel. "You guys got drunk and went swimming? What are you, a couple of high-school kids?"

"I told you, I wasn't drunk. And he's the one who jumped in the water. I was just the lifeguard."

"Madness," he said. "Absolute madness. You should have your head examined."

"Are you sure he didn't stop in? Just for a quick bite or something?"

"I think I would have noticed him. Are you sure you even brought him back last night? He didn't drown in the lake?"

"No, he did not drown in the lake. Now can you make me an omelet, please?"

"Unbelievable." He picked up his towel just so he could throw it back down on the bar. "You're a piece of work, you are."

"He'll be fine," I said. "Although I'm sure he'll be having a tough day. You better have a good hangover cure ready for him. You got some Bloody Mary mix?"

"You really are trying to kill him, aren't you. . . . You don't give a man with a hangover a Bloody Mary. You give him gin with lemon and a little Tabasco sauce."

"And you're calling *me* crazy? That's the worst thing I've ever heard."

"I'll take care of him," he said. "In fact, I don't even want you in the building when he gets here. I think you've done quite enough damage to the poor man."

We went on like that for another few minutes. My tried-and-true hangover cure versus his horrible mixture of death. I mean, anything that *starts* with gin. Just forget it. Then more about what a supposedly irresponsible friend I was in the first place.

I finally did get my omelet. I always do. But some mornings, I really have to earn it.

I had some renters leaving that morning, and with new renters coming in the next day, I wanted to make sure I had fresh supplies in the kitchens. That meant a drive to Sault Ste. Marie. "The Soo," as the locals call it. It's a good fifty miles away, but that's nothing up here. People drive a hell of a lot farther just to get to a real grocery store.

I have this bad habit of driving insanely fast when I'm on the open road. It's hard not to do when you see maybe one car every ten minutes. On top of that, every law enforcement official up here knows me by now. At least every Chippewa County deputy and every Michigan State Trooper who happens to be stationed up here. They know that I was a Detroit police officer for eight years. They know I took three bullets on the job, and that I still carry one in my chest, just behind my heart. It's not like I told every cop personally, but word gets around. This guy got shot on the job, he's still even got one slug in his chest, right next to his heart, and now he happens to drive a little bit over the speed limit once in a while. So if they happen to see a certain old F-150 truck coming down the road, they make a point of leaving me alone.

Reason enough right there never to buy a new vehicle. But lately I'd been trying to tone it down a little bit. Like maybe speed limit plus twenty, no matter where I was driving.

I thought about stopping in at the casino, just to see how Vinnie looked. But then I figured no, if the roles were reversed I wouldn't want him coming into the place just to see what shade of green I was. So I kept driving down that straight empty road. That's right about when the first county car came screaming toward me, going the opposite way. Lights flashing, siren on, the full treatment. About a minute later, a state car came down the same way, again with the lights and the siren. I was thinking an accident. More than one car if both the state and county were responding. I kept going.

When I hit the Soo I drove up the business spur to the hardware store. I bought a few more fans to put in the cabin bedrooms, even though I knew I'd wonder why I bothered the minute the weather went back to normal. Then to the grocery store for bottles of water. When I was on my way back to Paradise, another state car came ripping by me. Yet another cop going due west as fast as he could. I don't know if I was starting to feel slightly anxious yet. It's hard to pinpoint the exact moment when it all started to turn, but this time I definitely thought it would be a good idea to stop in at the casino, just lay eyes on Vinnie one time.

So I cut north along the lakeshore and went through Brimley to the reservation, past that one little sign that lets you know you're on sovereign land. I pulled in to the Bay Mills Casino lot. As always, there were plenty of cars there. I got out and walked inside, hearing the hollow sound of the slot machines as I made my way through the lobby to the casino itself, that huge stuffed moose looking out over my head as I passed beneath it.

I went back to the blackjack area and took a quick look around. I didn't see Vinnie anywhere, but I knew the dealers rotated frequently. I poked around for a minute or two, checking out the restaurant at the back of the place, where Vinnie usually took his breaks. Still no sign of him.

Eventually, I went to one of the tables and waited for the dealer there to take a shuffle break.

"Hey, is Vinnie around?"

The dealer was a woman. She looked too young to even be allowed in this place, let alone to deal cards. "Vinnie LeBlanc? No, he's out for a while. On bereavement leave."

"Today's his first day back," I said. "I just wanted to say hi to him."

"I haven't seen him. I didn't even know he was working."

When the pit boss came over to break it up, I motioned him aside.

"I'm just looking for Vinnie," I said. "I know he's working today."

The pit boss shook his head. "Nope, haven't seen him. I thought he was due back today, too, but I know he's had a tough week. Don't worry, we can manage without him."

"You really haven't seen him today at all?"

"No, sir."

I thanked the man and left. When I was in the parking lot, I took my cell phone from the truck and turned it on. I had just enough juice left to try Vinnie's number. He uses his cell phone about as often I do, but I figured it was worth a shot. It rang through and went to voice mail. I told him to call me if he got the message, but as I threw the phone back into the truck I knew that would work about as well as sending up a smoke signal.

As I worked my way back through the reservation, I kept an eye out for Vinnie's truck. He could be here, I thought, doing more family stuff. That was entirely reasonable. But I didn't see his truck anywhere.

I stopped in at both sisters' houses. They were right up the street from each other, first Mary and then Regina. Their kids were running around between the front yards, trying to throw water balloons at each other. None of the kids had any kind of arm strength yet, not to mention accuracy, so only my shoes got wet.

I didn't want to alarm either woman, so I simply told them I was passing by on the way home and was just wondering if Vinnie wanted to grab some lunch. I didn't mention him not showing up for work and neither of them seemed even aware he was due back today. So I think I got away with it, not spreading any more anxiety than I had to. I did pick up that same vibe I always got from them, that I was somehow responsible for keeping Vinnie off the reservation. But that I would have gotten no matter what. I thanked them both and kept going.

When I got back to the Glasgow, I didn't see his truck in the parking lot. Even so, I felt myself expecting to see him sitting there by the fireplace when I walked in. The truck is broken down, he'd say. Had to be towed to the shop, now I'm stuck here all day. That's how I wanted it to go, but as soon as I opened the door I saw Jackie look up at me with expectation written all over his wrinkled face.

"Did you find him?"

"I didn't realize it was a search party," I said, and then I stopped myself. Jackie was no more anxious than I was. He was just more ready to show it.

"You're telling me he wasn't at work."

"No, he wasn't."

"How often does he miss work?"

"You know the answer to that as well as I do. Once every thousand years."

"So where the hell could he be? It doesn't make any sense."

"I know," I said, "but I'm sure he's out doing something important. Something to do with his family. That's the only explanation."

I sat down at the bar. Jackie kept up with the muttering to himself and the head shaking.

"Hey," I said, "what was with all the police cars? They were all going west, full speed, lights, sirens. . . ."

He looked at me and I could see his anxiety go into second gear.

"I'm sure it's just a coincidence," I said. "Vinnie hardly ever goes out that way. None of us do."

"There's something going on in Newberry," Jackie said. "Guy came in for breakfast after you left, said there were police cars all over the place out there. I didn't even think about it at the time."

"Newberry? But I saw Chippewa cars going out there. Why would they go out to Luce County?"

"If it's something big enough. You know how it goes up here."

Neither of us said a word for a few seconds.

"Okay," I finally said. "We're gonna sit here and wonder if Vinnie's out there, right? Until one of us actually goes out there to see what's happening?"

"Go," he said. "Call me as soon as you find out either way."

Newberry's a little town in the middle of absolutely nothing, about forty miles southwest of us, across the county line. The back road out from Paradise hits the main highway across the state, and as far as I can tell, that's pretty much the only reason there's a town there in the first place. It's a little bigger than Paradise—it even has its own little airport—but the Soo is a lot bigger and just about as close. So bottom line, I never have any reason to go to Newberry, unless I happened to be driving through it on my way to Marquette.

The same goes for Vinnie, which is what I was telling myself as I drove. Then I remembered the other reservations to the west, including the little Sault outposts in Christmas and Manistique. Different tribe, but what the hell, I could easily imagine some reason for him going out that way.

I was driving eighty before I even realized what I was doing. I made myself take a breath and slow down. He's not out there, I told myself. The chances of him being in Newberry right now are a million to one.

I drove through the desolate pine barrens west of Paradise, past the Lower Tahquamenon Falls, where the tannins from the cedar, spruce, and hemlock trees turned the water the color of root beer. There were three or four cars lined up at the gatehouse, waiting to get in. Then past the Upper Falls. I was in Luce County now. A long winding stretch through the trees and nothing else until I finally hit the straightaway going due south. About ten miles to go.

I saw the first state car as soon as I hit the main part of town. The trooper was pulled over on the opposite side of the road, silent but with his lights flashing. He was busy talking into his radio. He didn't even look up at me as I drove past.

The traffic got heavier as I came to the highway, passing the little strip mall and the farm-equipment store with all the tractors lined up out front. Everybody seemed to be wanting to take a left onto the highway to see whatever there was to see. It was clearly the biggest event in Newberry in years, and probably the first actual traffic jam in just as long. I didn't feel like waiting, so I parked the truck behind the gas station on the corner and got out.

I walked down the side of the road about a mile, past all the cars and trucks that were sitting there at a dead stop. As I got closer to the airport in Newberry, I saw the troopers out on the road, waving the traffic past and trying not to spend too much time answering the same questions over and over.

When I got close enough to the fence, I saw a good fifteen to twenty cars parked inside, some Michigan State cars, some Chippewa County, some Luce County. I saw two Newberry Police Department cars, which was a surprise because I didn't even know they had their own department.

"What can we do for you, sir?" It was one of the troopers directing traffic.

"I'm just trying to find out what's going on."

"You're gonna have to keep moving, sir. We've got a lot of vehicles coming in and out of here."

I was about to go talk to him, even if that meant standing in the middle of the road, but then I saw a couple of other troopers standing by the gate. One of them I recognized, Sergeant Coleman, a man I'd had only one conversation with, but I was hoping he would remember me.

"I need a word with the sergeant," I said to the guy on the road, and then I walked over to the gate before he could stop me.

Sergeant Coleman looked up from his conversation as I approached. He had his official trooper face on until the quarter dropped and he recognized me.

"Mr. McKnight," he said. "What's going on?"

"What happened?" I looked past him at the runway. There was a small Cessna at one end. One truck with big off-road tires, one SUV, then all of the police cars. I saw two different tarps covering two different things shaped like human bodies, and from the way the cops were buzzing around it looked like there were more down the runway.

"We're real busy here," he said. "You're gonna have to read about it in the paper."

"I'm looking for a friend of mine, Sergeant. I just need to know he's not here. Then I can sleep tonight."

"What's your friend's name?"

"His name is Vinnie LeBlanc. I can't imagine why he'd be here at the airport, but I haven't seen him today and—"

"Vinnie LeBlanc." I could tell he was filing away the name. "Is he Bay Mills?"

"Yeah. Why?"

"I just figured. Lots of LeBlancs over there. You say he's missing today?"

"I wouldn't say missing. I just can't find him."

"Well, we've got five dead bodies in here. I don't think any of them are your man, but—"

"Five dead bodies? What the hell happened?"

He hesitated for a moment, looked behind him at the scene, then took a step closer to me. "All right," he said. "Quick version, it looks like a drug delivery gone bad. That plane over there is Canadian registered, and it's stuffed to the rafters with bags of marijuana. Like more than I've seen in my whole life. Two men were probably waiting for the plane, another two men showed up. They handcuffed the first two men, then shot them in the head."

"Okay, that's two dead. How did it get to five?"

"The pilot had a gun, apparently. After he landed, he must have seen he was in trouble. It looks like everybody started shooting at the same time. One of them was crawling back to one of the vehicles and almost made it."

"A night delivery," I said. "They find an airfield out in the middle of nowhere. The plane comes in low and turns on the runway lights automatically."

"How come you know so much about it?"

"It was in the paper. Last month, remember? Downstate somewhere."

"Yeah, I remember," he said. "The state police down there think it probably happened a dozen times until that one went bad. Now we've got *this* one. Right here in Newberry? Why'd they pick this place?"

"If they're looking for the middle of nowhere, I think this qualifies."

"Just what we need," he said, shaking his head. "But as far as your friend goes . . . I mean, we don't have any IDs yet."

"I'm sure he's not in there," I said. "He doesn't even smoke the stuff."

"You don't have to smoke it to sell it."

"Seriously. I can promise you, Sergeant. Unless you've got a black Ram truck in there, and an Indian with long hair down his back."

"No, that much I can tell you. We don't have that."

"All right then," I said. "I'll let you get back to it. Thanks for taking the time. I feel a lot better now."

"No problem, Mr. McKnight. Good luck finding your friend. I'm sure he'll show up somewhere today."

"I'm sure he will." As I walked away, I looked back through the fence. One airplane. Five dead men on the ground. Nothing to do with Vinnie. Obviously.

But I still didn't know where he was.

Jackie was waiting at the door for me when I got back to the Glasgow. "You were supposed to call me," he said.

"Sorry. I don't think my cell phone would have worked out there, anyway."

"What did you find out? Was it an accident?"

"No, some kind of drug deal gone bad at the airport."

"At the Newberry airport? That one little runway that gets like one plane a day."

"It can happen anywhere," I said. "Especially when you're this close to a border."

"That kind of stuff happens down in Arizona," he said. "Not in Michigan."

"You'd be surprised."

"Yeah, whatever. As long as it wasn't Vinnie getting flattened by a truck or something."

"It wasn't," I said. "So you know what? I think we're both being a little ridiculous. Vinnie's an adult. He went somewhere to do something and when he's done he'll come back. Hell, if we didn't know he was having the first hangover of his life, we wouldn't have even thought twice about it. Am I right?"

"Well, everything he's been through this week, too."

"Of course. But how many times has he taken off for a few days? He never tells us where he's going. He shouldn't have to."

Jackie thought about it. "Well, no. But—"

"But what? What else are we supposed to do? When he comes back home, we'll smack him a few times and ask him where the hell he went. Until then, we've both got work to do."

He had to agree with me. Maybe not one hundred percent. But then I wasn't one hundred percent sold on the idea myself.

We didn't talk about Vinnie anymore that day. I delivered my fans and my water and did a few fixes on the cabins and eventually ended up back at the Glasgow for dinner. It was me and Jackie. Still no Vinnie.

When it was dark, I finally went home. As I drove by his cabin, I could see that it was still empty.

"Sorry," I said out loud. "I gotta do this, Vinnie."

I stopped the truck, got out, and went to his front door. I knew it would be unlocked, like always, like why would you ever lock your door when you live out here in the woods? I opened the door and went inside. When I flipped on the light, I saw the broken glass all over the floor. It crunched under my feet as I made my way to the back of the cabin. I couldn't breathe. I imagined him lying on the floor in the bathroom, or in his bedroom, or anywhere. Everything coming together in one instant. The simple reason why he never went to work, why nobody had seen him.

But no. The place was empty. I started breathing again. Then I got the broom out and swept up the broken glass.

The rest of the cabin was immaculate, as always. It made no sense that he'd drop a glass or a vase or whatever the hell this was, and then leave it.

"What the hell?" I said. "How did this happen? Were you that drunk? Even so, you'd clean it up the next morning, right? Who leaves broken glass on the floor?"

The answer came right back at me. Somebody in a hurry, that's who. Somebody rushing out the door.

When the place was cleaned up, I turned off the light and closed the door behind me. I left the door unlocked, because that's what Vinnie would be expecting when he finally came home.

I stayed up late that night. I wasn't exactly waiting for him, but I know I would have heard his truck coming up that road.

I never did.

CHAPTER FIVE

The next morning, Jackie didn't even bother asking me. He could see it on my face. I had a quick breakfast and then I headed out into the day. Sometime during the night it had come to me, that I would get up the next morning and go out and find him. So that's what I did.

I looked for Vinnie's black truck wherever I went, starting at the northwest end of the reservation. When I got to the casino, I took a minute to look through the employees' section of the parking lot. No black truck there, but then I walked through the whole inside of the place anyway.

I drove by Vinnie's mother's house. The unofficial command center for the whole rez and yet now it was strangely empty. I parked and looked inside her garage window, picturing the truck there and Vinnie inside the house, maybe looking through old pictures or something. But I didn't see either.

I knew what I had to do next, but I was already dreading it. I stalled for a few minutes by driving by Buck's house. He was one of Vinnie's many second or third or whatever the hell cousins, and a frequent sweat host. The lights were on in the house and there was a beat-up old car in the driveway and an all-terrain vehicle parked in the grass, but when I knocked on the door there was no answer. That's when I noticed the steam coming from the sweat lodge. I walked around to the entrance. Buck had taken branches and formed them into a semicircle, then he'd taken every old blanket and towel he could find on the entire reservation and stacked them all over the top. There was a small fire pit inside and when he poured water over the hot stones the entire room would fill up with steam. I'd been in it more than once myself, and I knew Vinnie had done his sweat sometime this past week. Sitting in there while Buck put the healing medicines on the stones and feeling the steam fill up his lungs.

It didn't sound like a lot of fun in the summertime, but when you need your sweat, you need your sweat.

I didn't want to interrupt anything, but I figured I could be forgiven. I found the one big blanket that served as the doorway and peeked inside. I let in just enough light to see that the lodge was empty, and that the fire was low. Buck was just getting started or just finishing, but either way he wasn't here at the moment. So I decided I'd come back later. Right now, it was time to go see Vinnie's sisters again.

Mary LeBlanc Teeple was the older of the two. A little more fair-haired and less classically Indian, and maybe a little quicker to smile at people. Not that it mattered much to me. I knew she didn't like me that much and she didn't try real hard to hide it. Never mind that I'd done a few things over the years for her whole family. She seemed to have a short memory when it came to that.

I'd already been there once the day before, of course. Back when I said I was just wondering if Vinnie happened to be around for some lunch. Now I had to go back and tell her I hadn't seen the man for a day and a half, and that he had missed his first shift back at work. Which was about as un-Vinnie-like as you could imagine.

"I don't want to alarm you," I said to her, knowing even as I said it that it's probably the most alarming thing you could ever hear. "I haven't seen Vinnie since a couple of days ago, and I'm just trying to make sure he's okay. Wherever he is."

"You didn't say anything about that yesterday."

"Well, no. Because that was yesterday. He didn't come back home last night, so I started to get a little worried."

"Did you check the casino?"

"Yes, I did. He was supposed to be at work yesterday. His first day back."

"You didn't mention that, either."

"I know, I know. I just didn't want to—" I came to a full stop, amazed at how badly I had done with this in just a matter of seconds. "Look, I know he's had a tough week. You all have. He probably shouldn't have gone back to work so soon in the first place."

"I agree," she said. "If he lived here, I never would have let him try."

We were still standing there in the doorway. The kids ran into the house, slipping past us like we were just a pair of obstacles in their great summer game. Mary didn't even look down at them.

"Look," I said, "as long as we're beating up on me, I might as well tell you something else: Vinnie had a lot to drink the other night."

"My brother doesn't drink."

"Yeah, I know. Except maybe when his mother dies."

I stopped myself again.

"I'm sorry," I said. "I mean *your* mother. I know it's been—"

"So you took him out drinking."

"No, I didn't. It was his decision. I just kept him company. I was looking after him."

"Were you drinking with him?"

I hesitated, resisting the urge to say something completely out of line and downright sexist, that her question was the kind of thing only a woman would ask.

"Yes," I said. "A little bit. Like I said, I was keeping him company."

"You were keeping him company and drinking with him. And now he's disappeared. That's what you came here to tell me."

"I'm sure he's fine. I just wanted to know if you've heard from him. That's all."

"I haven't. We don't see that much of him lately. As you know."

Wow, I thought. A few more minutes of this and I'll need an ice bag on my face. "If you hear from him, will you have him call me, please? I'll do the same for you and your sister, I promise."

"That's very kind of you," she said. "I'll tell Reggie you were thinking of us."

"That's okay. I can tell her. I think I'll go see her right now, too."

"Oh good, she'll enjoy that."

"Listen," I said, "I mean, come on, Mary."

"Understand one thing," she said. "I know it was my brother's choice to leave the reservation. I don't blame you for that. I really don't. But I also know that my brother doesn't drink alcohol. Ever. Not after what it did to our father. He doesn't drink, period, end of discussion. So if you're telling me that this was his choice completely, him just deciding one day to go get drunk . . . Well, I do not believe you."

I put up my hands in surrender. I didn't know what else to say.

"I'll have him call you if I hear from him," she said. "I promise." Then she shut the door in my face.

Well, that was fun, I thought. Now I get to go do it again.

I walked down the street to Regina's house. Reggie, as her sister called her. She opened the door with the phone in her hand, her sister already briefing her on what was about to come. We had a condensed version of the exact same conversation, with the same punch line. If Vinnie was drinking, it clearly must have been my fault.

Then I got another door shut in my face.

I got back into my truck and spent a full minute just sitting there, my hands tight on the steering wheel. Then I started the engine and took off.

I had one more destination in mind. Up that long hill to Mission Point, the way we came up to the graveyard so Vinnie could talk to his mother one more time. He could be up there again, I told myself. He really could be. Although spending a full day and a half up there seemed a little farfetched.

The place was quiet and empty when I got up there. I stopped the truck and got out, walked over to the overlook, that same view we'd had that night, but brightly lit by the sun now, the lakes below capturing the light and breaking into a thousand little pieces.

"Vinnie," I said out loud, "where the hell are you?"

It was hours later, the sun gone down, another day nearly out of reach with nothing to show for it. There was a knock on my door. When I opened it, I saw a man in a uniform. I had no idea who he was.

"Mr. McKnight? Can I have a few moments? I'm Chief Benally from the Bay Mills Police Department."

"Oh, you're the new man in town," I said. "Come on in."

I'd known they had a chief coming in, some high-profile Ojibwa lifer from a tribe out in Wisconsin. This was obviously the man and he did look like he kept his boots shined just right. It's a strange position, actually, being the chief of a small reservation police department and also being deputized at the county level simultaneously. You have only a handful of officers, and if you arrest someone you have to coordinate with the county and keep the suspect in the holding cells in the Soo. On top of everything else, the community you serve is basically one big extended family, and even your officers are members. I could only imagine how complicated that could get.

I indicated the chairs and offered him something to drink. He declined. He took off his hat and put it on the table in front of him.

"I stopped by Vinnie LeBlanc's cabin on my way up here," he said. "Doesn't look like anybody's home."

"No, I haven't seen him since night before last."

"So I understand. I had a visit from his sister Mary today."

"Okay," I said. "Here we go."

"She indicated that you and Vinnie were drinking the other night. Is that true?"

It had been a long day and I had already gotten raked over these same coals twice. I was in no mood to make a third trip.

"Chief, please listen to me," I said. "This isn't about Vinnie getting drunk, all right? He lost his mother, he wanted to have a drink. And yes, I joined him. I was just keeping him company and looking after him. The only reason I mentioned it to his sisters is because I thought they should know. Obviously a big mistake on my part, because that's all they seem to care about right now."

"No, that's not true. They're very concerned about their brother missing his shift at work. Apparently this is the first time in several years. Their worst fear is that Vinnie suffered some kind of alcohol poisoning, and that perhaps he left his house and lost consciousness somewhere."

"Oh, for God's sake. When Vinnie gets back, I'm gonna have him come see every one of you guys, tell you the whole story. I really can't wait for that to happen."

"Well, I hope that happens, too," the chief said. "I really do. In the meantime, I've got all of my men keeping their eyes open. Unless you've got any other ideas about where he might be."

"If I did, I'd tell you."

"Okay, then. You'll let me know if something else occurs to you?"

He kept sitting there, just looking at me. I knew the drill, having done it myself a time or two. I looked right back at him.

"I understand you were a police officer yourself," he finally said. "Back in the day."

"I was."

"Chief Maven over in Sault Ste. Marie, he's got some interesting things to say about you."

"I'm sure he does."

"He started out by telling me you were the biggest pain in the ass he's ever had the misfortune of knowing."

"I can't imagine why," I said, even though I could have spent the rest of the night counting the reasons.

"He also told me you were a big help to him, not that long ago. He says he owes you a favor."

"Chief Maven said that? Seriously?"

"He did," Benally said, "which makes me inclined to give you the benefit of the doubt. You'll let me know if you hear from Vinnie LeBlanc, okay?"

"I will, Chief."

He stood up and put his hat on, squaring it up just so. He wished me a good night and then he was gone.

The next morning, I rolled by Vinnie's empty cabin and went down to the Glasgow for breakfast. Jackie had the *Soo Evening News* from the night before. I sat there and read all about the dead bodies in Newberry. The police still weren't giving them many details, but drug-related executions don't happen every day up here. I could only imagine what people would be saying about it all over the county.

"What's next?" Jackie said to me. "What's the plan for today?"

"I don't know," I said. "If you got any ideas, I'm all ears."

"Get back out there and look for him."

"He's not on the rez. Where else do I start looking?"

"We can't just sit here."

"The Bay Mills police are all on alert," I said. "If he's around, they'll find him."

"Yeah, Indians are good at that sort of thing."

I looked up to see if he was kidding, but he had already walked away. That's when I remembered the one loose end from the day before. I got up, went out to the truck, and drove straight to the rez.

I went back to Buck's house, with the beat-up old car out front and the carefully made sweat lodge in back. I knocked on the front door.

Nobody was answering, but I heard music from somewhere inside. I knocked again. Still no answer.

I walked around to the back of the house, wondering if maybe somebody was getting ready to use the sweat lodge. Kind of early in the day for it, I would have thought, but what the hell. I didn't see any steam coming from the lodge, but I opened up the flap anyway.

"What's up, dude?"

The voice came from behind me. I turned around, blinking in the sunlight. I couldn't make out where the voice was coming from.

"Right here, man! In the hot tub."

I went up to the back deck. I hadn't noticed the hot tub the last time around, but here it was. It was big enough for four people at least, about seven-by-seven, and as the man turned a dial the water came to life and started bubbling away like a cauldron. Why you'd need to soak in hot water on one of the few warm days of the year, or for that matter how Buck could drive around in a rolling junk heap and still find a way to buy a hot tub. Yet more of life's mysteries, but whatever. The man in the water was vaguely familiar in the way all faces here were vaguely familiar, from seeing him in the casino or at the Cozy or just walking down the road. But he definitely wasn't the man I was looking for.

"Sorry to bother you," I said. "I'm looking for Buck."

"Bucky's not here right now. I just came over to use the tub."

"I see. Do you know when he'll be back?"

"No, man, he's been gone a couple of days."

"Wait a minute," I said. "I was here yesterday and he had a sweat going out back."

"Nah, that wasn't him. That was me and a couple other guys. He lets us use all his stuff, even when he's not around."

The true Indian way, I thought. And as I looked around the rest of the back deck, I saw beer cans and pizza boxes and wadded-up empty potato-chip bags. It looked like the whole neighborhood had been using the back deck as Party Central.

"How long did you say he's been gone? Two days?"

"About that, yeah."

"Hasn't anybody been looking for him? From work or something?"

"No, not really. He was working at the casino for a little while. But then he was at the gas station. I'm not sure he really has a job at the moment. He kinda takes the summer off usually."

This part of the story was starting to make sense to me. A man like Vinnie, with a steady job, a steady life . . . If he disappears, people notice right away. But a man like Buck, who's apparently floating in his own little boat with the motor turned off . . . No, he's not gonna have people looking all over for him. Not for a while, anyway.

"He'll be back eventually," the man said. "Can I give him a message or something?"

"You really have no idea where he could be right now?"

"Not really. Like I said, if you want to leave a message . . ."

"No, that's all right. Thanks for your time."

I was about to step off the deck. Then I stopped.

"Wait a minute," I said. "What's Buck's last name, anyway? Is it LeBlanc?"

"No, it's Carrick."

"And Buck is his real first name?"

"Buck or Bucky. Take your pick."

I wasn't sure if that really answered my question, but I let it go. As I went back around to my truck, I ran through everything I knew about Buck. It wasn't much. I hadn't even known his last name until a few seconds earlier.

He was bigger than Vinnie. He had that not-really-fat but barrel-chested body you see in a lot of men on the reservation. Usually when they're more middle-aged, but I imagine Buck was that size when he was a teenager. Beyond that, I knew he lived by himself here, and that this house was sort of the local hangout for guys around his age. Buck was the kind of guy who'd make his sweat lodge a work of perfection, but I'm sure his kitchen would qualify as a toxic-waste site. I remembered seeing him drive around Brimley in that beat-up old car, probably unregistered.

A good guy. A fun guy. A guy you'd love to hang around with even if he wasn't your cousin. That was Buck. But at the same time, I had to figure he was probably broke most of the time. If he did lay his hands on some money, he'd obviously blow it on something impractical like a hot tub. Either way, he'd be the guy who'd come in your door and sit down at your kitchen table and eat your cereal. He'd wish you a good morning and he'd help you out in a second if you had to move some furniture, but yeah, now that I thought of it, Buck must have represented everything Vinnie had to get away from, that day he made the unforgivable decision to move away from the reservation.

But even now, I knew Buck would do anything for Vinnie. And Vinnie would do anything for Buck. They still had that family bond, something I could appreciate and even marvel at but probably never understand. Not completely.

They're gone together, I thought. That has to be true.

I just wasn't sure if this was good news or bad.

The Bay Mills Tribal Police Department is located in the Waishkey Building, right in the center of the reservation. I pulled into the lot and went inside. It was a small enough place that I could see through into Chief Benally's office. He was sitting there at his desk and he looked up when he heard the front door open.

"Mr. McKnight," he said, getting up. "Good to see you again."

I let the sentiment, real or not, sail right by me. "Vinnie's cousin Buck is missing, too," I said. "They both disappeared around the same time."

"Bucky Carrick, you're talking about?"

"Yes."

He ran this around in his head for a moment. He had both hands resting on his belt, the classic cop pose.

"How did you come to find this out?" he said.

"I went by, looking for him. The guy who was staying there said he's been gone for two days. Doesn't know where he is."

"Well, we've had an eye out for Vinnie today. Guess I should add Buck to the list, huh? You're thinking they're together?"

"It would be a big coincidence if they're not."

He nodded. The way he was standing there, not quite at ease, his body language saying, You don't really belong here, even if you come with useful news.

"Look, it's been a strange couple of days," I said. "And speaking of coincidences . . ."

"The business at the airport," he said, with no hesitation at all.

He was already thinking the same thing. "That's the other coincidence."

"In Vinnie's case, I know there can't be any kind of connection. Even with Buck, I mean, I don't know him that well at all, but he doesn't strike me as the kind of guy who'd do anything more than just smoke a joint now and then."

I knew it was probably more often than now and then, but I wasn't going to get into that. The Ojibwa had their own views about tobacco, how it was part of the land, one of the four sacred medicines. Cigarettes weren't frowned upon around here, not nearly as much as in the general public, and I had to figure that extended to other things you could smoke, as well.

But that was still a world away from gunning down drug dealers and hijacking their shipments.

"No, I'm sure you're right," the chief said. "But it does make you wonder just what the hell's going on around here."

"Yeah, well, I just wanted to let you know about Buck. That's all I had."

"I appreciate it, Mr. McKnight. Why don't you let us take it from here now? We'll have our officers looking out for them, like I said. We'll put in some calls to the other reservations in the state, in case they're both off visiting somebody."

"Okay," I said. "That makes sense."

"Okay, then. Yes. Thank you."

I left the place. I got back into my truck and drove off the reservation. These past couple of days, I was really feeling like a stranger here. You forget about it for a while, but then a few things happen and people say things to you in a certain way, and it all adds up. You may be welcome here, but at the end of the day, you're not part of this. You never have been and you never will be.

Back to Paradise for the rest of another long day. Dinner at the Glasgow. Jackie fussing with things at the bar and clearly more worried than he would admit.

They went on a trip, I told him. Vinnie and his cousin Buck.

They got into his truck and drove somewhere to see somebody. Somebody we don't know. They didn't tell anyone because it didn't even occur to them. When they get back, they'll be surprised we let ourselves get this worked up about it. In the end, we'll even laugh about it.

That's what I told Jackie. That's what I told myself.

It was late when I drove back up my road, past Vinnie's cabin. Dark and empty. I went into my own cabin, got undressed, and lay down on the bed. I tried to sleep.

I was just dozing off into some sort of half dream when a knock on my front door jarred me awake. It took me a second to find my bearings. I got up, put on some clothes, and went to the door.

When I opened it, I saw Chief Benally standing there. He was holding his hat in his hands, and in that one instant I flashed back to my own time as a cop and how I'd felt compelled to take my hat off while I was standing on a doorstep in Detroit, waiting to deliver the worst news imaginable.

"Chief, what's going on?"

"Sorry to bother you again. Can I come in?"

I backed up and he stepped inside. He'd been here the night before, so I didn't have to point out where the furniture was.

"Mr. McKnight, have a seat," he said. "I need to tell you something."

I sat down and waited for him to take the chair across from me. I was already anticipating his words. I was wondering exactly how he'd say it. Would he give me the preamble and ask me to prepare myself? Or would he launch right into it? Vinnie LeBlanc's body was just found about an hour ago. . . .

"Before I say anything," he said, "I have to ask you something."

"Okay . . ."

"What I'm about to tell you must remain in complete confidence. At least for the time being."

"I don't understand."

"I'm asking you to promise me that nothing said here will leave this room."

"I promise," I said. "But what—"

"We heard from Vinnie. He's with Buck, and apparently they're all right. So obviously that's good news."

"Wait. How did you hear from him? Where are they?"

"Well, that's the strange thing about this. You see, all he did was leave a message on the voice mail at the station. He said they were fine and that they'd try to call back again later. He didn't say where they were."

"Come on, Chief, he had to say something else. Nothing about why they left? Or when they'd be back? Or anything?"

"Well, he did ask me to let his sisters know that they were okay. So I've just been to see both of them. To let them know. Even though it's a pretty vague message, I realize. And then of course he also mentioned you."

"He mentioned me."

"He did, yes. Tell my sisters. Tell Alex. We're both okay. We'll be back as soon as we can. Don't worry."

"That's it. That's all he said."

"Yes, and because he mentioned you specifically, I made a point to come and tell you."

"Because if it was just up to you, I'd still be in the dark, right?"

"You're not being fair now. I would have told you."

"Okay, so then why the big secret?" I said. "If they're okay, why can't I tell anyone else?"

"It's kind of a delicate situation right now. With this business at the airport and all. Them disappearing the same night."

"So it's definitely connected."

"I don't know that for sure. Nobody does. But I think we need to keep a lid on things until we can get them back home."

"Meaning that they're definitely *not* okay. That's what you're really telling me."

"No. You've got this all wrong."

"Tell me the truth," I said, staring him straight in the eyes. "Where are they and what the hell is going on?"

He stared straight back at me. "I honestly don't know where they are," he said. "All I know is that they're safe, and . . . Well, I think somebody is helping them."

He put his hand up before I could speak.

"I don't know exactly who is helping them. I'm not going to speculate. But I think I heard a voice in the background. Somebody who didn't sound like Buck. That's all I can say right now. When I know something else for sure, I'll tell you. I promise."

I leaned back in my chair. I wasn't sure what else to say.

"Look, you're an ex-cop," he said.

"Yes. Long time ago."

"Doesn't matter how long, you still think like a cop. I get that. Believe me, I'll probably be the same way myself when I finally hang it up. But right now, I need you to stay here close to home, and to keep your eyes and ears open. Are we clear?"

"I'm not sure what I'm gonna see or hear. Aside from Vinnie's truck coming up that road . . ."

"I'm dead serious, Mr. McKnight. If you see anything suspicious. Somebody you've never seen before. You know, just nosing around maybe."

"Nosing around."

"Yes. Nosing around. You see somebody like that, I need you to call me."

"Chief, who are we talking about that would be—"

I stopped myself. I waved it away and made myself take a breath.

"Okay," I said. "I'll call you if I see anything unusual."

"Thank you. I'm going to go now. For right now, I'm afraid all we can do is wait."

He got up. He shook my hand. He put his hat back on and then he left.

I went outside and stood there in the night air. I listened to him drive away. That word still ringing in my ears. *Wait.* My least favorite word ever.

"Vinnie LeBlanc," I said. "Wherever you are, you might want to think about staying there. Because the next time I see you I'm going to kick your ass."

CHAPTER SIX

There was a time when Vinnie and I weren't speaking to each other. A young Ojibwa woman had asked me to help her, and I tried to do that. But because she was a member of the tribe, it was the tribe who came to her in the middle of the night. They took her away, they helped her, and yeah, I suppose she was probably better off with a whole community on her side instead of one aging ex-cop.

But they didn't tell me. That was the thing that burned me. I still haven't forgotten it, and I don't imagine I ever will. Vinnie wasn't one of the men who actually stole her away, but he knew about it. He had to know. Even now, if he were here, I could ask him about it one more time and once again he'd try to deny that he had one hundred-percent knowledge of what had happened. But there would be no point in doing that because it would just push us back, closer to that point where we couldn't be in the same room together.

In the end, we got over it. We got over it the way men get over things, not by talking things out heart to heart but by working on something together. He showed up one day to help me rebuild the cabin at the end of the road. The next day he showed up again. By the time the walls were up, we were talking again and eating dinner at the Glasgow. Which is a good thing because it's hard to avoid a man when he's your one and only neighbor.

That feeling, though . . . Damn it all. That feeling of being the outsider, of being totally excluded from everything that's going on around you, even if you want to help. Even if you *know* you can help. That's the feeling that always stayed with me.

Now here was Vinnie, hiding away somewhere with his wayward cousin. Obviously in some sort of trouble. If the situation were reversed, he'd be the first person I reached out for. We'd been down enough roads together over the years. We'd faced so much trouble. So much death and brutality. Hell, the man had once taken his own blood and painted stripes on my cheeks. Like we were brothers.

So when it's his turn to be in a real jam, what does he do? He sends a message to the rez. I get it thirdhand, almost as an afterthought. Tell Alex I'm okay. Tell him not to worry. As if he'd even think for one second that would be possible.

Not to worry. I mean, come on.

When the chief's taillights disappeared down the road, I went inside and sat back down in that same chair. I ran over everything in my head. Finally, when I thought I might punch a hole right through the table, I got up and went through my desk instead and found a business card. I dialed the number.

"Agent Long. What." The voice of a woman who had been in a deep sleep just a few seconds ago.

"Hi," I said. "It's me, Alex. I woke you up, didn't I?"

"Alex? What time is it?"

"It's about midnight, I think. I'm sorry."

"It's okay. I have to be up in five more hours anyway."

She laughed, and something came all the way through the phone line, over all those miles, and went right through me. Agent Janet Long of the FBI, stationed in Detroit. We'd spent all of two weeks together, when she had come up here to help track down a killer. When she had left, I had promised to call her sometime. I never did, until now.

You are a goddamned fool, I told myself. All this time you could have reached out, and you pick now, in the middle of the night. Just because you can't think of anyone else.

"I'm sorry," I said. "I shouldn't have called. I mean, I *should* have called. But not like this. I should have—"

"It's okay, Alex. What's the problem? I can tell you're upset."

"I just need to talk to somebody. I'm going to go crazy if I don't."

"So talk."

"You remember Vinnie LeBlanc," I said.

"Your friend, yes. I met him at that bar."

"He's gone. He and his cousin. They're in some sort of trouble."

"What kind of trouble?"

"I just broke a promise, by the way. I wasn't supposed to tell anyone. But I figure you don't count."

"Thanks a lot."

"No, I mean, being on the job and all. Which, by the way . . ."

"Yeah?"

"Tell me everything you know about this thing that happened up here. At the Newberry airport."

"Whoa," she said. "Time out. Are you serious?"

"I'm not saying they're involved. I'm just asking you to tell me what you know, beyond what was in the paper. I know five men were killed, but—"

"Alex, if they're not involved, why are you asking me this?"

"I can't see Vinnie having any connection to this, but as far as his cousin goes . . ."

"Do you think he was there? At the airport?"

"I can't rule it out. I mean, I didn't think it was possible, but I guess I don't know him that well. If he was actually there, well, let's just say it would explain some things if he was."

"You need to talk to somebody up there," she said. "Right away. If you have any information that could—"

"I already have, okay? There's a new police chief on the rez up here. He was just sitting right here at this table. He knows everything I do, and in fact, hell, he's the one who received the message from Vinnie."

"What kind of message?"

"Just that they're both okay. As if they were, I don't know, hiding out and figuring out what to do next? I'm not really sure, but that's the only scenario I can imagine."

"So you've had no contact with Vinnie yourself?"

"No," I said, tapping my fingers on the table.

"And that bothers you," she said. "You want to go get yourself right in the middle of it, don't you?"

"It wouldn't be the first time. We seem to do that for each other."

She laughed again.

"This is so weird," she said. "I was just thinking about this case when I went to bed, and then you wake me up to talk about it. I'm not dreaming, right?"

"So you do know about it."

"Of course I do. Marijuana flying in from Canada in the middle of the night? People shooting each other?"

"So it did come from Canada. I was reading about that last month. This isn't the first time, right?"

"No, I should say not. It's almost impossible to stop them, unless we want to station somebody at every tiny little airport in Michigan, every single night."

"They fly in, drop it off, fly right back."

"They're on the ground for five minutes," she said. "Ten minutes tops. It's kind of ingenious."

"Wait, didn't they actually handcuff some people to the fence last time?"

"They did, yes. We found them a few hours later. Good thing it was summertime or they would have frozen to death. Not that things ended up any better for them."

"What, are you saying—"

"I didn't just tell you that," she said. "But yeah, we ended up letting them go. They weren't in possession of anything, after all. The drugs and the money were long gone by the time we got there. As well as the airplane and the hijackers. All we had were two men handcuffed to a fence. We figured they'd be good leads to follow, anyway. So that's what we'd been doing. Up until this week."

"They didn't get the message, you're saying. So this time around they ended up in a shootout."

"Just like the good old days," she said. "Only replace the booze with marijuana."

"So who were the other guys? You must have them ID'd by now."

She didn't say anything. There was nothing but a distant hum on the line.

"You know I can't go there," she said. "But I can tell you this. The pilot was Canadian. The receivers were just your average local dealers. Maybe a little bit above average, because it was a pretty big quantity we're talking about. And maybe a little bit crazy, because after what happened last time—"

"Local as in where?" I said. "Were they from up here?"

"No, from downstate. That's one of the mysteries, why they'd go so far north to do this. It's the first time they've connected in the Upper Peninsula, as far as we know."

"Okay, so what about the hijackers?"

"That's where I have to stop you," she said. "I can't talk about them at all."

"You're saying, what? It's not just some other group of pot dealers who found out about the party and decided to crash it?"

"No, this isn't just another bunch of pot dealers. Look, Alex, you know how bad it's been getting down on the Mexican border. This is a long way from there, but the idea is still the same, right? Even if those cartels are not directly involved in this, you have to know that they're setting a standard for how you run a drug trade. Other groups see how well it works and then use the same approach. One warning, then absolutely no mercy after that. Just flat-out appalling violence. That's how you move in and take over."

"So these new people, they're from where again?"

"I didn't say, and I'm not going to. I'm dead serious."

"Okay. I understand. You can't talk about it."

I heard her let out a long breath. "Just be careful. That's the one thing I can say. If your friends really are mixed up in this . . ."

"Is it that bad?"

"Yes," she said. "As bad as it gets."

We both let that thought hang in the silence for a while.

"It's good talking to you," I said. "I'm sorry I called so late."

"It's okay, Alex. It's good talking to you, too. No matter what time it is."

I wished her a good night. She wished me one right back but I think we both knew that was impossible at this point. I certainly wasn't going to sleep through any of it.

I may have dozed off for an hour. Maybe two. But I snapped awake around eight in the morning with a sudden thought. I took a shower and got into the truck. As I drove by Vinnie's, I took a quick look, knowing exactly what I'd see but hoping against hope anyway. I shouldn't have bothered.

When I got to the reservation, I drove right to the Waishkey Building. I had been running through my conversation with the chief, over and over again. I kept feeling like I had missed something important. Maybe something we had *both* missed. But I couldn't put my finger on it. I figured if I talked to him again, it would come to me.

I parked by the police department entrance and went inside. The officer on duty told me Chief Benally was unavailable. That got my mind racing again. He's with Vinnie right now, I thought. Vinnie contacted him again and the chief has raced off to go help him.

"Just tell him to call me," I said to the officer. "As soon as he gets back."

I left my cell phone number. I thanked the man. The whole transaction was perfectly polite and reasonable, but as I walked out, there were two other officers coming in. They held the door open for me. I know I was just imagining it, but it felt like they were giving me a little extra space. Like right this way, sir. Have a good day and don't hurry back.

I am my own worst enemy. I realize that. I get something in my head and I can't let go of it and I drive myself and everyone else around me absolutely crazy. Even when I know I'm doing it, I just can't stop. That's what led me to drive into the Soo and to stop in at the multiplex. I wasn't there to see a movie, God knows. I was there to see Leon Prudell.

When I did my little ill-fated stint as a private investigator, working for a local lawyer, Leon was the man whose job I took. He paid me a visit at the Glasgow one night and tried to take me apart in the parking lot. From that auspicious beginning, a strange sort of friendship grew. I hated being a private eye, even before the whole thing blew up in my face. On the other hand, being a private eye was the only thing Leon ever wanted, ever since he was a kid. He even tried to set up his own practice in a rented office on Ashmun Street. There just isn't enough business around here, even if you double as a bail bondsman. He'd been working a string of odd jobs ever since. His latest was right here at the multiplex, serving popcorn with yellow sludge on top to teenagers.

You look at him and you see an overweight local guy in a flannel shirt, with that wild orange hair on his head, and you might think this kind of job is the only thing he's qualified to do. But he has a nose for investigation. He still knows how to break down a situation and look at it from every angle. That's why I still go to him whenever I need help.

The lobby was pretty much empty, with another sunny July day going on outside. I asked the kid at the ticket booth if Leon was going to be around today, but he seemed not to know who I was talking about. We circled around that point for a while, because how many orange-haired adult men could actually work there? Eventually, I got passed off to a manager who told me that Leon had quit about a week ago.

Good for him, I thought as I walked out. I got back into the truck and drove out of town, just south to Rosedale. I pulled up in front of the Prudell house, with that tire swing in the front yard, hanging from the lowest branch. The car was gone, but I knocked on the door anyway. Nobody answered. As I stood on the front porch, I looked around. Something seemed out of place. That's when I remembered the camper that was usually parked next to the driveway. One of those fold-up things you tow behind your car. It was gone now, which could mean only one thing. Leon and his entire family were on vacation.

After I got back into the truck, I just sat there for a while, staring out the windshield at nothing. If Leon was really your friend, you'd already know he was on vacation. You would have talked about it. He would have told you where he was going and how excited his kids were. You would have wished him a great trip. Maybe you'd even be stopping by his house just to make sure the mail was stopped and the newspapers weren't piling up at the front door.

But no, you come see him only when you want something from him. When you need his help, you know he'll be only too willing to oblige. Then you forget about him until the next time.

Hell, you did the same thing to Janet last night. You called her up in the middle of the night because you wanted information. Did you spend more than two seconds asking her how she was doing?

That leaves two other people in your life. Jackie and Vinnie. Are those your only true friends? The only two people you can really talk to?

If so, then it's no wonder you go so crazy when one of them is missing. One friend means half your goddamned world right there.

I started to think about other people who had meant the world to me, once upon a time. The father who raised me on his own. My ex-wife. My dead partner. A certain Ontario Provincial Police-woman. All of them gone now. Is that why I didn't want anyone else to get too close to me?

Okay, I thought, enough with the psychoanalysis. Just find Vinnie. Or hell, maybe Chief Benally is right. Maybe you just have to wait for him to show up on his own. That's when you can tell him you don't have enough friends left to be losing one.

I put the truck in gear and took off.

I was sitting at the bar. Jackie put a cold Canadian in front of me.

"Thank you," I said.

He hesitated for a moment, looked at me before walking away.

"How are you doing?" I said.

"Excuse me?"

"I asked you how you're doing."

"Why?"

"Because I want to know."

He came back to my end of the bar. "What's going on? Since when do you need to know how I'm doing?"

"I didn't say I *need* to know. I'm just . . . Look, forget it."

He walked away again, shaking his head. I sat there and slowly emptied the bottle while the sun went down. There was a Tigers game on, above the bar. I watched it for a while without paying attention to it at all.

When Jackie came back to take my empty bottle away, I asked him if he had a map of Michigan. He went to the kitchen and came back with the standard road map, with the blowup of metropolitan Detroit on the back. I spread it out on the bar, squinting in the fading light.

"I'm wondering where the rest of the reservations are," I said. "Can you make them out?"

He came around and squinted next to me.

"You think Vinnie's there," he said. A statement, not a question.

"Vinnie and his cousin. One of the other reservations."

"It would make sense. That's the best place to go if you're in trouble."

He stood there and looked at the map with me for another few moments.

"You can't find him," he said. "Not in a million years."

I kept looking. Then I folded up the map.

"You're right." I gave him back his map and left.

Outside, the air had cooled, but the sky was clear. An amazing night in the Upper Peninsula, but I couldn't let myself enjoy it. I got into the truck and drove up the road. Took my left and knew I'd see Vinnie's dark cabin again. Came around that bend and stopped dead.

There was a car parked outside his cabin. There was a light on inside.

I slowly backed up the truck until it was out of sight, then I swung it crosswise so it was blocking the road. I grabbed a flashlight and made my way back toward Vinnie's cabin, moving as quietly as I could. The car parked in front of the cabin was a white Camry with a Michigan plate. I snapped on the flashlight and took a quick look inside. There was one suitcase in the backseat, a rental agreement on the front seat, next to a road map just like the one I'd been looking over at the Glasgow. I saw the Thrifty sticker in the corner of the windshield and started putting some things together. Thrifty and Avis were the only two rental companies at the airport in Sault Ste. Marie. Somebody flew in, rented this car, and drove here. He came up this road and found Vinnie's cabin, and from here he might not even have suspected that there were more cabins beyond it. He wouldn't know that I'd be heading up this road and that I'd see his rental car parked out front.

Don't let me stop you, I thought. Just keep doing whatever it is you're doing.

I crept up to the door and listened. Then I moved to the nearest window and stood with my back against the rough wood of the cabin. Then I turned and moved slowly, until I could finally see through the edge of the glass.

A figure. One male. Standing at Vinnie's counter, holding Vinnie's phone. His back was to me, which gave me the chance to give him a good look from top to bottom. He had black hair streaked with gray, just long enough to tie into a tight ponytail. He was wearing a beat-up old leather jacket. Jeans and black cowboy boots with metal tips.

He turned around just then, quickly, as if startled by something.

Even though I had not made the slightest sound. I held my breath and kept my back to the wall. I heard him moving inside.

A gun would be nice right about now, I thought. Or at least something big to hit this guy with.

The door opened and a wedge of light hit the ground, inches from my feet. I saw his face, his eyes widening as he recognized what was about to happen. I had to act fast to keep any advantage, so I went right at him. I put the heel of my hand to his chin and drove him backward. He stumbled back into the cabin but did not fall. I grabbed his right wrist and spun him around, twisting the arm behind him. He bent over and I thought I had him dead, until he tripped me and turned himself free. Perfectly using my own momentum against me. Clearly this wasn't his first tango.

He tried to kick me in the ribs and just grazed me. I rolled over and grabbed something to throw at him, anything, a book from the coffee table, flying open like a great wounded bird as it hit him in the face. I drove my shoulder into his chest, taking him all the way into the kitchen until his back hit the edge of the counter. I could tell that hurt him bad. He sagged like he was about to go down, but I was ready for the bluff this time. He came right back with a big swing. I ducked it and put one right in his gut.

He reached back to the counter, grabbing for a knife or anything else he could use to defend himself. I slid open one of Vinnie's kitchen drawers and grabbed the heaviest thing I could find. A good old-fashioned rolling pin, something right out of the movies, but what the hell. It was as good as a bat and I knew I could knock his teeth out if I had to.

"Who are you?" I said. "What the hell are you doing here?"

"Peace," he said, putting his hands up. "Please, friend. Peace."

I was breathing hard. So was he. Now that we had stopped moving, I got a better look at him from the front. To say that he was tanned would be an understatement. He was more like a walking public-service announcement for sunscreen, so absolutely ruined by the sun that it was hard to tell how old he was. I was betting a little older than me, anyway. He was breathing just as hard as I was, so that was another clue that his best fighting years were behind him.

"I asked you a question," I said, still ready with the rolling pin. "Now start talking."

He looked me straight in the eye for the first time. That's when I saw the resemblance. The years had not been kind to him. All those hard years in prison, much of it obviously spent outside in the sun, maybe on a road crew. Or God knows what. But I could see the answer to my question even as he answered it.

"My name is Lou LeBlanc," he said. "I'm Vinnie's father."

CHAPTER SEVEN

"Put down the rolling pin," he said. "You look like a housewife get-ting ready to brain her husband for coming home late. Like in that old comic strip. What was that guy called, Andy Capp?"

"You're supposed to be in prison," I said. "What are you doing here?"

"Vinnie told you that? That I was still in the joint?"

"Who else would tell me?"

"He's got old information. I've been out for almost two years."

"And you're here now for what reason?"

"It's been a while, I grant you. I never thought I'd get back to Michigan. But then I heard about Vinnie being in trouble."

"Heard from who?"

"One of the old-timers. Sometimes he lets me know how my kids are doing up here. I think he just wants to rub my nose in it, you know, how well they're doing without me. Or if they're not doing so well, how it must be my fault. But either way, that's how I keep up, at least."

"Because there's no way you could contact them yourself, right? It's been, what, how many years?"

"They don't want to hear from me," he said. "I know that. And I sure as hell wasn't gonna come back here. Not while their mother was alive."

I still had the rolling pin in my hand. I felt like hitting him just on general principle.

"I got run out of here pretty good," he said. "There's no way she would have let me come back."

"That's not my understanding of how it happened," I said. "I don't think it's Vinnie's, either."

"Yeah, well, I'm not surprised. She could spin it any way she wanted if I wasn't here to defend myself."

"Say one more disrespectful thing about her and I'll put this thing right up your ass."

"Okay, okay, take it easy. There's two sides to every story, right? Let's just leave it at that. Now will you put the bakery equipment away? I wasn't kidding, you look ridiculous."

I put the rolling pin back in the drawer and slammed it closed.

"Is this really his house?" the man said, looking around. "This is my son's kitchen? What does he do, make pastries for a living?"

"He built it himself. You'll have to excuse him for having a nice place to live."

"He really lives here. All by himself."

"Yes, he does."

"Why isn't he on the reservation with the rest of his family? And who are you, anyway?"

"My name is Alex. And Vinnie moved off the rez for his own reasons. You can ask him if you see him."

"I will," he said, nodding his head. "You're a friend of his?"

"Yes, I am."

"Are you a good friend?"

"I'd like to think so."

"So you know he's in trouble."

I hesitated. "I don't know much of anything. I know he's gone. I know his cousin Buck is with him."

"Yeah, Buck Carrick. I hear they disappeared together. Nobody knows where they are."

"How'd you hear that?"

"I told you, I'm still plugged into things. I may live out West now, but I'm still a member of the tribe, whether they want me to be or not."

"When did you hear about it?"

"Yesterday. I hopped on the first plane to the Soo."

They all know, I thought. Every single person on that reservation, and even people who've been gone for years. They all got word of this before I did.

"The chief led me to believe this was some kind of secret," I said. "I guess it's not."

"A *secret*? Are you kidding? On a reservation?"

"Okay, whatever," I said. "You still haven't answered my question. Why did you come all the way out here?"

"He's still my son," he said. "He's in trouble. Isn't that enough reason?"

"They haven't heard a thing from you in how many years? Hell, you didn't seem to care that much when your *other* son was in trouble. I don't recall seeing you at his funeral, either."

I could see that got to him. He flexed both of his fists and for a second I wished I were still holding that rolling pin. He was probably ten or fifteen years older than me, but he looked like he'd spent at least a few of those years in the prison weight room.

"I was doing my time at Ironwood," he said, "so it's not like I had any choice. Besides, like I told you, I don't think I would have been welcome up here."

"But now is different."

"Now is different, yes. Now Nika is gone and I can come here without breaking my promise to her, to never step foot in this state while she's alive. Now maybe I can actually do something good for Vinnie, who I understand probably wants nothing to do with me. But if he's in trouble, I can probably find him and help him. I'm pretty good at finding people. That's why I was here when you walked in and jumped me. I was trying to find out who might have called him on this phone."

He picked up the phone and hit a few buttons.

"Look," he said. "In the caller-ID record. This call three nights ago. Just after two A.M. Do you know this number?"

"It's probably Buck's cell phone," I said. "But we can double-check."

"Okay, good. You see, now we're working together. We might even make a good team."

"Who says we're a team all of a sudden?"

"Do you want to find him or not? Or are you not that good a friend?"

"I helped him find your other son, okay? Did you hear about that one on your grapevine? When Tom disappeared in Canada? I helped Vinnie bring him back and bury him. So lay off with the friend business."

He turned away from me and rubbed his forehead. "Okay, I apologize," he said. "God, I can't even believe I'm back here."

"I know you came a long way," I said, "but I don't know how you expect to help find him. You don't even know him anymore."

"Where do you think he is?" he said, turning back to me. "Right this second?"

"If I knew, I'd be on my way there."

"In general, I mean. What kind of place?"

I thought back to that map I'd looked at on the bar. "On one of the other reservations," I said. "That's probably how he got word up here to the chief."

"Okay," he said, nodding. "So let me ask you one question. If he's on another reservation, who do you think they're gonna talk to first, you or me?"

He had me on that one.

"While I'm at it, let me ask you something else. I know I've been gone a long time, but everybody on the plane was saying you guys have been having a big heat wave up here. People passing out on the street, having to go to the hospital . . . Is that true?"

"It almost hit ninety a couple of days ago. So yes."

"When I left Vegas, it was a hundred and fifteen. You realize you're all pussies up here, right?"

"Come back when there's six feet of snow on the ground," I said. "We'll see who's a pussy."

He laughed at that one.

"Ah yes," he said. "That part I don't miss. But if I can ask you one more question. Last one, I promise."

"Go ahead."

"Is there anyplace we can get a drink around here?"

That's how I ended up back at the Glasgow. I surprised Jackie, who'd already written me off as an early departure that night. I surprised him even more when he got up close to me and looked at my face.

"What the hell happened to you?" he said. "And who's your friend?"

I wiped at the scrape I seemed to have received over my left eye. "Meet Lou LeBlanc."

"You look even worse," he said as he gave Lou the once-over. "What were you guys doing?"

"What do you think?" I said.

"LeBlanc, did you say? Any relation to Vinnie?"

"I guess you could say he's related. He's Vinnie's father."

Jackie stopped dead, halfway into his crouch to get down to the refrigerator under the bar.

"Are you kidding me?"

"He's not kidding," Lou said. "Pleased to meet you."

Jackie finished his mission, coming up with two Molsons and putting them down in front of us. A bad idea, I thought. I should have stopped him before he went for the fridge.

"Let's get it out of the way," Lou said. "I don't imagine either of you think that much of me. Running out on my family, never coming back. I'm sure people still think I'm a total monster around here."

"To tell you the truth," I said, "they don't think about you at all.

Or if they do, they don't say anything. I don't think I've heard Vinnie mention you more than two or three times, up until a week ago, when his mother died."

"Ouch," Lou said, nodding slowly. "That's even worse."

Now that I was sitting next to him, I could see all the scar tissue around his eyes and ears, and the long scar running along the left side of his jawline. With all of the sun damage on top of that, he looked a little unreal. Like he had spent a couple of hours in a Hollywood makeup chair, getting ready to play an old, ravaged warrior.

"I think maybe we should put these away," I said, collecting the two beers. "How about a Coke or something?"

"It's fine," Lou said, taking one of the bottles from me. He had quick hands. "It's just one beer."

I was about to say something else, but he cracked it open and took a hit.

"What brings you back here?" Jackie said. He was eyeing the man like he still wasn't quite sure what to make of him. Which made two of us.

"Damn, what is this?" Lou said, looking at the label. "Molson doesn't taste like this back home."

"He says he's good at finding people," I said to Jackie. "He thinks he can find Vinnie."

"I said I wanted to try," Lou said. "I know it's a little late to be doing something for one of my kids."

"Twenty-five years late," Jackie said. "No, wait, almost thirty?"

Lou put the bottle down and raised his hands. "I'm not defending myself," he said. "If you want me to get up and walk out of here, I'll do it right now."

"Let's hear your angle first," I said.

"My angle, huh? Okay, fair enough."

He took another long draw from the bottle and appreciated it for a long moment, maybe flashing back to a lot of thirsty days in a hot prison cell.

"Let me start this way," he said. "Put yourself in Vinnie's place. Why did you go to the airport?"

"Because my cousin called me and asked me to come get him."

He looked at me while he thought about it.

"You seem pretty sure about that part. There's no way Vinnie could have been there himself? I mean, when everybody started shooting each other?"

"I can't see that."

"No," Jackie said. "No way."

"Okay, let's say I'm with you on that one. We're saying it was just Buck who was there when it all goes down. What kind of player is he? Is he a shooter?"

I had to smile at that one.

"I don't know Buck nearly as well as I know Vinnie, but I can't see him playing the heavy in any of this. Maybe it was just a case of wrong place, wrong time?"

"What, you mean he just happened to stumble onto the airport runway in the middle of the night? Like he took a wrong turn or something?"

"Look, I don't know. I'm just saying, he always seemed pretty harmless to me."

"Yeah, I did time with some guys who seemed pretty harmless. But either way, the bullets start flying, and he's the one guy who walks away. So he calls Vinnie, right?"

"Right."

"Vinnie's the kind of guy who would go get him? In the middle of the night?"

"He's that kind of guy, yes."

"You both are," Jackie said. "There's not a lick of sense in either one of you."

I shot Jackie a look, not that it would have slowed him down one bit.

"Okay, so he's an easy touch," Lou said. "He goes out and picks up Buck. Then what? Where does he take him?"

"Maybe to another reservation," I said. "We've already been over this. How many are there?"

"There's a few. Some of them are pretty big. Hell, the Saginaw rez is like two hundred square miles. But why did they run in the first place?"

"Because they're freaking out," Jackie said. "Why else?"

"Alex, is Vinnie the kind of person who would freak out like that?"

"No," I said, "but I don't know about Buck."

"Maybe he got shot," Jackie said. "Maybe Vinnie's trying to take care of him."

"I think you have to take him to the hospital right away," Lou said. "Don't you? Unless you're a complete idiot."

"Yeah, he would know better," I said. "Vinnie probably just took him away to calm him down. To figure out what to do next."

"Everybody's dead now," Jackie said. "What's he afraid of?"

"If they find out he was there and that he walked away alive," I said, "then he must think they'll be coming after him."

"Who's they?"

"Anybody," Lou said. "On either side of it."

"There's three sides," I said. "The delivery side, the receiving side, and the hijacking side. I don't imagine any of them are real happy right now."

"Damn," Jackie said. "Poor Buck, he might be right in the middle of all these guys."

"That's exactly right," Lou said. "So now if you're Vinnie and you're looking after him, what are you saying?"

"I'm saying you have to turn yourself in," I said. "It's the only thing you can do."

Lou was already taking another swallow and he just about spit it right up. "Are you serious?"

"It's the only safe play. Turn yourself in. Explain why you were there."

"You sound like a cop or something."

"I was," I said. "For eight years."

He took a long look at me, like he was seeing me for the first time. "This is getting better and better."

"How do you mean?"

He put the bottle down and wiped his mouth with the back of his sleeve. "You really think he'd be safest if he turned himself in?

If he ended up sitting in a holding cell somewhere? Where everybody in the world would know exactly where he was?"

"Okay, I understand, just because he's in a cell . . ."

"You really think that's what Vinnie's telling him? Like right now, wherever they are? 'Hey, Buck, let's go turn your ass in to the authorities? And oh by the way, me too? Because I was an accessory to helping you run away?'"

"Look . . ."

"Don't take this the wrong way, Alex. But if you're gonna approach this like an ex-cop, then maybe we should part ways right now. No use having us get in each other's way if we've got completely different ideas."

"So what's your idea?" I said. "If you find them, I mean. What would you suggest they do?"

He picked up his bottle again. "That," he said, "is something we'd just have to play by ear."

"So let's start by finding him," I said. "Let's not even worry about what happens next."

"Fair enough." He looked at me. "You were really a cop?"

"Yes."

"I should have known. You fight like a cop. Totally clean. No cheap shots."

"I'll take that as a compliment."

He smiled. "Whatever you say."

Jackie looked at me and I just shook my head. I was already past having second thoughts and was well into the third thoughts. But I decided to let him keep talking.

"Tell me more about Buck," he said. "Start with where he buys his weed."

"What good is that going to do us?"

"Follow the weed," he said. "Right back to the seller. Right up the supply chain, from the seller to somebody else, to maybe somebody who might know something."

"Okay," I said. "I guess that makes sense."

"So you know where to take us?"

"I think so."

"Then what are we waiting for? Let's go."

It was close to midnight now. We were both in my truck, on the way down to Brimley. As we passed through the reservation, he sat up straight and stared out the window.

"This is seriously one place I never thought I'd see again."

"I'm sure it's changed a lot," I said.

"I forgot how you just drive down the road and all of a sudden you're on the rez. Out West, you gotta drive for miles through absolute desert. There's not much doubt about it when you finally get there. Out of sight and out of mind."

"That's the King's Club," I said as we passed the first casino. "Was it even here when you were here?"

"They were just building it," he said. "Although I thought they were gonna call it something else. I understand it was quite the bust when they first opened it. They had to close it and try again, right?"

"So I'm told. I wasn't here yet."

"You're not a native Yooper?"

"Born and raised in Detroit."

"Is that where you were a cop?"

"Yes."

There were a few cars on the road, most of them gamblers on a warm summer night, or Bay Mills members who were driving to or from work.

"They got nice houses here," he said. "I don't see one place I recognize."

"All the shacks are gone. But again, that was before my time. Which reminds me. Your daughters' houses are coming up on the right."

I slowed down.

"Who lives there?" he said. "Mary?"

"No, this is Regina's house. Mary is a few doors down. You want to go say hello?"

"Wow, I don't know. It's kinda late, isn't it?"

"Yeah," I said. "It's late."

"I mean, even so. Maybe after we find Vinnie. Maybe we can all sit down together."

"They have kids, you know. Both of your daughters. I just saw them the other day."

He nodded his head at that. But he didn't say anything. I kept driving.

When we passed the big Bay Mills Casino, he looked it over. Then he turned to take in the Wild Bluff golf course on the other side of the street. The back of Mission Hill rose into the darkness.

"My God," he finally said. "I can't believe what I'm seeing."

"Sorry you left now?"

He just shook his head again.

"We're almost there," I said.

"There's a rez out by Las Vegas," he said. "It's called Moapa Valley. You ever hear of it?"

"No."

"Instead of a golf course they've got a coal-burning plant. Right next to the houses. Down the road there's a place called Yucca Mountain. It's sacred to the Paiutes, so of course you know what the government is trying to do? They're trying to use it as a storage area for nuclear waste."

"Why are you telling me this?"

"I don't know. I'm just thinking, I hope these people know how good they've got it up here."

"These people work hard," I said. "They earned everything they've gotten."

I could feel him watching me for the next few moments. Then he gave out a tired laugh.

"Now I know why you're not a cop anymore. You had to quit so you could get into politics."

I fought off the urge to slam on the brakes right then. Bounce this joker's head right off the dashboard.

"Listen," I said, "you want to know why I'm not a cop anymore? Because I got shot." I was about to tell him about my partner lying dead on the floor next to me, and then about another cop who died on another floor, a lot closer to home. But I swallowed the words. It was none of his goddamned business.

"Just knock it off with the cop jokes," I said. "Okay?"

"Easy, friend. I didn't mean anything by it."

"We're not friends, Lou. But if you really came all this way to help Vinnie . . ."

"I did, man. I swear."

"Okay, then let's find him."

I kept going down the road. Neither of us spoke for a while.

"Vinnie says you went to prison because you got drunk and ran into a car," I finally said. "Is that accurate?"

"It's not polite to ask that."

"I'm asking anyway."

"It's accurate," he said. "I would give anything to take back that night."

"I also understand this was not your first brush with the law."

He let out a long breath. "You understand correctly. I've done a lot of things I'm not proud of, before I got clean."

"Did I not just watch you drink a couple of beers tonight?"

"I didn't say clean and sober. Just clean."

"I won't even ask," I said. "But you've been out for two years now, you said?"

"Coming up on two years, yeah. I'm already on the other side of sixty years old now. I don't figure I have much chance to do something good with my life. So when I heard about my son being in trouble, well, I just figured I should try doing one thing right."

"Okay," I said. "I get it."

"By the way, you didn't have to point out the fact that I've got grandkids sleeping in those houses back there. You don't think I know that? You don't think I recognize that that's the saddest thing in the world, that they've probably never even heard of me?"

"Fair enough," I said. "Sorry I got a little sensitive about the cop business."

"It's all right. I was out of line."

We passed the sign letting us know we had just left the reservation.

"This place we're going," Lou said, looking behind him, "it's not on the rez?"

"No, it's in Brimley. Just around the bay here."

"You gotta leave the rez to drink?"

"You can drink at the casino, or hell, you can drink at home if you want. But yeah, most of them seem to end up at the Cozy."

"The Cozy! Are you kidding me? That place is still around?"

A minute later, I pulled up in front of it. There were a good dozen cars in the lot. When we got out, Lou took a quick walk across the street, stopping over at the guardrail where the river came out from under the road and fed into the bay.

"Good old Whiskey River," he said, "and Whiskey Bay."

"You better not let Vinnie hear you say that."

"What do you mean?"

"It's Waishkey," I said. "Not whiskey."

"So what's the big deal about that?"

"Try drinking a few shots while he's in the same room. You'll find out."

"I can't wait." He turned back and looked out over the water.

"The water's pretty calm tonight," I said.

"I know that can change in a second. That's something you don't forget. But we didn't come here to gaze out at the lake, huh? This is the place where you figure Buck might buy his weed?"

"It's where he drinks most of the time. So I'm just guessing."

"All right, then. Let's go see if anybody's holding in there."

As we crossed the street, he stopped dead in the middle. It's the kind of thing you can do in a place like Brimley, Michigan. After midnight, or hell, pretty much anytime of the day for that matter.

"Something's not right here." He looked back and forth from one side of the road to the other.

"They dragged the Cozy over to this side a few years ago," I said. "Then they added on to it."

"So I'm not crazy," he said. "At least not in this particular case."

We finished crossing the street and went inside. As you step into the place, you're greeted by the heat and the noise, and you can see where they built on to the one side of it, turning the place into a genuine restaurant and not just a corner bar. Although you can eat dinner there with your family only up until nine o'clock. Then they kick out everybody who's underage and the only thing you can do there is drink. Either that or play pool on the one table in the middle of the room.

We picked out an empty table and sat down. A waitress came by and we ordered a couple of beers. I knew they wouldn't be real Canadians, but we didn't have much choice. As we sat there drinking, Lou looked the place over.

"How many Bay Mills' you figure are here right now?"

"Maybe half."

"Seriously? What about those guys right there?" He nodded to a table where six young men sat quietly. The empty bottles were gathered in the center of the table like bowling pins.

"Those are all guys who work at the casino," I said. "I saw them at the funeral."

"I forgot how much the blood gets mixed up here, man. A couple of them look whiter than you do."

"So, what next?"

"I think you should stay right here for a minute," he said. "No offense, but I don't think these guys are gonna believe you're really looking to score."

I couldn't argue with him. He walked over to the table. "Hey, little brothers," he began, putting on a big smile and talking so loud I could hear him across the room. "I'm from out of town, wondering if you can help me out."

He bent down for the rest and I couldn't make out a word. From the body language at the table, it didn't look like he was getting anywhere. But he was smiling when he wished them a good night and came back to our table.

"What happened?" I said.

"Not a damned thing. But I mentioned a sum of money that will get them thinking. At least one or two of them. Now all we have to do is wait."

It started getting a little too noisy to talk, so we just sat there for a while. That was fine with me, anyway. I still wasn't sure what to make of this guy.

I had to admit, though. His plan was solid. If Buck was involved in that drug ring, this was the best way to find out more. And there was no way I could do this on my own, even if I had thought of it.

We waited there another thirty or forty minutes. The group of six men got up to leave. They all went outside, and for a moment it looked like the whole thing had been a waste of our time. But then about two minutes later, one of the men came back inside. He looked over at us and gave us a little head bob. We got up and went to the side door.

When we were outside, he came out and joined us.

"Who's this?" he said, pointing at me.

"He's my friend," Lou said. "Don't worry, he's cool. He looks pretty straight, but he needs his herb, man. Helps him with the nausea."

"What, like you mean he's sick?"

Lou put a finger to his lips. "Let's not even go there," he said, "but yeah, it's pretty bad. You're really helping him out."

He reached into his pocket and pulled out a wad of money. It went into the young man's hand before I could see the bills, and something else was passed from the young man to Lou. For one brief second, I flashed back to the streets of Detroit. This was where I'd make my move, handcuff them both and call for backup.

"My man Buck says this is the place," Lou said. "I'm glad he was right."

"You know Buck?"

"We go way back. Haven't seen him in a while. Have you?"

"Not lately. He was supposed to be here tonight, but he's been gone for like three days."

"Ah, whatever," Lou said. "He'll turn up. You know how Buck is. So listen, if we need a little more of this, where can we go?"

"You come right here, man. I'm here most every night."

"No, no, I mean if we *really* need more, you know what I'm saying? There's gotta be somebody else up the line, right?"

"I don't know, man."

"Come on, be a good friend to a couple guys in need," he said. "Do it for Buck. Or hell, do it for a little finder's fee, eh?"

Another wad of money came out of the pocket and disappeared into the man's hand.

"All right, man. I'll give you an address. But it can't come from me, you got it? Tell him Buck sent you or something, but you can't give him my name."

"You haven't even told me your name," Lou said. "So how could I pass it along? You're as anonymous as the wind."

That seemed to satisfy him. Lou produced a folded receipt from his pocket, along with a pen. The man wrote down a name and address on the back of the receipt and passed it back to him. They exchanged a complicated handshake, then the man looked at me like he still wasn't sure what to make of me. Then he was gone.

"How much money did you give him?" I said.

"Don't worry about it," Lou said, holding the paper up in the cheap light. "If this works, it'll be a bargain."

"I'm serious. You already flew out here on short notice. That had to run a couple thousand dollars. Now you're here throwing money around like some kind of big shot."

"I got some saved," he said. "So what? What else am I gonna spend it on?"

Maybe child support, I was thinking, going back a number of years. But I let it go.

I looked at my watch. It was after one o'clock now. Inside the Cozy, somebody started the jukebox and the bass notes came rumbling out under our feet.

"I haven't been to the Soo in years," he said, handing me the paper. "You think you can find this address?"

"I'm sure I can." I didn't even bother looking at it.

"Then it's your turn," he said. "Mr. Ex-cop. Let's go pay this guy a visit, see how good you are at sweating a suspect."

CHAPTER EIGHT

I drove east through the darkness, with Vinnie's long-lost father sitting in the passenger seat. I looked over at him more than once just to confirm to myself that this was really happening. He sat there in complete silence, looking out the window at the landscape he hadn't seen in almost thirty years.

We were alone on the road until a car finally came toward us. He had his high beams on and it woke Lou from his trance. He patted his shirt pocket and took out the bag he had bought from the young seller at the Cozy. He flipped on the interior light, held the bag up, shook the contents in the harsh glare for a few seconds, then turned the light back off.

"Good stuff?" I said.

"It's not ditchweed, that's for sure."

"From Canada, you think?"

"Definitely hydro. Very clean. So yeah, maybe Canada."

"It could have come over on one of those planes," I said.

"Not the last plane, I'm thinking. The cops are smoking that stuff right now."

I let that one go. He didn't.

"You ever do that?"

"Do what?"

"Find a big ol' load of the green stuff."

"Not a big load," I said. "Maybe an ounce or two in somebody's car."

"Did it all go into evidence?"

I looked over at him.

"I won't tell anybody," he said. "I'm just wondering."

"Yes, it all went into evidence."

He made a clicking sound and shook his head. Like, what a waste.

"What's the big deal with this stuff, anyway?" I said. "Why fly it over from Canada when you can grow it in your own basement?"

"Who says you can do that?"

"Well, it's not legal, of course. But, I mean, I don't know what it's like out in Nevada. Here, people are getting pretty loose about it."

"You think so? They're getting loose?"

"Overall, yeah."

"So you probably won't have the Michigan State troopers knocking on your door, is that what you're saying?"

"I'm just saying—"

"How about the feds? Are they 'pretty loose' on it, too?"

"Not the feds so much, no."

"Yeah, not so much. If they get you in their sights, they'll still come to your door, right? But instead of knocking they'll bust it right down. Shoot your goddamned dog right in front of you. Then they'll take your house. Take your kids away, even. Burn your whole life down, leave nothing but a pile of ashes. All because you've got three pot plants in your basement."

"I don't think that—"

"I've seen it happen, Alex. Not to me personally, but I know people who've lost everything. Got sent away for a decade or more. So I don't have to wonder why these guys would rather just fly the stuff in from Canada. There you don't have the Mounties breaking in your door with their guns blazing. In fact, it might as well be legal."

"Okay, I understand what you're saying. I'm not defending what the feds do. Not if they're breaking down the door and shooting your dog."

"You even it up on both sides, at least, then you don't have people moving stuff across the border. You realize it doesn't matter what the stuff is, right? It could be bubble gum, for God's sake. As long as people want it and it's more legal on one side than the other . . ."

"I know," I said. "You don't have to tell me."

"It's kind of the golden age for sellers right now. More general acceptance means more people smoking it. Which means a lot more sales for them until it finally becomes legal and Phillip Morris puts them out of business."

"How come you know so much about selling pot?"

"I don't sell, if that's what you mean. Never did."

Then my cell phone rang and I had to spend the next few moments locating the damned thing on the floor.

"Mr. McKnight, I'm returning your call." It was Chief Benally.

"Hello, Chief," I said, trying to remember why the hell I had called him. This was earlier in the day, before I had found Vinnie's father and everything had taken such a sudden left turn.

"What's going on? My officer said you wished to speak to me."

"I guess I was just wondering if you had heard anything from Vinnie yet." I sensed Lou sitting up straight and leaning closer.

"I told you I'd be in touch if I heard anything. Where are you right now, anyway? You sound like you're in your vehicle."

"I'm just heading into town," I said, looking over at Lou. He gave me a double wave of his hands, like a man signaling to the bartender not to tell his wife he's there.

"Kinda late, isn't it?"

"I'm a night owl, Chief. But I appreciate you calling me back."

"I'm dead serious," he said. "You're not out there trying to find Vinnie, are you?"

"I'm driving to the Soo. I can't imagine why he'd be there. Unless there's something you're not telling me."

The line was silent for a few seconds. I could picture him on the other end, closing his eyes and counting to three.

"I think I've been very up front with you," he finally said. "I was hoping for the same in return."

"I'll try to do the same," I said, not quite sure what else to say. "Not that I'm in the loop here. At all."

He hesitated again, but then he let me off the hook and wished me a good night.

"Which chief are we talking about?" Lou said as I put the phone down.

"Bay Mills. Chief Benally."

"Benally? I don't know that name."

"He's not a local. They brought him in from Wisconsin."

"Are you kidding me? A foreigner is running the Bay Mills police?"

"I said Wisconsin, not France."

"That's been a steady gig for *somebody* on the rez ever since they formed the department."

"Maybe getting some new blood is a good idea, then."

He shook his head at that one. "I can't believe it."

"I notice you didn't want him to know you were in the truck with me. You were assuming he'd remember you?"

"There'd be a few of the old-timers who'd be surprised to see me around, put it that way. Even if this guy didn't grow up on the rez, I'm sure he's got a few other guys around him who have."

"So what's the big deal? What happens if some of these old-timers find out you're back after all these years?"

"I think we'll probably find out eventually," he said. "I just don't see any reason to flag down the welcome wagon."

I looked over at him, wondering just how high the pile of ashes was from all of the bridges he had burned in his life. I kept driving down that dark empty road, listening to his breathing. He sounded tired. It was a long, long day for him, one that had started on the other side of the country, but I didn't figure he was ready to rest. Not quite yet.

I hit the highway and gunned it north until we reached the first exit.

"Sault Ste. Marie, Michigan," he said as we pulled onto the side streets. "I spent a few years drinking in the bars there. I wonder how many are left."

"I'm guessing one or two of them are still around." I looped up to Ashmun Street and headed into the downtown area, or what you'd call downtown if the Soo were big enough to have one. We were looking for a Mr. Andy Dukes, apparently the man to see for high-quality marijuana if you're in Sault Ste. Marie. He lived on Hursley Street. I vaguely remembered that street hitting Ashmun somewhere around the power canal.

We passed a few cars coming in the opposite direction. It was just after 1:30 A.M. now. Almost closing time, but all of the good bars were down this way on Portage Street so this would be the one part of town still awake. As if to make that point, a solitary Soo police car sat still and dark in front of the theater, waiting for somebody with beer-dulled senses to come roaring by.

The bridge over the power canal was just ahead of us. That's when I saw the turn for Hursley Street, the very last turn before the canal. I took the right and drove down the street. Once we had put Ashmun behind us, it quickly became two parallel rows of sub-urban houses, not much different from any other street in any other town. Although even now on a warm July night, you could see how the long winters had taken their toll on these houses. There wasn't a single sheet of siding or a single window frame that didn't bear the scars.

"Not the ritziest street in the world," Lou said. "Not for a suc-cessful pot dealer."

"This town doesn't do ritzy."

"You're right about that. Some things don't change."

"Pot dealers like to stay under the radar, even if they *can* afford a mansion."

Lou looked at me and laughed. "Okay, Detective Friday. What-ever you say."

I shook my head.

"That was from *Dragnet*. Gannon and Friday."

"Yeah, I got the reference."

"Which house are we looking for, anyway?"

I slowed down and began checking the house numbers. We found the one we wanted a block and a half down, on the north side of the street. I rolled to a slow stop, turned off my lights and then the ignition. We sat there for a while, letting our eyes adjust to the darkness and listening to the warm engine ticking.

The house was one of several in a row that seemed to have been built with the exact same plan, probably by the same builder in the same year. Dukes' was two stories high, and it looked tall and narrow as it stretched back to make the most of the lot. There was an enclosed front porch, pretty standard for any house this far north, and there was just enough room on each side of the house for a driveway, with a detached garage in the back. Two beat-up old lawn chairs sat empty in the front yard.

The house was completely and utterly dark. There was no car in the driveway or parked immediately out front on the street. We couldn't tell if there was a car in the garage.

"Doesn't look like anybody's home," Lou said.

"It is kinda late. Maybe he's asleep."

"This is prime time for a pot dealer."

"What do you say we go knock on the door, just to make sure?"

"You cops don't have any manners at all," he said, but he got out and went right along with me. I knocked on the exterior front door first, then opened it and stepped onto the porch. A distant memory told me this wouldn't technically be illegal entry, although I may have had that wrong. Not that it mattered anyway. There was a doorbell next to the interior door. When I pushed it, I heard the bell ringing somewhere deep in the house. Then there was nothing but silence. As I left, I looked around the porch and saw a great mess of old furniture, broken-down antiques and toys and God knows what else.

I looked around the side of the house and spotted Lou out back by the garage. He was peeking through the window.

"There's just junk in there," he said as he rejoined me. "No car. You think he ran?"

"If he knows what happened at the airport, I guess I wouldn't be surprised."

"But he'd only run if he thought it would come back on him, right?"

I nodded, thinking it over.

"Either the cops connecting him to it," Lou said, "or somebody else. Somebody a lot worse."

"I don't know," I said. "Seems like you'd have to have a pretty active imagination to think they'd be coming after you, just because you happened to be in the same supply chain."

"Unless he was a little more involved in it."

"Or maybe *we're* the ones with the active imaginations," I said. "He could just be out at one of the bars. They don't close for a few more minutes."

"We could wait," Lou said, "unless you feel like talking to one of his neighbors."

The porch light was on in the house to the left, but otherwise the place was dark. The house on the right had no exterior light at all, but we could make out a flickering blue glow coming through the side window.

"Looks like somebody's still up over here," Lou said, "watching a little late-night TV. Think he'd mind a visit?"

I crossed the front lawn and driveway. I was just about to knock on the door when I saw that this house actually had a doorbell on the exterior. An amazing innovation. I pressed it and heard a two-tone chime going off inside the house. Lou was standing right next to me, and for a moment I wondered what we'd look like standing there at somebody's door at almost two in the morning, my beaten-up ex-catcher ex-cop white face next to Lou's sun-ravaged version of an old Indian. If it was a woman here in the house alone, say, then I could imagine her being scared right out of her socks.

A light came on outside, just about blinding us. The exterior door opened and the late-night television watcher looked out at us. It was a man, and then some. He had to go around two hundred and a half, a lot of it beer gut, but he also had hamhocks for arms, with faded tattoos on either side. He was wearing an almost-white undershirt and black pants that sagged under his belly.

"Who are you guys?" he said. He was unshaven and the hair he had left on his head was slicked back. "What the hell do you want?"

"We're looking for your next-door neighbor," I said. "Andy Dukes. Do you happen to know where he is?"

"He left," the man said. "He drove to Texas a couple of days ago. I got no idea when he'll be back. If ever."

"Do you know of any way to get in touch with him?"

"I told you, he's gone. I got no phone number. No address. No nothing."

"I'm smelling a little something in the air," Lou said. He took a step closer and tried to peek around him, into the house. "I take it you're a loyal customer of Mr. Dukes?"

"I don't know what the hell you're talking about," the man said. "I think you guys should leave."

"If you're not a customer, then maybe you sell some yourself? What do you say?"

The man was flexing his forearms and looked about ready to jump on us both at the same time. But Lou stepped even closer to him.

"Come on, friend," he said. "We're just looking to take the edge off, okay?"

"I'm not your friend," the man said, "and I still don't know what you're talking about. So why don't you get the hell out of here?"

"Can we leave a phone number in case you hear from—"

"I told you, he's gone and I don't expect to have any contact with him."

"Okay," Lou said, nodding slowly. "Whatever you say. Sorry to disturb you, friend. Please have a nice night."

The man took a step backward and closed the door in Lou's face.

"Charming gentleman," Lou said as we walked back to the truck. "It's a shame we didn't have more time to talk."

"Why were you trying to buy off him?"

"I was testing him. I wanted to see if he'd sweat. Hell, maybe he *does* sell. Maybe his next-door neighbor is his partner."

"Or maybe he just gets paid by the ounce," I said, "for being so good about taking messages."

"He'd make a great receptionist, wouldn't he?"

When we were back in the truck, we sat there for a while longer, looking at the two houses. Lou leaned his head back against the seat. It was obvious he was running out of gas.

"You've had a pretty long day," I said. "Let's get some sleep. Tomorrow morning, we'll figure out what to do next."

He banged his fist against the dashboard, but he didn't argue with me.

I pulled out onto the street. He looked at the two houses one more time as we drove by. He didn't say a word as we drove through Sault Ste. Marie, the streetlights flickering across his face. He stared straight ahead and stayed silent as we left town and found that empty road back to Paradise, running across the hayfields and through the trees, then rounding the bay with the water stretching out into the darkness.

I took us back on the northern route, through the reservation.

"Let's stop at the casino," he said. "The one where Vinnie works at."

"I've already been there. Nobody could help me."

"Even so. I wouldn't mind seeing where my son works. Get a feel for the place. Hell, maybe something new will occur to us."

It sounded like another lap around a track I'd already been on. But I had no better ideas at the moment, so I slowed down as we came around the bend and pulled into the parking lot. The Bay Mills Casino was lit up and shining in the darkness. Not Vegas level, of course, but as bright as anything else you'll ever see up here. The lot was mostly full at the end of a beautiful summer day. Plenty of visitors to the Upper Peninsula who find out there's not a whole hell of a lot to do after dark aside from drinking. I parked and we went inside. Instead of going right into the gaming area, Lou wandered around the lobby for a minute, looking up at the giant moose head mounted over the fireplace, then going down the line of pictures in the hallway. There were portraits of the Bay Mills Executive Council going back a few years, and Lou studied each quintet carefully.

"I went to school with a couple of these guys," he said, more to himself than to me. "Looks like they're doing just fine."

I sensed some movement to our left, turned and saw two old-timers watching us. I elbowed Lou, but as soon as he turned to see what I was looking at, the two old-timers did a quick 180 and disappeared.

"Old friends of yours?"

"I kinda doubt it. But whatever. What exactly does Vinnie do here?"

"He's been a blackjack dealer here for years. He'll move over to pit boss if they need him, but he still likes dealing. He's probably the best they've got here."

"Taking money from white tourists. That's quite a gig."

"Nobody's making them play. Sometimes they even win."

He looked at me. "Yeah, sometimes. Look at this place and tell me just how often you think that happens. Hell, come to Vegas sometime."

"Do you want to see where he deals, or not?"

"Yes, I do."

I led him around the corner, past the slot machines, to the table games. There was a circle of people around the roulette table, another playing craps. Then we hit the line of blackjack tables. Most of them were full. Lou found two empty seats at a two-dollar table and he sat down.

"Couple of hands," he said to me. "Just to clear our heads."

I took the spot next to him. Lou took out a hundred-dollar bill and put it on the table. I went for my wallet and he stopped me.

"I've got you covered," he said. "We won't be here long."

The dealer was a woman in her thirties, a tribal member of course, although like most people up here you could see the European influence on her features. A little German here, a little Finnish there, the intermarriages going back through the generations.

Her name card said "Jennie." She gave us an all-business smile and made change for Lou's hundred. He slid half the chips over to me without looking at them.

She was close to the end of her decks, so we got only two hands in before she had to shuffle. That was Lou's chance for a little small talk.

"Nice place you got here, Jennie."

"Where are you from?" She handled the cards like she'd done this a few thousand times before.

"Vegas."

"You must play a lot out there."

"I try not to. I know it's a losing proposition."

She smiled and shrugged that off, offering Lou the yellow cut card. Lou placed it in the deck and she completed the cut.

"You know Vinnie?"

She paused at that. There was a subtle change in her body language, then she was right back to all-business again. "Vinnie LeBlanc?"

"Yeah, Vinnie LeBlanc."

"He's a dealer here, too. I haven't seen him in a while. His mother died."

"You must be a cousin," Lou said.

"Everybody's a cousin up here. But maybe you want to talk to Phil, sir."

She tilted her head and called his name without taking her eyes off the cards. A dealer never takes his or her eyes off the cards when they're in play, after all. We finished up the hand and then Lou thanked her by sliding her the rest of his chips. I did the same. As we stood up, the pit boss came out with his head cocked, waiting for our story. I knew him well enough to say hello to, and in fact he was the exact same pit boss I had taken aside just a few days ago.

"You're Alex," he said to me, looking right past Lou. "Vinnie's friend, right? We already had this conversation, remember? I have no idea where he could be."

"I guess we're just stopping by again," I said, "on the off chance you might have heard something new."

"No, not a word," he said, looking back and forth between us. His eyes narrowed as he focused on Lou. "Have we met before?"

"Maybe a long time ago. Last time I was here, this place wasn't even built yet."

"You're Bay Mills?"

He took a few seconds to answer that one. The pit boss and I both waited while everyone else around us kept doing their casino business.

"No," Lou finally said. "I'm not. I thought I still might be, but no."

The man gave him a strange look.

"I appreciate your time," Lou said. "I'll let you go back to making money. That's a nice golf course you've got across the street, too."

The pit boss kept waiting for the punch line, or for Lou to start making some kind of sense maybe, but Lou just turned and walked away.

"Don't mind him," I said to the man. "He's had a long day."

When I caught up to him I grabbed his arm.

"What the hell?" I said. "Was all of that really necessary?"

"Did you notice?" he said, shaking his arm free. "As soon as I said his name, it was like a big red flag went up. Like I'm under suspicion all of a sudden, just for asking about my own son."

"Nobody in there knows he's your son. They're just looking out for him."

"I wanted to find him," he said. "*Today.* I wanted to get off the plane and find Vinnie."

There were a dozen comebacks I could have made to that one, but I let it go. Whatever the circumstances, however belated the effort, he was here to help Vinnie, and that was the one thing we could agree on.

"Let's get out of here," he said. "Figure out what to do next."

We went outside. We weren't ten steps from the door when a car pulled up. A black four-door sedan that looked sort of like an unmarked police car, and I was already getting our story ready. But when the car stopped, the driver's-side door opened, and I recognized the man who stepped out. He had long gray hair tied behind his head, like a lot of the old-timers around here. I'd see him over at Vinnie's mother's house every time I went there. He would nod to me once in a while, but I don't think he ever said one word to my face.

"Lou LeBlanc," the man said, coming around the front of the car. "It *is* you. I thought those guys must be losing their minds."

"Henry," Lou said. "It's good to see you."

"Yeah, like hell. What are you doing here?"

"Alex, this is Henry Carrick," he said to me. "One of Buck's uncles, I believe."

"I'll ask you again," the man said. "What are you doing here?"

"I'm looking for my son," Lou said. "Excuse me, I'm looking for my son *and* your nephew."

"I'm amazed you'd even show your face around here," the man finally said. "I mean, hell, I'm amazed you're still walking around with all your teeth. If some of the other guys see you here—"

"Yeah, go give them a call," Lou said. "Round up every last one of them. In the meantime, I see you're all talk. Just like always."

"You're banned from the reservation, LeBlanc. You know that. Hell, you're banned from the whole state. I thought that was made clear when you got run out of here."

"I didn't get run out of here," Lou said, stepping closer to him.

"Okay, you ran away with your tail between your legs," the man said. "Like a beaten animal. However you want to put it, the result was the same. You were supposed to leave and never come back."

"I stayed away for as long as Nika was alive. I kept my promise."

"Don't you even dare say her name. Not anywhere on this reservation. Do you understand me?"

"She was my wife, Carrick. She chose me. Not you."

"And look how well that turned out."

Lou grabbed him by the collar. I took a step forward and Lou put out his other hand to stop me.

"This is between two old friends," he said to me. "Just stay out of it."

At that point, I would have been happy to do so. Hell, I would have just driven home and left the two of them there to have it out. But we were starting to draw a small crowd of people coming in and out of the casino. I couldn't just let him kill this guy, anyway. Which is exactly what would have happened if they'd started swinging at each other.

"We don't have time for this," I said. "We've got more important things to do."

Lou finally let the man go and tapped him lightly on the cheek.

"It still must hurt," Lou said. "What is it, forty years now? The love of your life and she dropped you like a hot rock."

"You've got five minutes to get off the rez."

"Yeah, I know," Lou said, walking away. "And then you'll call the whole gang to come beat me up. I heard you the first time."

"You got a lot of nerve, too," he said. "Talking about Vinnie and Buck, like we're not doing everything we can to find them. This from a man who abandoned his whole family."

Lou stopped. Mr. Carrick finally found some degree of sense and went around to the other side of the car, putting two and a half tons of metal between himself and a prison-hardened man who probably could have taken him apart with his bare hands.

"You've been warned," the man said. He got into his car and drove away. The people who had gathered around us continued on, into or away from the casino.

"You did mention the welcome wagon," I said as we walked back to my truck. "I guess that was it."

"I'm obviously not welcome here," he said. "But can we make one more quick stop?"

"Where's that?"

"I just want to say hello to her. And goodbye. One more time."

I stopped there in the middle of the lot and looked at him. This was exactly what Vinnie had asked to do.

"Come on," I said. "Get in."

A few minutes later, we were up on top of Mission Hill. It was just as dark and empty as that night I had brought Vinnie up here.

Once again, I stayed by the truck and watched a lonely LaBlanc man make his way through the graveyard to find the stone next to the freshly turned earth. Once again, it was a clear summer night and I could see all the way across to the blinking lights on top of the wind turbines in Canada.

When he was done, he got back into the truck and we rode down to the bottom of the hill, then off the reservation. To Paradise.

He was already reaching for his bag as I drove up toward Vinnie's cabin.

"I've got an empty cabin just down the road," I said. "I think you should stay there."

Either he agreed with me or he was too tired to fight about it. He sat back as I drove him around the bend to the first of the five rental cabins. I went inside with him and showed him where everything was. He put his bag down and sat in one of the chairs. Then he took out little plastic baggie from his coat pocket.

"Is it cool if I smoke in here?"

"A joint, you mean? You're gonna smoke a joint now?"

"I just need one," he said. "It's been a hell of a day."

"This is none of my business, but you started out as 'clean and sober,' and then that got downgraded to just clean, right? So now you're what? Neither?"

"I'm still clean, Alex. Clean inside and out. It's just marijuana."

"Yeah, just marijuana," I said. "Tell that to those dead men on the runway."

He just looked at me. I knew we were about two seconds away from more of the ex-cop versus ex-con routine, so I decided to bail out and let us both get some sleep.

I drove back down to my cabin. Before going inside, I stood there for a while and let the darkness and the silence close in around me. There were clouds moving quickly across a tilting half-moon. The air was still almost warm. Then the wind picked up and as it hit my face it brought along an unmistakable message. It may be July, and it may feel like summer just got here, but the end is already on its way. The cold, the snow, the ice, the natural basic state of this place, it is right around the corner.

I took a quick walk back to Vinnie's cabin. Nothing had changed. I walked back to my own place, hoping this much exercise would help me get to sleep. I was expecting a losing battle on that front, but I must have been exhausted because I dropped right off. I had all the bad dreams I would have bet money on having, but somewhere in the night a brilliant idea came to me. Brilliant for me, at least, and thank God it was still with me when I woke up.

As I opened my eyes to the sunlight, I still had no idea where Vinnie was. But I knew exactly where Lou and I needed to go.

CHAPTER NINE

It was almost eight o'clock in the morning when I got into the truck and drove down to the next cabin. I knocked on the door, but there was no answer. I knocked again, then pushed the door open and peeked inside. I could see Lou's bag still on the table, and it looked like he had been making coffee in the kitchen. There was still a strong scent of marijuana in the air, just what I needed for the next rental guest.

"Lou, are you in here?"

I gave the place a quick once-over, including the bathroom. He wasn't in the cabin. I opened all the windows on my way out.

I was just about to go down to Vinnie's cabin to see if the rental car was still there, but then I saw Lou walking down the road toward me. He was coming from the dead-end direction. The other cabins were up that way and then the road just gave up and the forest took over.

"Good morning," he said. "Are all those cabins yours?"

"Yes."

"I didn't know you had renters. There were some nice old ladies in the next cabin up, but I believe I probably scared them to death."

The bird-watchers, I thought. They were here to observe the piping plovers or some such thing, and Lou was probably right about scaring them.

"I'll go tell them you're harmless later," I said. "But never mind that. I've got a question for you."

"Shoot."

"When we were talking to that guy last night, Mr. Dukes' next-door neighbor, did his whole speech sound a little . . . rehearsed to you?"

"Like he had it in a can, ready to go? Yeah, of course it did. I thought that was obvious."

"He didn't even ask us why the hell we were ringing his doorbell at two in the morning. Did you notice that? He was too busy giving us the party line. But why did he even do that? Why tell us that Dukes drove to Texas? What's the point?"

"Probably because Dukes wanted to cover his tracks. He skipped town and he wanted his neighbor to feed people a false story."

"You mean, he's not really in Texas."

"I would bet he's not, no."

"Okay, so we agree on that. Let's go."

"Where are we going?"

"To go talk to Mr. Dukes," I said. "But I think we should take your rental car."

I had Lou drive through the McDonald's in Sault Ste. Marie to get us some breakfast to go. I looked at my watch and wondered when your average pot dealer would get out of bed.

"So tell me why we're back here," Lou said to me as he went through the bags of food. "I'm not quite seeing it yet."

"Put yourself in his shoes," I said. "A couple of people in your supply chain get murdered. If you're scared enough by that, and if you're smart enough, what do you do?"

"I get the hell out of town."

"Do you really pack up everything in your car and drive a thousand miles to, say, Florida? Leave a fake story behind to make people think you're in Texas?"

"Maybe. Although hell, I probably wouldn't even try to bother with that last part. I'd just go."

"All right, so what if you're not quite scared enough? Or not quite smart enough? Or both?"

"I'm still not following you."

"Look, you *live* here. You've got a good business going. You know something bad happened, but what if you're not absolutely sure it's going to find its way to you."

He mulled it over for a while. Then it came to him.

"You don't go anywhere," he said. "You just make it look that way. You get your neighbor to act as your beard for a few days, and you see what happens."

"Maybe you even keep the sales going," I said. "No need to shut down the cash flow, right?"

"Okay, so your neighbor's selling for you, you're saying. As long as the customers are people he can trust. If it's a stranger who shows up, then he just sends the bastard packing, tells him you're long gone and you're not coming back."

"That's how you'd play it halfway," I said. "You stay in business, but you keep your eyes open for trouble."

"So while your neighbor's keeping the business going, where does that leave you? Where are you hiding?"

"Where else?"

He thought about it, and this time it took him only a second.

"Dukes is in the neighbor's house," he said. "He was there last night when we knocked on the door."

"That part I'm just guessing. But how else are you gonna keep the customers straight? He was probably watching us from a window."

"God damn," he said. "You just might be right."

A few minutes later, we were on the other side of town. We drove down that same street, the modest rows of houses looking all the more threadbare in the light of day. We stopped a few houses short, pulled over, and made sure we had a good sight line. This was why we had the rental car that day, in case the neighbor had noticed my truck well enough to remember it. I wouldn't have put money on him being half that sharp, but there was no reason to take any chances.

Dukes' house still looked abandoned, and the neighbor's house looked just as quiet. But then it wasn't even nine o'clock yet.

"That car in front," Lou said, pointing to an old gray beater. "That's gotta be the neighbor's, right? Dukes' car is probably in the neighbor's garage."

"If we knew what kind of car he had, we could check."

"Yeah, we just have to wait to see what happens."

"That's the part I'm gonna hate," I said. "I never did like stakeouts."

"Well, if prison teaches you one thing, it's how to wait. Unless you have another idea."

"We could go break the door down and start counting heads. One, I'm wrong. Two, I'm right."

"I'm pretty sure that could get us arrested," he said. "Unless they've changed the laws around here."

"Arrested or killed. I wouldn't be surprised if they're armed."

"Oh, I'm sure of it."

"I've already been shot twice," I said. "I think that's probably enough."

We sat there for a long time. I don't know exactly how long, because I was doing everything I could to turn off the clock in my brain. I leaned back in the passenger seat, my eyes just high enough to see over the dashboard. For all of his talk about learning how to wait in prison, Lou seemed even more anxious than I was. In the end, we agreed to take turns watching the houses while the other closed his eyes for a while and recharged his batteries. It made it a lot easier, but it still wasn't going to rank as one of my favorite ways to spend a summer morning.

"Did it really happen twice?" he said, finally breaking the silence.

"What's that?"

"You said you got shot twice."

"I shouldn't have brought it up."

"Fair enough. Whatever."

More silence.

"The first time was on the job," I said after a few more minutes. "I let my guard down. We both did, my partner and I. He didn't survive it."

"But you did. And you blame yourself."

I looked over at him.

"Which is only natural," he said. "Even though I'm sure it's wrong."

I didn't try to argue. It was a thousand sleepless nights' worth of old ground for me, and I had no desire to go over it again.

"That was the first time," he said. "What about the second?"

"That was pretty recent. In fact, I'm not sure my doctor would love me doing this right now."

A car came by. It was going slow, but it didn't stop. A few minutes later, it came by again, obviously having taken one lap around the block. We both kept our heads down as the car pulled over a few spots ahead of us. The driver got out. He was young and white and he had a ratty blond ponytail down his back. He wasn't actually wearing a ratty denim jacket with a big embroidered cannabis plant on the back, but something told me he had one at home.

"And here we go," I said. "If anybody's sleeping late in there, they're about to be woken up."

He went to Dukes' door and knocked. When nobody answered, he started looking around the place like his dealer might be around the side of the house, washing his car or something. That's when the door to the neighbor's house opened. Our big friend stood in the doorway. He was still wearing the same outfit, undershirt and black pants. Hell, he'd probably slept in it. Maybe right there in front of the television set, after Lou and I had left. He called over and the customer just about jumped out of his skin. A few words were exchanged. Then the customer went over to the other house and went inside. The neighbor took a careful look up and down the street. Then he closed the door.

"Good call swapping the vehicles," Lou said. "This guy probably would have made us in the truck."

As we watched the house, I tried to imagine each step of the transaction. You make your buy. Then you get the hell out, right? You don't stick around and chat afterward.

"So far your theory is holding up," Lou said. "Now as soon as this guy leaves, we go knock on the door again, right? Have you figured out what you're going to say yet?"

"Something friendly yet persuasive," I said. "My specialty."

Before another word was spoken, we saw a man moving between the two houses. It wasn't the neighbor. It wasn't the customer. It was a third man, taller and thinner than the other two. He moved quickly, glancing out at the street as he disappeared behind the other house.

"That's gotta be Dukes," I said. "What do you say we call an audible?"

"I'm right behind you."

We both got out of the car and walked down the street, trying to be quick and smooth and unassuming all at the same time. He's going into his house to get some of his product, I thought. Then he'll come right back out and retrace his steps to the neighbor's house. That'll be our chance to stop him, and once we do that, we have to convince him as quickly as possible that we're just here to talk.

We got up to the neighbor's house. I willed the front door to stay shut, the neighbor and the customer safely inside, waiting for Dukes to make his way back with a bag of the good stuff. When we got to Dukes' house, Lou gestured to the far side and went across the front lawn, keeping his head down. Now we were split up and approaching him from both sides of the house.

I heard the back door opening and I had to make a quick decision. There was no need to give the man a heart attack, but at the same time it would be better to surprise him than to give him time to react.

Okay, maybe you didn't quite think this through, I told myself. Maybe you're about to force the man to do something stupid.

I kept my back pressed against the side of the house. Wait until he's close, I thought, then step calmly around the corner. Hands up, showing him you're unarmed, but still ready for anything. Tell him you just want to talk to him. Nobody gets hurt. Piece of cake, just like that.

I waited for the sound of his footsteps. Where the hell was he? Was he walking on the grass? Hell with it. Time to move.

I stepped around the corner and saw him standing a good eight feet away from me. Not the distance I had planned.

"Mr. Dukes," I said, barreling right ahead. "I need a word with you."

He was tall and gangly enough to do a good Ichabod Crane impression, complete with the expression of wide-eyed, pants-pissing shock. He was wearing an untucked striped rugby shirt with the sleeves rolled up, and as he took one step backward he reached under his shirttails and drew out a revolver.

"Don't shoot!" I said, already bracing myself for what I knew was coming.

He barely had time to raise the gun when Lou was already on top of him. Lou spun him around and grabbed the gun with his left hand, giving Dukes a quick chop to the throat with his right. It wasn't deadly force, just enough to surprise him and to loosen his grip on the revolver. As Dukes doubled over, Lou gave him a little hip check and knocked him to his knees.

"This thing is cocked," Lou said, as he carefully let the hammer down. Then he flipped open the cylinder. "And loaded. What were you just about to do?"

Dukes was trying hard to catch his breath, one hand on his throat and the other on the ground.

"I asked you a question," Lou said. "Were you seriously going to shoot us just now? Was that your plan?"

Dukes shook his head, but he still couldn't speak.

"Not to mention having a cocked pistol stuck down your goddamned pants," Lou said. "You're lucky you didn't blow your own dick off."

"Lou, take it easy," I said. It was finally starting to catch up to me, the simple fact that this man on the ground probably would have shot me if Lou hadn't stopped him.

"Take it easy yourself," Lou said. "We could both be lying dead on the ground right now."

"I didn't mean it," Dukes said, finally finding his voice. "I'm sorry. You guys just scared me. I didn't mean to hurt anybody, I swear."

"Oh just shut up," Lou said. "I oughta put one through your head just for being such a dumbass. We came here to talk to you, all right?"

Dukes swallowed hard as he looked back and forth between us. That's when his neighbor came bursting out his back door, holding a baseball bat.

"Put the bat down!" Lou said, pointing the gun at him. "What the hell is wrong with you?"

"Put it down, Eddie!" Dukes was making no effort to get up yet. "For God's sake, put it down!"

Neighbor Eddie did as he was told. He stood there on the other side of the driveway, his hands in the air and the bat at his feet. I looked around and wondered if the police cars would be here in two minutes or just one. But the street looked quiet.

"Can we take this inside," I said, "before we all get arrested?"

We led them back into Eddie's house. The customer took one look at us and the gun in Lou's hand and bolted out the front door. Which was fine by me. Lou told the two men to make themselves comfortable on the sofa. I stayed on my feet, pacing back and forth across the room and trying to bring my heart rate back into double digits. Lou just stood there glaring down at both men, his arms folded and the gun still in his right hand. Never mind the fact that we had just spent most of the last twenty-four hours together . . . The way he had disarmed the man, and now the absolute calm on that ageless weathered face, made me realize how little I really knew about him.

"Lou," I said, "you can put the gun away."

"I'll keep it right here, Alex. We don't want these gentlemen to get any funny ideas."

"Okay, now you sound like a gangster. We all need to turn it down a notch."

"This clown brought the gun into the equation," Lou said, nodding toward Dukes. "It wasn't our idea."

"The man is scared out of his mind," I said, and as I looked down at him I could see how true that was. His hands were shaking so badly that he could barely keep them together. Beside him, Eddie was trying to look small and inconspicuous, probably for the first time in his life. He was failing miserably.

"What are you scared of?" Lou asked Dukes.

He started fumbling around for an answer, but it was like he just couldn't put the sounds together into words.

"Okay, stop," I said. "We're not here to hurt you, I swear. Just take a breath."

He nodded his head and did his best to compose himself. As he did, I took a good look around Eddie's house. It was the house of a man living alone, that much was obvious. The furniture was ugly and simple. There was a big-screen television across from the couch and a collection of empty beer cans on either side table. The carpet needed vacuuming. *Everything* needed vacuuming, including the air itself. On what passed as a dining room table, there were newspapers and magazines and a small scale. Something told me it wasn't a Weight Watcher's scale for measuring out food portions.

I grabbed one of the dining room chairs and positioned it in front of the two men.

"Let me start," I said. "My name is Alex. I know your name is Andy Dukes and this man here is Eddie, right?"

They both nodded.

"We're looking for two men. One is named Vinnie LeBlanc, the other is Buck Carrick. They're both from Bay Mills. Do either of those names mean anything to you?"

"No," Dukes said. "No, I swear." He looked me in the eye for the first time since sitting down. He didn't look away. I would have bet everything I owned that he was lying to me.

Lou obviously had the same impression, because he went right over to Dukes and put the revolver to his temple.

"You know how much I hate liars?" Lou said.

Eddie made a move to get up.

"Sit down or I'll shoot both of you."

Eddie sat back down and closed his eyes. He was shaking just as badly as Dukes now.

"Lou, for the last time," I said, wondering how many felonies we'd actually end up committing that day, "put the gun away before somebody gets killed."

This was not going the way I had planned it, to say the least. This was light-years away from any possible way I would have imagined it. But we were here and the gun was in Lou's hand and I figured, what the hell. If there was ever a time for a little game of good cop/bad cop . . .

"I don't want him to shoot you," I said, "but I honestly think he might if you lie to us again."

"What do you want from me?" Dukes said. "Who are you guys?"

"I told you, I'm a friend of Vinnie LeBlanc's. This is his father. He's going to try to cool it for a minute so you can talk."

Lou looked over at me for a moment, then he took a step backward.

"Buck Carrick is Vinnie's cousin," I said. "We have reason to believe that Buck may have been at the Newberry airport the other night when those five men all had their shootout. We know that the airplane was carrying in marijuana from Canada, and we know that you're a dealer."

"Who told you that?"

"One of your customers. It doesn't matter."

"Who was it?"

"I told you, it doesn't matter. What matters is that you're obviously connected to what happened at the airport. If you weren't, you wouldn't be hiding in your next-door neighbor's house."

"I'm not connected to it. I swear I'm not."

"Here's a little tip," I said, sneaking a quick look at Lou. "Every time you say, 'I swear,' you give yourself away."

"I'm not," he said. "I'm not really connected. I just . . ."

He let out a long breath and looked down at his hands.

"You just what?" I said.

"I didn't think anything like that would happen. I just helped them with an idea. That's all I did."

"Who are we talking about?"

"Some people," he said. "From downstate."

"All right, we'll come back to who those people are. Tell me about this idea you helped them with."

"They wanted to find another airport, after what happened the last time. With those guys ripping off the delivery in Sandusky. Or wherever that was. When the plane landed, the regular pickup dudes who were going to meet the plane, they were handcuffed to the fence. These other guys took all the bags and they told the pilot to fly back to Canada and to tell the growers over there that they had new contacts in the States."

"That part I know about," I said. "So you're telling me your friends decided not to stand by and let this happen?"

"They're not my friends," he said quickly. "Come on, this is all business. I just get my supply from them. But when I knew they were looking around for another airport, I told them they should think about up here."

"So it was *your* idea, you're saying. You weren't just *helping* them with the idea."

"Yeah, I guess it was. It was my idea."

"It got five people killed," I said. "You realize that, right?"

"Those guys weren't supposed to find out. It shouldn't have happened."

"Whatever you say. Keep talking. What happened next?"

"These people from downstate, they came up here to check it out, and I was showing them around, you know, and at first they weren't too sure about it, because for one thing you gotta take everything back down over the bridge. But I was like, hey, you just pull up and pay your three-fifty toll. It's not like they're gonna search the truck or anything. So then they were like, okay, let's see some of the airports, and I took them around to Saint Ignace and Sanderson, and then I finally took them out to Newberry. And they were like, this would be perfect if it wasn't so deserted."

"Wait," I said. "I thought that was the whole point. I thought you *wanted* it to be deserted so nobody would notice the plane landing."

"You don't want anybody to notice," he said, "but you also need to have more than one road out of there. That way, if somebody *does* see you, you can still get away. With Newberry, you just got the one road going east–west, or maybe you could take the cross-road north, but then you'd just be driving all that way up to Paradise and then you'd still have to loop back around. It wouldn't take more than two cop cars to totally nail you."

"All right," I said. "I guess I see the logic there. If it's forty miles to the next turn, they can seal you right off. So what changed their mind?"

"The off-roads. There's hundreds of them, all over the place. Hell, we got more off-roads up here than regular roads. I even got this map out and showed them. Right there at the airport, you can jump right on a trail and go to another trail, and pretty much go wherever you want to go, all over the UP. You practically never have to hit a main road once."

"I'm sure they appreciated your creative thinking," I said, "and that would explain that truck I saw at the airport. I'm sure it was four-wheel drive, big tires, perfect for getting down those trails, right?"

He nodded.

"So let's get to the part of the story where Buck gets involved."

He didn't say anything for a moment. He didn't have to. I was already racing to the answer, picturing that all-terrain vehicle parked on the grass next to Buck's driveway.

"Oh, don't even tell me," I said. "I don't even want to hear this."

"What?" Lou said. "What happened with Buck?"

"He's the guy who knows the trails," I said. "Am I right?"

Dukes nodded again.

"And you actually hooked him up with those people? Is that what you're gonna tell me?"

"Buck was always riding out there," Dukes said. "He talked about it a few times. So I just introduced him."

"You just introduced him," I said. "To a gang of drug dealers from downstate."

"It's not like that. You don't know these people."

"Oh, am I misrepresenting them? Are they not a gang of drug dealers who fly in massive amounts of pot from Canada and sell it to people all over the state? Is that not an accurate description?"

"They're not a gang, for one thing. There's just two of them, and they're old. Like in their fifties."

As if I didn't already have enough reason to smack him in the face.

"Two old pot dealers," I said, trying hard to maintain my composure. "So those were two of the dead bodies at the airport? Is that what you're saying?"

"No, they don't take the deliveries themselves. They don't do that kind of stuff anymore."

"On account of being in their fifties and therefore so old and decrepit," I said. "Is that it?"

"They just don't. They always have these guys hanging around them all the time, working on the farm or whatever. Which kinda explains why they took such a shine to Buck."

I looked over at Lou. He didn't seem to be understanding this any better than I was.

"What in holy hell are you talking about?" I finally said. "Who are these people?"

He kept quiet then. Maybe he was thinking he had already said too much. Not that I cared at that point.

Eddie raised his hand like an elementary-school student. "Can I go now?" he said.

"Shut up and don't move," I said to him. Then I turned my attention back to Dukes. "Tell me who these people are."

"I can't."

"I'm pretty sure you can."

"No. Really."

"Really, you can. Lou, shoot him in the hand. Either hand will do."

"I really need to use the bathroom," Eddie said.

"If Eddie says one more word, shoot him in the hand, too."

Lou took one step forward and that was all it took. I didn't like having to threaten these men, but I was getting sick of everything and I just wanted to get the hell out of there as soon as possible. With some answers.

"Okay," Dukes said, "just take it easy. Let's not get crazy here."

"Their names. Now."

"Harry and Josephine!"

"I swear to God, Lou—"

"That's their names! Harry and Josephine Kaiser!"

"These are the major drug dealers we're talking about. Harry and Josephine Kaiser."

"Yeah, they're like old hippies or something. They have this farm downstate. They used to grow themselves, but they don't do that anymore. Now they just import."

"Old 'hippies' don't run major drug rings, I'm thinking."

"That's what they *look* like. I'm not saying they're really hippies. They just wear hippie clothes and they have hippie hair. That kind of thing."

I dropped my head and rubbed my forehead for a while.

"Okay, you've already proven that you're a terrible liar," I finally said, "and coming up with those names and the dress-like-a-hippie angle would be absolute genius if it wasn't true. So I'm gonna have to believe you. So tell me about how Buck got hooked up with these people."

"I told you, as soon as they took one look at Buck, they just ate him up, man. A real *Indian*, you know? Oppressed by the white man, driven off his land . . ."

"I'm pretty sure Buck never got driven off his land. In fact, he recently bought a hot tub."

"I know, but it's just the idea. That's the way these people are. Everything's about freedom and not having the government telling you what you can do or what you can smoke. That whole trip they're on. So having a real Indian guide on this deal . . ."

"All right, I get the picture," I said. "These people, the Kaisers, you say? These Kaisers fall in love with Buck and that's how he ends up doing this little favor for them at the airport. The regular couriers probably picked him up in their truck. They drive out there in the middle of the night, expecting not to have any company this time. But surprise, the hijackers show up. What can you tell me about *them*?"

"Nothing," Dukes said. "They're just people who are trying to take over."

"Come on, you gotta know more than that."

"I'm telling you, I don't. I don't know anything. In fact, I thought you guys were probably hooked up with them. That's why I was carrying the gun around."

"So you're expecting them to find you?"

"I don't know what to expect. It's just all getting turned upside down right now. I didn't sign up for this."

"Yeah, nobody did. But surprise, the hijackers show up, and this time everybody starts shooting. Buck's the only one left standing, apparently. But instead of driving the truck away, he calls his cousin Vinnie."

"That part makes sense," Lou said. "I wouldn't drive the truck, either."

"Or maybe he just runs for a while," I said. "He runs and maybe he ends up in town. Or wherever. He calls Vinnie and says you gotta come pick me up. Vinnie gets out there, he hears the story. Hell, maybe Buck's got blood all over him. Who knows? The one thing we do know is that he takes Buck away somewhere. To hide out, to figure out what to do next, whatever they think they have to do."

"They went to another reservation," Lou said. "We already know that."

"We *thought* we knew that," I said. "But now I've got another idea."

"What's that?"

"If these old so-called hippies downstate, the Kaisers, if they took such a shine to Buck and they're the ones who got him into this mess . . ."

"Then maybe Vinnie and Buck went down there," Lou said. "That's what you're saying."

"It's the best idea we've got right now."

I pulled my chair up closer to Dukes. I leaned over so that I was just a few inches from his face.

"We just need a couple more things from you," I said to him. "And then we'll be gone. I promise."

Ten minutes later, we were back in the car. Lou was driving. He had kept the gun and it was tucked under the driver's seat. I was keying in a number on my cell phone. It went right to voice mail, and, oddly enough, there was no recorded message telling me I'd reached a full-service wholesale marijuana distributorship. Just a beep.

"I'm a friend of Buck's," I said. I gave them my number, told them to call me back.

"How long to get there?" Lou said. "Two and a half hours?"

I turned the page over and read it again. Dukes had written down the street address, along with some rough directions. It could all have been fake, but something told me he was just as bad a liar on paper as he was in person.

"Maybe closer to two hours," I said, "if you gun it."

He gunned it. We crossed the bridge and kept going straight south. Next stop, a farmhouse just outside Cadillac. We were going for some answers, but hell, maybe Vinnie and Buck would be there. Maybe we'd pull up and they'd all be sitting there in the shade, Harry and Josephine Kaiser and their two guests from the UP.

Maybe, just this once, we'd catch a break and this whole thing would be over.

I wasn't betting on it.

CHAPTER TEN

I had two hours to think about things. I wasn't even driving, so I put my head back, closed my eyes, and played it all back in slow motion. I had come way too close to getting my ass shot off, that was the first thing that hit me. I had jumped in front of a drug dealer who was obviously scared out of his mind, and I had done this completely unarmed. If Lou hadn't stepped up behind him, I might well have been still lying on that asphalt, looking up at the sky with yet another bullet in my chest. If there really is a place you go after you die, where you need to justify your life, surviving two shootings and yet somehow dying in a third was something I would have had a hard time explaining.

I opened my eyes and looked over at Lou. He was staring dead ahead, both hands on the wheel. That scar on his jawline went all the way back, under his ear, into his hair, and it was just one more reminder that this man had led a hard life I knew very little about. Like him chopping that man right in the throat, or later, pulling out that gun and pressing it against the man's head. I mean, I knew these were extraordinary circumstances. The man was looking for his only remaining son, after all. But some things you make your-self do because you have to, and some things you do because you've done them in the past and you know they work. It's so easy and immediate, it's practically muscle memory.

"That gun," I said, finally making a sound after sixty or seventy miles. "I'm just thinking . . ."

"You didn't expect me to give it back to him, did you?"

"No, I didn't. But I'm not sure keeping it under the car seat is such a hot idea."

"You may have a point," he said. "As a convicted felon, I'm not supposed to be in possession of a firearm. That's what you're say-ing, right? I guess maybe I shouldn't have taken it away from him? I should have just let him shoot you?"

"That's not where I was going. I was just thinking there might be a better place for it. Like in the glove compartment. Unloaded."

He worked that over for a mile, mile and a half. Then he reached under the seat and brought out the gun. It was a Smith & Wesson .357, now that I was finally getting a closer look at it, and it looked a lot like the service weapon I'd carried in Detroit. He passed it to me handle first without taking his eyes off the road. I swung open the cylinder and emptied the six rounds into my left hand. I opened up the glove compartment and put the works on top of his rental agreement. Then I closed it.

"I should probably thank you at some point," I said. "If that thing really was cocked and ready, he could have shot me without even thinking of it."

"Buy me a beer later," he said. "You would have done the same thing."

Another mile went by.

"Besides," he said, "it was your idea that got us here. I was just doing my part. But now that we've got something to go on, I mean, what do you think we're gonna find at this farmhouse? You think the Kaisers will be there?"

"Only one way to find out."

"What kind of people do you think we're talking about, anyway?" he said. "A couple of heavy hitters pretending to be hippies? Does that make any sense at all to you?"

"I don't even care," I said. "As long as we get some answers."

A point he couldn't argue with. We were into the Lower Peninsula now, still making good time down I-75. We passed by Gaylord and then Grayling, then we got off the expressway around Houghton Lake and made our way west. It was yet another flat and empty part of the state, and we passed through small towns named Merritt and Lake City. We drove right into the center of Cadillac, where the road came to a T on the shores of Lake Cadillac. There were restaurants and people walking down the sidewalks with ice cream cones. Historical markers and an old locomotive sitting right in the middle of a park, but we had no time for any of it. We were looking for a street just north of town, so we made our way up the main road. As we cut back west, we drove right past the Wexford County Airport.

"You think they ever flew in here?" Lou said.

"It's right in their backyard," I said. "Kinda dangerous, you'd think. But who knows? It was probably easy the first few times, no matter where they did it."

"Yeah, funny how the wrong people always seem to notice what you're doing, if it happens to be making you some money."

"Even around here," I said as we passed the little airport and saw nothing but small houses and open fields ahead, "I bet it's hard to keep a secret."

We kept driving west. The few houses dwindled to almost nothing. We crossed some railroad tracks and then they fell into line just off the right side of the road, even as we cut north and drove through a tiny town called Boon. The tracks left us as we cut west again. The road was so thin and empty now, it felt like we were back in the Upper Peninsula, the trees getting thicker on each side of us until I began to doubt we were being sent to the right place after all. Then finally we saw a lone, nameless mailbox with the number we were looking for and an opening in the trees just wide enough for a car to fit through.

The branches scraped against both sides of the car until we broke through into a clearing. A lone, tall house stood at the end of the gravel driveway. It was a classic farmhouse with rough wooden siding, and there were two separate outbuildings, one on either side of the house. There were no signs of life, and I didn't see any vehicles until we got closer to the house. That's when I saw the bright red sports car parked over by one of the sheds, and then in the next second as we came around the bend I saw the black truck parked next to it.

It was Vinnie's.

Lou slammed on the brakes. I had the door open before we even came to a complete stop. I ran out through the cloud of dust kicked up by the tires and opened up Vinnie's driver's-side door. There was a thick layer of pebbled glass all over the front seat, with a long piece of metal protruding from what had once been the windshield.

"Is that his?" Lou said, coming up behind me.

"Yes."

I pulled out the hunk of metal. It was a heavy, galvanized U-channel, the kind of thing you'd use to mount a road sign. As I let it drop to the ground, I noticed the faint odor of bleach. I went over to the other side and opened that door, and the smell was stronger. I felt the seat.

"What is it?" Lou said.

"This seat is damp."

"Not this side," he said, his hand on the driver's seat.

"Vinnie's a fanatic about keeping his truck clean. He was obviously washing something off the—"

I stopped and bent down to look at the edge of the floorboard.

"What is it?"

"It looks like a drop of blood," I said. "This is what he was cleaning up, but he didn't quite get it all. So now we know Buck was bleeding, probably because he got shot at the airport. But it couldn't have been too bad."

"Why's that?"

"Because he was able to clean it up," I said. "He had *time* to clean it up. If Buck was bleeding seriously in here, it would be a goddamned mess, and Vinnie would have had more important things to do."

"Okay, so then who smashed his windshield? And where the hell is he? If somebody was home, you'd think they would have noticed us by now."

"I think you're right about that."

"What's this?" Lou said. He picked up a crumpled bag from the floor and opened it. "Looks like they stopped for hamburgers."

"That's not like Vinnie to leave garbage in his truck. Hell, if he spent all this time cleaning up the blood . . ."

"He cleaned up the seat and then they stopped for hamburgers later," Lou said, slamming the door shut and sending a few more pieces of the windshield onto the seat. "Then apparently he got somebody really mad at him. Or at least at his truck."

I closed the passenger's-side door and looked up at the farmhouse. It was just past the middle of the day now, and the sun was out from behind the clouds and casting a blinding hot light on everything around us. There was only the hum of insects in the grass and no other sound. That's when I noticed that the front door to the house was ajar.

"What's going on here?" Lou said as he spotted the same thing. "Why is that door open?"

I stepped forward, a sick feeling already rising in my gut. I was afraid to look inside the house, but I knew we had to. We were set on this course the moment we left Dukes and his neighbor in Sault Ste. Marie, and here we were almost two hundred miles away, about to find some answers whether we wanted them or not.

I saw the debris on the floor as soon as I got close to the doorway. I was looking into the kitchen, where someone had apparently taken out every single drawer and upended the contents on the tile. Silverware, paper, pencils, hand tools, electrical cords, a thousand different things all scattered around the place. I stood there in the doorway and was about to knock on the frame. As if somebody would come shuffling through from another room to greet me with a smile and to apologize for the mess.

"We have to go in," Lou said. "You know we have to."

I didn't say anything. I just nodded my head.

"Don't touch anything," he said.

Normally, this would have set me off. Like maybe I shouldn't sign the guest book, either? But my mind was already running ahead of me and I couldn't help imagining the worst. I took a step inside and heard a sudden pop that made my heart leap out of my chest, followed a millisecond later by the crunch of a tiny Christmas tree light bulb under my shoe.

"Let's split up," Lou said.

He went left, around a staircase. I went straight through the kitchen, around the butcher-block island, marveling at the thoroughness of the job done by whoever had been here. Besides every drawer, he or she or they had opened up every cupboard and swept the contents clean. There was a big pantry with the door half open and when I looked inside I saw a riot of food boxes and cans all covered with a thin coating of flour. This was more than just a ransacking of the house. It was an annihilation.

I opened the door next to the pantry. It led downstairs to a finished basement. There was a steady hum from a dehumidifier sitting in the corner, and as I looked around the rest of the room I had to wonder how that particular machine had been allowed to keep running. The large-screen television had been pulled off the wall, and it was now lying facedown on the carpet with all of the stereo equipment piled on top of it. All of the pictures and posters and whatnot had been taken from the walls, the glass frames smashed and many of the contents ripped into pieces. As I looked closer, I saw the fragments of concert posters and photographs of old rock-and-roll musicians. I even saw the scrawled signature in one corner of one picture that I couldn't quite make out, but it was further proof that these had been some valuable pieces at one time. But no more.

I went back upstairs. I looped around the ground floor and didn't see Lou anywhere. What I did see was more carnage. Dining room chairs smashed over the table, a china cabinet literally tipped over with the contents spilling out into a million pieces of broken glass and porcelain.

I went up the stairs, hearing the old treads creak with every step. I found Lou in the master bedroom, looking down at a great pile of clothing that had been torn out of the closet.

"Did you find anything?" he said. "Any sign of Vinnie or Buck?"

"No. Just more wreckage."

"What do you think the point of all this was?"

"Trashing the whole house? Either they weren't real pleased with the owners. Or else they were just looking for something."

"Maybe both," Lou said. "But damn, this kinda goes beyond that, doesn't it? This looks like pure rage to me."

"Too bad we missed them," I said. "We could have asked."

Lou shook his head and scanned the clothing on the floor. There was a full-length fur coat ripped out of its protective bag. I would have bet anything it wasn't a fake.

"Look at this stuff," he said. "Does this look like something a real hippie would wear?"

"Yeah, I couldn't help noticing, everything in this house looks pretty expensive. Although I did see a lot of old stuff from the sixties in the basement. Concert posters, signed photographs, stuff like that."

"Maybe that's where they came from," he said. "A long time ago. But they seem to have gotten over it. I bet they own a lot of land here, to go with this quaint little four-thousand-square-foot house."

We left the master bedroom and checked out the rest of the top floor, finding three more bedrooms and three bathrooms, each with mirror shards in the sinks. At the end of the hall there was an office, and here, finally, the intruder's efforts seemed a little more focused. Every drawer in the desk and file cabinets was thrown open, but the papers weren't scattered to the winds. Instead, someone had apparently sat himself down and gone through everything page by page, stacking them on the floor when he was done with each handful.

"Now all of a sudden they're looking for something," Lou said. "What do you think it was?"

"Who knows?" I said, carefully moving some of the papers aside as I looked through them. It was all the usual stuff you'd find in any home office. Tax receipts, insurance policies, all the mundane details of modern life.

"Maybe bank records," Lou said, bending down to look through the papers on the other side of the room. "Or phone records. Or hell, it could be anything. Whatever it was, we don't even know if they found it."

I looked out the window. I saw the metal roof on one of the outbuildings. Lou looked out the same window and seemed to have the same thought.

"Why is Vinnie's truck still here, anyway?" he said. If he was trying to keep the dread out of his voice, he was doing a lousy job of it. "If he's gone, why wouldn't he—"

He didn't even finish. He didn't have to. We both went back down the stairs and out the door. Without saying a word, he went to one of the buildings, and I went to the other. Mine was either a small barn or a large shed or who the hell knows what. There was a door on the side with a bare light bulb mounted over it. When I opened it, I had a small heart attack when a chicken screamed at me and then came strutting outside. I went in and saw a few more chickens walking around the place. There were bales of hay and a work table piled high with rusted old farm tools. Sunlight streamed through the windows and there was no sound except for the chickens' clucking. On any other day the scene would have seemed downright peaceful.

I left the building and went to the other. As I walked through the lone door on the side facing me, I saw four bay doors that opened up in the other direction. It was a large garage, with two older cars taking up the spaces on the far end. I didn't see Lou anywhere, until he finally appeared on the wooden ladder mounted against the wall. He was coming down from a small loft, and he looked thoughtful, not horrified. A good sign.

"Did you find anything in the other building?" he said.

"Just some chickens."

"Were they alive?"

"Yeah, why?"

"Because whoever was here, they took it out on these cars, too.

It wasn't just Vinnie's. Which makes me wonder why he didn't do anything to the animals."

As I looked a little closer at the old vehicles, I saw what he was talking about. One was an old white Cadillac from the 1960s, the other an even older car, a mint-green Hudson from the 1950s. The windshields of both cars had been bashed in, spraying the front seats with a thousand pebbles of glass. That's when I noticed the metal signposts stacked in the corner of the garage. Whoever had been here had obviously grabbed one and gotten busy with it.

"There's room for four vehicles here," Lou said. "Counting that red sports car we saw outside."

"There's one unaccounted for," I said, looking down at the faint tire marks on both empty spots. "Wherever the fourth vehicle is, that's probably where the Kaisers are."

"And maybe Vinnie and Buck?"

I nodded, looking out the open door. All I could see was the gravel driveway and the woods in the distance.

"So how do we find out where they went?" Lou said.

"Hell if I know."

I went out the door and looked at the sports car. It was a bright red Chevy Camaro from the 1970s, just one more indication that these weren't exactly genuine hippies we were looking for. Not unless they were hippies with a lot of money and great taste in home furnishings and classic American automobiles. This one looked brand new, except of course for the missing windshield.

"They got this one, too," Lou said. "We didn't even notice it before."

"Yeah, Vinnie's truck just happened to be in the wrong place at the wrong time."

"Do you think he was here when all of this was happening?"

I looked over at his truck, then back at the house. It gave me a little shiver, the way those dark empty windows stood out against the brilliant sunny day.

"I don't know," I said. "If Vinnie and Buck went somewhere with these people . . ."

"They were probably long gone, you're saying."

"He's gonna be pissed when he sees this truck, is all I know. I've seen him spend half a day buffing out a scratch in the finish."

"Maybe he's got bigger things to worry about right now." There was a sudden edge in his voice. Yet another shift in mood for a man who already seemed as unpredictable as the weather on Lake Superior. "Maybe we do, too."

I wasn't sure how to answer that, so I didn't even try. He shook his head and walked away from me. As he stood there looking into Vinnie's truck, it occurred to me that this was just another secondhand impression of a son he hadn't seen in almost thirty years. Vinnie's house, now Vinnie's truck. Everything but the man himself.

"We're not doing anybody any good standing here," I said. "Not that I have any idea where we should go next."

He didn't answer me. He kept staring into the truck.

"We should move this," he finally said.

"What are you talking about?"

"His truck. We shouldn't leave it here."

"Are you serious? You want to call a tow truck or something?"

"No," he said, giving me a sharp look. "I'm saying we should take it back into town, drop it off at an auto-glass place. By the time we find him, it'll be fixed. Plus, it's probably not a good idea to have this here, you know, just in case . . ."

"Just in case what?"

"I don't know, maybe these Kaiser people are dead somewhere. The police come by here, check out the house . . . It'll look bad if his truck's sitting here, right?"

Maybe these Kaiser people are dead, he says. Not taking that one further step. Who else might be dead. But yeah, come to think of it, the man has a point.

"I watched a man hot-wire a truck once," he said. "Once he got the ignition cover off, it didn't take him more than two minutes."

"Or we could just use the key," I said, taking out my key ring. "You take the car and I'll follow behind you."

"You have the key to Vinnie's truck?"

"We both have each other's keys, yeah. It's a good idea in the winter, in case one of us gets stuck, or a battery dies, or you name it."

He gave me a little knock on the shoulder as he went to the car. I brushed off some of the glass, got into the truck, started it, and headed down the driveway. It's amazing how much wind you feel when you drive without a windshield, not to mention the pollen and the bugs and whatever the hell else was hitting me right in the face. But it was a short trip back to Cadillac and we pulled into the first auto-glass shop we found. I went inside, dealt with the paperwork, gave the man my credit card. He said he'd have it done in a couple of hours, but it would take a few more hours after that for the glue to dry. I told him I didn't know for sure when I'd be back, and he said he didn't want me to get there too soon and have to wait.

I'd take that problem any day, I thought to myself. Vinnie safe and sound, sitting in the lobby of this little auto-glass store in Cadillac, Michigan, waiting for the glue on his new windshield to dry.

Lou was waiting for me in the parking lot. "So what the hell do we do now?" he said. "We have to figure out where they went."

"How about where they *were*?" I said, holding up a crumpled paper bag. "This was probably the one day in Vinnie's life when he left garbage in his truck."

"Yeah? So?"

"Five Guys Burgers and Fries. One with lettuce, tomatoes, grilled onions, and mustard. The other with grilled mushrooms, bacon, mustard, and jalapeño peppers. Plus an order of fries."

"So they had hamburgers for lunch. I don't see how that helps us."

"They bought this at exactly 12:08 P.M. yesterday," I said, pulling off the receipt that was taped to the outside of the brown paper bag. "On East Pickard Street in Mount Pleasant."

"Mount Pleasant . . ."

"That's by the Saginaw Reservation, isn't it?"

"Right next door," he said. "Think it's a coincidence?"

"No, I don't."

"Then what are we waiting for?"

We got into the car and took off.

CHAPTER ELEVEN

Their official name is the Saginaw Chippewa Indian Tribe, and their reservation is just north of Mount Pleasant. It's by far the largest reservation in Michigan, more than two hundred square miles. It's technically called the Isabella Indian Reservation, maybe because it's in Isabella County. I don't even know. What I do know is that the Saginaws live there and most people up north just call it the Saginaw rez, and when they say it you can often hear a little bit of animosity. Or maybe animosity mixed with a little bit of envy, especially if the speaker's a member of either Bay Mills or the Sault Tribe. The reason is simple. Even though the Indian casinos started in the UP, it's the Saginaws who seem to be making the most of the idea.

They've got two casinos now. The Soaring Eagles, right in Mount Pleasant, and the Saganing Eagles Landing over by I-75, on a separate parcel of land overlooking the Saginaw Bay. Between the two properties the tribe makes enough money to pay each member something like seventy thousand dollars every year. It starts to get ugly when they start having to decide who's an official member and who's going to be left out in the cold, and it gets just as ugly when other members up north start to wonder why they're not getting the same kind of deal from their tribes.

But whatever. It wasn't my concern and I'd hear people talking about it at Vinnie's mother's house if I happened to be there. They were all Ojibwa at heart, whether Bay Mills or Sault or Saginaw or anywhere else. Michigan, Wisconsin, Minnesota, Canada, it didn't matter. When you got right down to it, they were all one people, and that was my original idea, thinking that if Vinnie and Buck were going to go hide somewhere, it would be on another reservation. Now, at last, we had one small clue to help point us in that direction.

It was only an hour from Cadillac to the Saginaw rez, through more open flatland until we hit the Au Sable State Forest and then finally the highway running south from Clare. A few more miles through the heart of the rez and we hit Mount Pleasant. We were in the middle of the mitten now. If you held up your right hand as a map of the Lower Peninsula and pointed to the center, that's exactly where'd we be. Pickard Street runs east and west through the center of town, and you can find just about any chain restaurant you want. We kept going a few blocks until we saw the Five Guys. We parked and went inside.

"We should eat something," Lou said, looking at his watch. It was past lunchtime by now. "It'll make us think better."

I didn't argue with him. We ordered a couple of hamburgers, and as we were waiting I looked around the place, as if Vinnie and Buck would be sitting right there at one of the tables. They called our number a few minutes later, and that's how we saw the way they ran their operation there. They'd tape your receipt with your magic number on it, right there on the outside of the brown paper bag.

I didn't feel like burning an hour sitting down for lunch. I would rather have taken the food in the car while we drove around the rez. But Lou insisted.

"Let's sit here and let it sink in for a while," he said. "Vinnie and Buck may have sat right here at this table. Just yesterday."

"Something tells me they didn't do that," I said. "If that bag was in his truck . . ."

"They ate on the run, okay. But just the same, let's watch out the window for a while, get the rhythm of this place. I bet you something will come to us."

So that's what we did. I don't know if we ever got into any kind of rhythm, or what the hell that even means, but we did get to sit there for a few minutes and plan out our next move.

And yes, we were both starving. Taking a few minutes to eat a couple of big hamburgers was the right idea.

"So imagine you're Vinnie," Lou said, wiping his mouth after a big bite. "You've got your crazy cousin with you, and you're trying to take care of him. He's bleeding—"

"So you take him to the hospital."

"But you're worried about him getting in trouble."

"You take him to the hospital anyway."

He waved that away. "If you go to the ER with a gunshot wound, they have to call the police, am I right? Isn't that the rule?"

"Gun, knife, anything deadly," I said. "Actually, any kind of violence at all. If you've been assaulted in any way, bad enough to go to the hospital for treatment, then they're supposed to call it in."

"Seriously? Anything?"

"That's the Michigan law. It might be different in other states."

"Damn," he said. "But okay. That makes my point even stronger. As soon as Buck walks in with a gunshot wound, the police are on their way."

"So where else would they go? And why all the way down here?"

"Because they know somebody. Buck, Vinnie, one of them. They come down here because they've got a friend on the rez who can help them without calling the cops."

"It's the biggest reservation in the state," I said. "Where would we even start?"

"We already have. We're retracing their steps. Backwards, maybe, but we know they drove to that farmhouse and left Vinnie's truck there. Before that, they were here."

He gestured to the counter.

"There's no drive-through here," he said. "Did you notice that? That means they were standing right there at that counter. Or maybe just Vinnie, I don't know. But he was *right there* like twenty-four hours ago."

"So what are we going to do, ask the cashier if she remembers seeing an Indian man with long black hair? She probably sees a hundred of them every day."

"I don't see a lot of long hair here," Lou said, looking around the place. "But no matter. It wouldn't do us any good even if she was here yesterday and even if she did remember him. I don't imagine they talked about much more than what he wanted on his hamburgers."

"Okay, so we've gotta take one more step backward. To wherever they were before they came here."

"That's the idea," he said, wadding up his wrapper and throwing it into the bag. "Let's go find it."

A simple enough plan, even if I had no idea where we'd begin.

There was a walk-in clinic just down the street from the Five Guys. It seemed way too much to ask for this to be the place where Vinnie and Buck had come for help, but we walked inside and right there on the wall was a board with all of the doctors' names. They were Indian names, all right. But we were just off the rez now and these were not the kind of Indians we were looking for.

"Patel, Singh, Alyeshmerni," Lou said, going down the list. "Yeah, I'm thinking we're not going to find our long-lost friend of Vinnie or Buck here."

"We need to find something on the rez itself," I said. "But even if we find the right place, how are we gonna know? If they came down here to get Buck treated off the books, how can you expect the doctor to talk to us about it?"

"That's the tricky part," Lou said as we got back into the car. "We'll have to rely on the old eyeball test."

I looked over at him.

"You know the eyeball test," he said. "I mean if you were any kind of cop . . ."

"I know the eyeball test," I said. "You ask them a question and you watch their eyes. If they're lying, you'll know it."

"So you've done it before."

"A few hundred times. Once in a while it even works."

We spent the next half hour driving around, looking for the clinic. We knew it had to be there. Any decent reservation would have a walk-in clinic and this one was so far beyond decent. We drove by the Soaring Eagles Casino and it was truly spectacular, even bigger than the Sault tribe's Kewadin. It even had its own entrance road, with a big sign arching over it. We kept going past that and finally found the clinic just a few blocks to the south. It was called the Nimkee Medical Clinic, and, no surprise, it looked so clean and new and state-of-the-art, you'd feel lucky to be wheeled through the front doors with a bullet in your head.

"I can't believe any of this," Lou said as he drove through the parking lot. There was a covered canopy you could stop under, complete with valet parking, so you could walk into the place without being bothered by the weather. "I told you about the Paiutes in Moapa Valley, right? With the coal plant next door?"

"You mentioned it, yes."

"You know what kind of . . ."

He took a breath.

"Never mind," he said. "If these people are making a good life for themselves, then more power to 'em. I'm gonna go talk to somebody."

"You're going to?"

"We're on the rez now, Alex. Besides being an obvious paleface, you look like a cop, too."

I didn't fight him too hard. Probably because I knew he was right. This was the one place I'd be of no use to anybody. I sat there and babysat the car while he walked through the front doors. I looked at my watch. It was almost three o'clock. This day had started up in Sault Ste. Marie, staking out Dukes, rousting him, getting his story. Then down to Cadillac to see just how badly one could trash a nice farmhouse, not to mention four vehicles. Now we were here on the Saginaw rez, still trying to retrace Vinnie and Buck's steps. It didn't feel like the longest day of my life quite yet, but then the day was still young.

A few minutes later, Lou came barreling back out the front door. He didn't look happy. He got into the car, slammed the door, and started the ignition. As soon as it was in gear, he laid down tracks and we were out of that parking lot in seconds.

"Slow down!" I said. "What the hell happened?"

"We're supposed to be one people," he said, sounding more like he was talking to himself than to me. "One big family, no matter what."

"Lou . . ."

"One people. That's what the word means, right? *Anishinabe.* The people. *One* people. That doesn't mean anything anymore?"

I let him burn it off on his own. A few minutes later he had stopped talking, but he was still driving a little bit too fast.

"I take it that didn't pan out," I finally said.

"I just asked them if anybody from Bay Mills had come down to the clinic. I told them there were two men, and that one of them was my son. 'He's my son,' I said. 'I'm looking for my son.' You think that would evoke a little empathy, right? But no. As soon as I walked up to the desk, that woman is already looking up at me like I'm some kind of criminal or something. I didn't even get to finish explaining and she had already called security."

"Are you serious?"

"A few more seconds, hell, I might have been arrested in there. Just because I was looking for my son."

"You mentioned that part about them being from Bay Mills," I said. "You said that before she called for the goons?"

"Why does it matter?"

"I'm just asking. Did you mention Bay Mills at the beginning of the conversation?"

"Yeah. I guess so."

"Somebody got the word out," I said. "You remember how antsy everybody got when you were asking about Vinnie yesterday? We might just get that same reaction on every other reservation in the state. If anybody comes snooping around, asking about two men from up north . . ."

"You might be right," he said. "I should have had you come in after all."

"Where are we going, anyway?"

He was driving back toward the center of town. But then as we were about to pass the entrance to the casino, he made a hard left.

"What are we doing here?" I said.

"You got any better ideas? This is where half the tribe is, probably. Somebody might know something. At the very least, we can put your theory to the test, see if every Indian in Michigan is really looking out for suspicious strangers. Besides, I could use a drink about now."

We parked in a lot filled with at least a thousand other cars. It was the heart of the afternoon, on a gorgeous Michigan summer day, so what better place to spend it than inside a casino, pumping money into a slot machine? We took the long walk across the hot pavement and went inside, feeling the sudden icy chill of the air conditioning. Lou found the bar in twenty seconds and the bartender in twenty-one. He ordered a shot and a beer. I asked the man for a Coke.

"You've been driving all day," I said. "When we go back outside, it's my turn, okay?"

He looked at me over his shot and then he downed it in one swallow. The bartender filled him back up and he downed that one, too. The beer was apparently just for show.

"Hey, friend," he said to the bartender. "How long you been working here?"

"Five years." The man had the wide face of an Ojibwa, along with the calm eyes and the black hair.

"You ever been up to Bay Mills?"

"Nope."

"You don't know anybody from up there?"

"Don't believe so."

"I was born there myself. Haven't been around for a while, but if I came down here looking for help, where would I go?"

"I don't follow you, sir."

"I'm just saying, if I was in trouble and I needed somebody to help me out. You know, patch me up and send me on my way?"

"I think I know what you mean," he said, sliding right into an acting job so blatant it was like he was reading his lines off a cue card. "I'm gonna go get somebody to help you. Wait right here."

He disappeared through a door at the far end of the bar. Lou took out a twenty-dollar bill, threw it onto the counter, and took off for the door. When I caught up to him in the parking lot, he was taking the keys out of his pocket. I grabbed them from his hand and got into the driver's seat before he could say a word. He got in on the other side and told me to get going. A minute later we were out on the main road, heading back toward town. I couldn't remember the last time I had driven a car instead of a truck. It felt strange to be so low to the road.

"You were right," he said. "The word is out. Anybody looking for two men from Bay Mills is an automatic red flag."

"I don't know what we can do now. Next place we stop, we're likely to be arrested."

"You don't carry an old badge or anything?"

We were back on Pickard, heading right back to the Five Guys. Presumably there was nowhere else to go but back to the freeway. And back home.

"I technically have a private-investigator license," I said. "But I don't use it."

"Excuse me?"

"It doesn't matter anyway. I don't have it with me."

"You never told me you were a private eye. We could have—"

"Look, it doesn't matter. It wouldn't have helped, believe me. It never does."

"I don't even understand what you're saying. How can you not—"

I hit the brakes and nearly sent him through the windshield. There was a horn blaring right behind me and the screech of tires, and I suppose I almost did get us killed right there. But I didn't even notice.

"What the hell is wrong with you?" Lou said.

"Look there," I said, pulling off the road. "We didn't even notice it the first time we came by here."

It was a low, squat building made of brick, not unlike a dozen other buildings all up and down the street. The thing that set this one apart was the statue of a dog out front. It was painted white with black spots, like a Dalmatian, and it was wearing sunglasses.

"I bet they take the glasses off that dog when it rains," I said, "and put on a raincoat."

He just looked at me like I had lost my mind.

"You still don't know why I stopped."

"No, I most certainly do not."

"Read the sign."

"Isabella County Animal Hospital."

"Keep reading."

"What, it's just the names of the—"

He stopped.

"Ronald Carrick, DVM," he said.

"You can practically smell the hamburgers from here," I said, nodding toward the Five Guys. "Perfect place to stop after you leave this office. And if I'm not mistaken, there aren't a whole hell of a lot of Carricks running around who don't belong to Bay Mills."

It was one of the family names that dominated the reservation, right up there with Parrish, Teeple, and LeBlanc.

"You realize," Lou said, "this means Buck got fixed up by a vet instead of a doctor."

"A vet *is* a doctor. What do you think the *D* in *DVM* stands for?"

We got out of the car and went inside. There was a diploma from Michigan State University's College of Veterinary Medicine on the lobby wall. Next to that were some newspaper clippings, all to the effect that Ronald Carrick was one of only a handful of Ojibwa tribal members in the state with such a degree. We didn't have to read any further. We knew we were in the right place.

"Can I help you guys?" The voice came from the receptionist.

She was sitting behind a high counter, and she looked young enough to be a student at the local college, Central Michigan.

"I need to speak to Dr. Carrick," Lou said. "It's very important."

"I'll see if he's free."

She left the room and I started to wonder how we should play this. That's when the doctor came out. He stepped around the counter and came right up to us. He was wearing the standard white coat, and he had that same barrel chest that Buck had. He was a Carrick, all right. Maybe even a first cousin.

He took one look at Lou, saw that old LeBlanc face, and all of a sudden we had a new version of the eyeball test, one that told us everything we needed to know.

He put us in a back room, like we were a couple of dogs who needed our annual checkup. As we sat there, I couldn't help wondering if the whole thing was a ploy to call the tribal police, no matter how much it seemed like the doctor was buying Lou's story out in the lobby.

We waited and we waited, until finally the doctor came in and closed the door behind him.

"I apologize," he said. "I had to finish up with some patients. But I don't have any appointments now, so we should be able to talk."

He sat down in the only remaining chair and smoothed his white coat over his knees. He looked rattled.

"Dr. Carrick," I said. "We need to find Vinnie and Buck. They were here, weren't they?"

He nodded, looking down at the floor for a moment.

"Buck must be your cousin, right?"

"One of many," he said, smiling. "I barely remembered him."

"They came to you for help," I said. "Buck was injured?"

"Right here," he said, pointing to his underarm. "In the axilla. He was shot once. The bullet passed right through. He was very lucky."

"Did they say how it happened?"

"If I had any idea they were in serious trouble," he said, "I would have acted differently. You have to believe me."

"It's okay," Lou said. "You helped them. We understand, and we appreciate it. Please just tell us what happened."

"Okay," he said, taking a long breath. "I'm sworn to secrecy, but I figure if you're really Vinnie's father . . . And it's not like I have any official doctor-patient confidentiality here. . . . Anyway, this was what, three days ago? They came down here, it was late at night. Like really late. I live in the house just behind the practice here. They knocked on the door and I was thinking it must have been an animal emergency. A dog hit by a car or something. I get calls like that all the time, but usually they don't come to the house. Anyway, I open the door and there's my old cousin Bucky, holding his arm against his chest. I can see that he had been bleeding. Vinnie was with him. I recognized his name, but I don't think I ever met him before. Although I guess technically Vinnie's my cousin, too, like a second cousin or once removed, or whatever. I only went to college for eight years and I still don't know how that works. Anyway, they came in and they told me that Vinnie was cleaning a gun at Buck's house and it accidentally went off. And that they were afraid to go to the hospital because they'd have to report it and Vinnie would get in big trouble. I guess he's been in jail before."

"Is that true?" Lou asked me.

"No. Not really." I was thinking of the one time Vinnie got charged with assault, when he went after somebody in the parking lot with his hockey stick. Somebody who definitely had it coming. But the charge was later dropped.

"It was just part of the story," the doctor said. "I see that now. At the time it made a certain amount of sense. In a bumbling sort of way. But anyway, I told him I was a vet and he said he didn't think it was serious, and fortunately he was right. The shell might have just grazed one of his upper ribs, but otherwise it was basically skin damage. I was able to patch him up pretty easily and I even had some antibiotics to give him. People pills, not animal pills. I thought it was the right thing to do."

"When did that feeling change?" I said.

"Well, they stayed at my house overnight. Buck was just lying around the next day, resting, while Vinnie was outside cleaning his truck. I guess there was a lot of blood in it. That's when I started wondering, I mean, it's like three hours to get down here. If he was really bleeding that much, it was a really stupid thing to do, no matter how much trouble you thought Vinnie might get into. I even asked him, I said, 'Is this really what happened?' He said yes, but I could kinda tell he was lying."

"Vinnie's a terrible liar," I said.

"Yeah, well, apparently he called somebody at the rez, told them everybody was okay and that they'd be home soon."

"When was that?"

"That was the next day. He asked if he could use the phone in my office, instead of at the house. Which sorta seemed weird. It's like he didn't want Buck to hear it."

"But you were there? You heard him on the phone?"

"I heard some of it. He just said, you know, we're both okay. Tell our family. Tell somebody else. I don't remember the name."

"Alex."

"Yeah, that's it. He said, tell Alex not to worry. Tell him not to do anything stupid. We're okay and I'll explain everything when I get home."

He stopped and looked at me.

"I'm sorry," he said. "This was all kind of a shock when you came in. I know you told me your name, but I don't think I caught it. So are you—"

"Alex, yes. Doing something stupid. But go on."

"Okay, so, later that night, it was Buck's turn to get on the phone. I don't know who he was talking to, but it was all about these people who wanted Buck and Vinnie to come see them, how they were going to take care of everything."

"That's gotta be the Kaisers," Lou said. "Harry and Josephine Kaiser. Do you recognize those names?"

"No, I didn't catch the names, sorry."

"But they said they were going to take care of everything? What were they going to do?"

"He didn't say. I was thinking maybe they must have had a good lawyer or something. But then I was thinking, no, not if it's just an accidental shooting. So I guess I really had no idea what he was talking about. They were just going to take care of everything, he said. That's it."

"Vinnie went along with this?"

"No, not at first. But I think Buck wore him down. They ended up leaving yesterday morning, and I know they weren't going home."

"What time did they leave?"

"Eleven thirty? Noon, maybe? They were just hanging around for a while, then Buck went to make a phone call. He came back and said they had to get going right away."

"Did he say why?"

"No. But all of a sudden they were in a hurry, and off they went."

I looked at Lou. I could tell he was thinking the same thing. Yesterday must have been the day when everybody involved in this situation got their wake-up call. It was time to run and not look back.

"So they left in a big hurry," Lou said.

"Yeah, they did. I guess that's when I sort of knew for sure. Not only was their story complete bullshit, but they were obviously in some kind of serious trouble. Vinnie kept saying they should just go home, but Buck was saying, no, these people were their only hope. Heck, I wanted them to stick around and have some lunch at least, but they just took off."

"Well, they stopped at the Five Guys down the road for some hamburgers," I said. "Something tells me Buck doesn't go that long without eating, no matter how much of a hurry they're in. But if you can think of anything else they might have said . . ."

Lou was pacing back and forth in front of the lab sink now. He pounded on the counter a few times before finally speaking again.

"If you were convinced they were in such big trouble," he said, "why did you let them go?"

"Take it easy," I said to him. "What did you expect him to do, tackle both of them?"

Lou put his hands up. "I'm just saying."

"I should have tried harder to stop them," the doctor said in an even voice. "I realize this now."

"No, I'm sorry," Lou said, rubbing his forehead. "It's been a hard day."

"Please go on," I said. "Is there anything else you remember from yesterday? If you can add one more little piece to the puzzle, it might be helpful."

We waited around for a few more minutes while he thought about it, but he came up empty. I gave him my phone number and asked him to call me if he remembered anything else. He told us to make sure we took care of Buck and Vinnie, assuming we ever found them. Then we thanked him and left.

"We need to find out more about the Kaisers," I said as we got into the car. "Find out where they might have taken Vinnie and Buck, once they were all together."

"Someplace safe, right? I mean, if they were nervous enough to be in such a big hurry yesterday . . ."

"So where is that? What's the safest place they'd go?"

"No way to know. We've never even met these people."

"I can only think of three people who *have* met them," he said. "Buck, Vinnie, and—"

"And the person who sent us down to that house in the first place," I said. "He's our only lead right now."

He nodded and looked out the window. "Sounds like it's time for one more visit."

That's how we ended up back on that same street in Sault Ste. Marie. It was almost dark by the time we got there. It was late and we were both hungry, and we had spent six good hours in the car running all over the state. The last thing we wanted to do was talk to Andy Dukes again. I don't imagine he felt much like talking to us, either. With or without his next-door neighbor, Eddie. But Dukes was the one man who might have more information about Harry and Josephine Kaiser. If we were finally due for that one lucky break, he would think about it for two seconds and then say, "Oh yeah, they must all be at their summer place. Here, let me write down that address for you."

But that lucky break was apparently still lost in the mail.

We made our way back to Hursley Street, taking that same turn just before the power canal. We pulled up in front of his house. It looked dark and empty, but that wasn't a surprise. We knew the drill. He was officially long gone, already in Texas by now. Just ask his neighbor.

The lights were on next door, and once again we saw the blue flickering glow from the television. We rang the bell and waited. I heard faint voices but figured they could be coming from the television. We rang the bell again.

"It's almost like they're not happy to see us again," Lou said. "Go figure."

"At least he won't be armed this time." I thought of the revolver we had taken from him, currently locked up, unloaded, in the rental car's glove compartment. Then I thought how foolish it would be to assume that was the only firearm Dukes owned.

Lou opened up the outside patio door before I could tell him what a bad idea that was. He went to the interior door and started pounding on it. I was already picturing the wooden door breaking apart, a thousand scraps of wood flying in the air as the gun blast turned everything inside out.

He stood there pounding on the door until finally he peeked inside through the front window.

He froze.

"What is it?" I said.

He didn't answer.

I went up the steps and moved him out of the way. I looked through the window and saw exactly what he saw.

I saw the two bodies on the floor. I saw the blood. I saw the damage that somebody had inflicted on both of these men.

Everything we had done that day, everywhere we had gone, it had all led up to this single moment.

"I knew it," Lou said. "I knew it. I knew it."

"Knew what?" I said, barely able to speak.

"This is what these people do," he said. "You screw around with these people, and this is what they do to you."

I came down off the steps. I tried to breathe. The sun was finally going down.

"We have to find them," he said. "We have to find Vinnie and Buck. Don't you see, Alex? We have to find them. Or they'll be next."

CHAPTER TWELVE

He pulled me to the street. I tried to push him away, not for any coherent reason, just a reflexive reaction to what I'd seen through the window.

"Let's get the hell out of here," he said through clenched teeth. "Right now."

"We have to stay here," I said. "We have to call somebody."

"Like hell we do."

I took him by the arm and was halfway into a wristlock, pure muscle memory from all of those years on the force. A suspect resists and you twist that arm right around and turn that wrist. All of a sudden he's a lot more cooperative.

"I'm calling the police," I said. "Then we're going to wait until they get here."

"Don't be an idiot. If we call the police, they'll lock us both up."

"Why would they do that?"

"Because that's what they do."

I knew that was the reality for him, at least. That was his own personal experience.

"No, Lou. Come on."

"We came here earlier today," he said, "and now we're back and those two guys are lying in there in a lake of blood. What do you think they're gonna do?"

"They're gonna talk to us, and we're gonna tell them everything we know."

"So you want them to take us down to the station, is that what you're saying? Best case, they put us in a room for the next twenty-four hours. Ask us the same questions over and over, which won't do anybody any good. Meanwhile, whoever it was who did this is getting closer and closer to Vinnie."

"He wasn't there, you realize that."

"What are you talking about?"

"Vinnie's not involved in this. He's never had anything to do with Dukes or these people from downstate, and he wasn't even at the airport that night. He just picked up Buck and—"

"And helped Buck get away," Lou said. "He's been with Buck ever since. Go ask Dukes' neighbor in there, what's his name? Eddie? Go ask Eddie how that one works. You think Eddie was a big player in this whole thing?"

I took a quick look up and down the street, expecting somebody to be watching us. Two men standing in the yard, having an argument. But the street was empty.

"You make a fair point," I said, "but we still can't just leave. We can't let somebody else find these guys like this."

"Then we call the cops when we're on the road. Give them an anonymous tip, tell them to come check out this house. It'll do just as much good, without jamming us up. We have to keep moving, Alex, don't you understand?"

"But we have no idea where we're going. You know that."

"We have to think. We have to figure it out."

I let go of him. I wasn't ready to leave with him, but what he was saying, it was starting to sink in.

"Whoever did this," Lou said, "if they get to Vinnie and Buck first . . ."

In which case it would be hopeless, I thought. In which case they're as good as dead. But I didn't dare say it.

Then it hit me. If Buck was really the next target . . .

"You win," I said. "Let's go."

I was back behind the wheel, driving hard from Sault Ste. Marie to Bay Mills. I had to remind myself that I wasn't driving my truck now. If I roared by a Michigan State Trooper going eighty, he wouldn't know it was me and he'd pull me over in a second. In the state I was in, I had no desire to explain why I was driving so fast.

I kept seeing it in my head, those two men on the floor. The blood, the unnatural positioning of the bodies. The way the television cast the whole scene in an otherworldly glow. And something else. One more detail.

"Those two men," I said, not using the names. They didn't have names anymore. They were just dead meat on the floor. "They weren't shot."

He thought about it. He brought up the same image in his mind and, assuming he had the same power of recall, went over the two bodies from head to toe.

"No, they weren't," he said. "There was a lot of cutting."

"But not the throat. Did you notice that?"

"They bled to death," he said, nodding. "It probably took a while."

"So whoever did this, there was probably more than one of them. With a gun you can kill them both single-handed. But not this way."

"Yes," he said, nodding again. "There's at least two of them."

I kept the car on the road. Going straight. Between the lines.

"So pull over at this gas station," he said. "Let me call it in. If I do it, they won't have your voice on the tape."

"We'll do that in a minute. We've got something else to do first."

"Wait, aren't you the one who insisted we call somebody? Where are we going?"

"To Buck's house."

"We both know Buck's not there."

"You're right. We know that. But we have no idea if *they* know that."

"I don't follow you."

"Whoever these people are," I said. "If you happened to be sitting in Buck's house and they rang the bell, do you think you'd be safe opening the door?"

He looked at me while he thought about that one.

"Are you saying there might be somebody at Buck's house today? Even though he's gone?"

"I'm saying there's almost definitely somebody there. It's the local party house, whether he's around or not."

He didn't say anything to that. He didn't have to. I kept driving as the sky got darker and the moon rose above the trees. When I got to the intersection in Brimley, we could see all of the cars in the Cozy's parking lot. We barreled down that road, around the curve of Waishkey Bay, until we finally got to Buck's house. There were no cars in Buck's driveway besides his old beat-up clunker, but that meant nothing. Not in a neighborhood where most of your extended family and every close friend is within walking distance.

We got out and went to the door. I knocked but nobody answered. I tried the door. It was unlocked. I pushed it open. Then I turned on the first light switch I could find. The living room was empty. There were beer cans by the dozen, lined up in rows on every flat surface.

"Good thing you're not a cop anymore," Lou said. "This would not be kosher, just walking in."

"It's not kosher for anybody. But I figure we can make an exception."

I went down the hallway to the bedroom. I turned on a light and saw an unmade bed and several loads of laundry all over the floor. There was a faint odor of marijuana in the air.

When I am done with this and Vinnie is home safe, I said to myself, I will make sure I never have to smell this stuff again. I don't care if it really is nonaddictive and the plant itself is the answer to every problem in the world, I swear to God I hate the sickly sweet smell of it so much right now.

I backed out of the bedroom and stuck my head into the next

room. A guest room, I suppose you would call it, on account of the folded-out futon, but really it was just another place to throw piles of clothes and a huge old tube television that probably weighed a ton and a half. The most important thing was that there were no dead bodies anywhere.

I poked my head into the bathroom and even pulled open the shower curtain. The tub needed cleaning, but at least it wasn't full of blood.

I met back up with Lou in the kitchen.

"Nobody here," he said. "I guess that's good news for once."

I was about to agree with him. Then we both heard it behind us and we froze. It was the unmistakable sound of a pump-action shotgun being racked, a sound that would turn even the hardest man's knees to jelly.

"Don't move," a voice said. "Either one of you. Now turn around slowly."

I wasn't about to point out that we'd have to move to turn around. I figured just keeping my mouth shut and following his last instruction was probably the way to go. As we both turned at the same time, I saw the man standing there. I was expecting a police officer. Hell, maybe even Chief Benally himself. In which case we could immediately begin explaining ourselves. But no, the man was not wearing a uniform. He was wearing a light windbreaker and a baseball cap. I had never seen him before.

"I suppose you're Buck," he said, pointing the gun barrel at Lou.

"No," Lou said. "You've got the wrong guy."

The man looked a little confused. Then the gun barrel came over to me.

"He's not Buck, either," Lou said. "Buck's not here."

"How do I know you're not just lying to me?"

Canadian, I thought. That accent. In a land of Yoopers, many of whom sound almost but not quite Canadian, this guy was the real thing.

"This man's name is Alex," Lou said. "Does he look like an Indian to you? And hell, I'm probably twice Buck's age."

"How would I know how old he is?" the man said. "I just know he lives in this house. That's all. So I figure that has to make you him."

"Well then, you don't know a thing about Indians," Lou said. "We walk into other people's houses all the time."

The man closed his eyes for a moment. He let out a long breath. "Where is he, then?" he said. "Where is Buck Carrick?"

"We're going to tell you the truth," I said. "And then I hope you'll put the gun down. Buck Carrick has been missing for four days. Lou and I have been trying to find him. That's why we're here right now."

Another long breath from the man. A few seconds ticked by. It seemed to me like he had no idea what to do next. Not a good idea when you're holding a shotgun. It looked like a Benelli to me. One of the sleek black models. But I was pretty sure even a cheap gun would have blown us both apart just fine.

"I need to know where he is," the man said. "That's the only reason I'm here. Tell me where he is and I'll leave."

"I swear we don't know," I said. "Please put the gun down."

He hesitated for a few more seconds. Then he lowered the gun barrel. Lou took a step toward him, but I grabbed his arm.

"It's not even loaded," the man said. "I apologize if I scared you."

Lou still seemed to want to get a lot closer to the man, whether to take the gun away or to smack him right in the face, I didn't know.

"Just put it down, please," I said. "You'll make us both feel a lot better."

He bent down and laid the gun down on the kitchen floor. He did it slowly and carefully. Then he just stood there rubbing his forehead, his eyes closed.

I went over and picked up the shotgun. It was indeed a high-end Benelli and it was unloaded.

"It's my brother's gun," he said. "I've never shot it before. I've never shot *any* gun. I hate guns."

"Who's your brother?"

"His name is Pete. I mean, his name *was* Pete. He's dead now."

"What happened to him?"

The man opened his eyes and looked at me.

"He was killed four days ago. At the Newberry airport. I assume you men know about what happened there?"

I let that fact sink in. I was about to ask the obvious follow-up question, but he beat me to it.

"He was the pilot," the man said. "He's the guy who flew the plane and never came back."

We sat down with the man, right there in the kitchen. He apologized a few more times. His first name was Perry. We never even got his last name. We found a bottle of cheap whiskey in the kitchen cupboard and poured him a drink. He sat there and nursed it for a while. Then he finally told us his story.

"My brother Pete and I," he said, "we've been making these flights over to the States, from Port Elgin. We were flying at night."

"We know that part of it," I said. "You find an empty airstrip in Michigan, turn on the ground lights from your cockpit."

"The PCL, yeah. Pilot-controlled lighting."

"That's how you deliver a whole planeload of marijuana across the border, without anybody catching you."

He just looked at me.

"We're not the police," I said. "We don't care at this point. Please, continue what you were saying."

"Yes, it's pot," he said. "Not hard drugs. Not even an addictive drug at all, if you want to get technical. Way less dangerous than tobacco or alcohol."

He raised his glass to emphasize that last point. I didn't feel like hearing the whole extended argument again, so I just waved him on.

"We were doing it for the money, I'll give you that much. These growers in Canada, they can make a lot of money moving it over to the States, and we get a good cut of that. Even though it's a pretty easy flight. Just fly low, right over the water. Light up and land. They're waiting right there, unload, boom, you're done. Back in the air in ten minutes. Fly back home. It was actually kind of an adrenaline rush. I really enjoyed it, I admit. Until the one night I landed and the wrong people were there waiting for me."

"Wait a minute," I said. "That was you? Earlier this summer?"

"That was me, yes. I landed and there were these two guys there, with guns. I told you, I hate guns. But they pointed them at me and they told me I would be working for a new organization now. Same schedule, same pay. Everything nice and friendly, they said. Which would have sounded a little better if they didn't have guns pointed in my face. Then they made me help unload the cargo. When I was going to their truck, I could see my regular contacts handcuffed to the fence. They were alive, at least. I mean, nobody got killed that time, right? That should have been enough of a warning."

"Who were these guys who hijacked the cargo?"

"They weren't exactly wearing name tags. But they said they were working for a man named Corvo."

"Corvo," I said, looking over at Lou. He shook his head. The name was just as new to him.

"I think they were from Chicago," Perry said, "if I know my American accents. But whatever. I didn't care. As far as I was concerned, that was my last flight. I tried to convince Pete of that, too. But, well, he wasn't there with me when the men with guns showed up, first of all. And second of all, he always was a little more crazy than me."

"Was he doing the flights all along?"

"We both were, yeah. Mostly me, because I had a lot more hours in the air and visual flying by night can be a little tricky. But once he got his license, I started bringing him along once in a while. I figured he could start spelling me if I didn't want to make a run, and hell, he could start making some money, too. He'd already done like three or four solo flights by the time this happened. I told him, hey, that's it for us, we're done. No sense getting killed over it. But then when Harry and Jo kept calling. . . ."

"Those are the Kaisers you're talking about," I said. "Harry and Josephine Kaiser."

"To tell you the truth, I never did hear their last name. They weren't calling us directly, they were calling the growers and then they'd put the product together and they'd say like, 'Harry and Jo will have a couple men waiting for you. Go to this airport at such-and-such a time.' That kind of thing. I never met Harry and Jo, because they'd always have their guys there doing the unloading."

"Would they give you the money, too?"

"No, that was all done separately, between Harry and Jo and the growers. Then the growers would pay us. But anyway, when this thing happened with Corvo and his men, like I said, I was all done. But then Harry and Jo got this idea that they could move the drops way the hell up north, in the Upper Peninsula. I said no way, because we'd have to fly over Lake Superior instead of Lake Huron, which means taking off from a different airport, like maybe Batchawana. You need something small but not too small. But even if you got that worked out, it would only be a matter of time until the wrong people found out about it again. And this time they wouldn't be so 'friendly.' "

"So he did the flight to Newberry," I said. "You tried to stop him."

"I didn't get the chance. I didn't even know about it until he was gone. The growers came right to him, told him they had this new route worked out. Harry and Jo were gonna pay more, and it was a longer flight so Pete would be paid more, and everybody would be happy. It's four days later and I still don't even know which airport he took off from. None of the growers will talk to me. They've all disappeared. Their phones are disconnected. Finally, I remembered I had this one number for Harry and Jo, an emergency number in case their men ever didn't show up. I called and I talked to them. To Jo, actually. She sounds like a real charmer. She was all like, oh my God, we're so sorry, we had no idea. We lost two of our own men here, they were like family to us. And I was like, I just need to know what happened. Why did they have to kill Pete? He was just the pilot. What on earth were they thinking of that they had to kill the guy flying the plane?"

He stopped talking for a while. He sat there in the kitchen holding a half-empty glass of whiskey with both hands. He stared down at the floor.

"Please keep going," I said. "Did they mention Vinnie and Buck?"

"They mentioned Buck," he said, looking up at me. "Buck and his getaway driver. I assume that's Vinnie you're talking about."

"His getaway driver?" Lou said. He'd been leaning back in his chair, listening intently to Perry's story. Now he was halfway to his feet.

"Jo said it was all Buck's idea," Perry said. "This whole new plan. Buck was working with this other dealer up here, some guy named Dukes."

"Andy Dukes," I said.

"Yeah, she said it was Buck and this guy Dukes who were really running the show now. Harry and Jo didn't even want to be in the business anymore, not after what happened. That's what she said. But then these guys went behind their backs and made the new arrangement to keep things going."

Lou sat back down, but he was leaning forward in his chair now. I could see him flexing his forearm muscles as he made two fists.

"I know it was a lie," Perry said. "Okay? I'm not that stupid. I know she was trying to cover her ass. I know this was all Harry and Jo and that these other guys were just the hired help. Like always."

"So why are you here?" I said. "If you know they weren't behind this . . ."

"They told me Buck was there," Perry said. "At the airport. They told me he was the only guy who walked away. Whether this other guy, this Vinnie, whoever he is, if he was the man who drove him away, I don't care. Whether *any* of this other stuff they're saying is true, I don't care. I just want to know if that one part of the story is true. If this one man named Buck Carrick was there that night, and if he really lived to talk about it. That's why I'm here. I just wanted to look him in the face and ask him what happened. Why my brother got killed. Or if he was, I don't know, if he was even alive when Buck just walked away from it. If he left him there dying on the ground."

He stopped again. I watched him stare at the floor for another half a minute.

"Even if this guy Buck is a walking dead man," he finally went on, "I had to hear it from him, face-to-face."

"Why did you say that?" I asked. "Why is he a walking dead man?"

"That's what Jo said. Him and Vinnie both."

I looked at Lou, waiting for him to react. But he just sat there like someone had slapped him across the face.

"She said Corvo would carve them all up like Thanksgiving turkeys," Perry said. "Her exact words. She told me I should stay out of the way, in fact, or I might get caught in the middle of it. She said I should just lay low for a while, wait for Corvo to get it out of his system. That's what Harry and Jo were going to do."

"Do you know where they are?" I said. "Do you know where Harry and Jo are *right now*?"

"No, I don't."

"Please think," I said. "This is very important."

"I promise you. I don't. I just had the one phone number. Here, I'll find it."

He took out his cell phone and did a quick scroll through the memory. He read me off a number and I recognized the 231 area code. It was almost certainly the number at their farmhouse in Cadillac. Either that or a cell phone. He tried calling the number, right then and there, but there was no answer. There wasn't even voice mail. Another dead end. Lou kept sitting there, watching both of us but not really seeing anything. I could tell his mind was somewhere far away.

In the end, when all the words had been said and his story was done, we took him and his unloaded shotgun back outside to his car. He had been parked down the street, where he could watch Buck's house. I told him that if we found Buck, I would have him call him. I told him Buck would tell Perry everything he knew about that night. About his brother Pete and the way he'd died. I figured that was the least I could promise him.

"I was thinking maybe I should go talk to this guy Dukes," he said, just before he got into his car. "Maybe he can tell me something."

"Don't bother," I said, and then I put up my hand before he could even pursue it. "Please, just go back home. You look exhausted."

"So do you," he said. "Both of you."

He was right, of course. But we were far from done. We watched him drive away.

"Come on," I said to Lou. "We still have to call the police."

I drove back down off the rez to the gas station next to the Cozy. I figured that was the closest pay phone. Lou sat in silence while I drove, then he got out and went to the phone. He had a quick one-sided conversation with the 911 operator. Then he got back into the car.

"What did you tell them?"

"I gave the woman the house number on Hursley Street," he said, "told her to send a car over."

"That's all?"

"I told her to send someone with a strong stomach."

We drove back to Paradise, once again passing the two houses on the rez that held his two daughters, along with his grandchildren, all sound asleep at this hour. Lou looked out the window as we drove by, and I couldn't even imagine what he was thinking.

The moon was waning but still bright. The lake was there just beyond the trees and when the trees broke we could see far out onto the water's cold surface. I was tired, but I was even more hungry, so when we came to Paradise I pulled into the Glasgow Inn. Lou still hadn't said a word.

Jackie took one look at us and knew better than to ask how the day had gone. We ate some of Jackie's famous beef stew and we each had a cold Molson. When we were done we got back into the car and drove up my road. My road and Vinnie's road. We stopped in front of Vinnie's cabin and gave it a quick once-over. Nobody had been there.

We were standing outside under the stars and I don't think either of us knew what to do next. We both needed to sleep, but to give in to that would have been to admit failure. We had looked for Vinnie and Buck all day long and had ended up right here where we had started.

The only difference was, now we had much more to worry about. Including a man named Corvo, who apparently liked to carve up each of his victims like a Christmas goose.

"You had a good idea last night," Lou finally said.

"Did I? I don't even remember."

"It was your idea to go find Dukes. You thought he was probably still close to his home and you were right."

"Not good thinking on his part," I said. "But yeah, that's how we started the day, huh? Seems like a long time ago."

"I'm trusting that you'll have another good idea tonight. So go and get some sleep. We both need our strength for tomorrow."

"Okay. You're right."

"We'll find them tomorrow," he said. "I know we will."

I drove him to my second cabin and dropped him off there. Then I went back to my own cabin. Get some sleep, the man says. Like it's that easy.

As I lay down, the thought came to me. A whole train of thought, running through my mind as unavoidably as a real train roaring down a set of real tracks. This man Corvo came to Sault Ste. Marie to butcher Dukes and he happened to find his neighbor in the house, too. But he didn't come out here to Buck's house. And he didn't come to Vinnie's house.

He knows they wouldn't be here. Either one of them. If he knows where they're *not*, he probably knows where they *are*. Which can mean only one thing. The one unavoidable thing I must stop myself from thinking, no matter how hard that may be.

Vinnie and Buck, wherever they are . . .

They're probably already dead.

CHAPTER THIRTEEN

I slept more than I'd thought I would. But it was a thin troubled sleep born of sheer exhaustion, and I awoke the next morning feeling like it had done me no good at all. I got up and looked at the sunlight streaming through the window. It was another goddamned beautiful useless day in Paradise.

When I was cleaned up and ready to go, I drove down to the second cabin. Lou was gone, just like the morning before. Only this time he didn't come walking up the road. So I got back into the car and drove down past the other cabins, past the cabin with the four women from downstate, up here on their quest to help protect the nesting plovers. Right about then I would have paid big money to have that as my biggest problem, to be going out on the beach and looking for nests instead of whatever the hell the day had in store for me.

I drove past the next cabin, with the family here to visit Tahquamenon Falls and the Shipwreck Museum. Past the next three cabins, all empty that week. I finally found Lou sitting on a rock, just past the last cabin, on the edge of the woods. There was a slight wind that morning, and it was well past black-fly season. Otherwise he would have been sitting there on the rock being slowly eaten alive.

His eyes were closed. He opened them when he heard me coming closer.

"Good morning," he said. "You've come to tell me your great idea for the day."

"I wish I was. I've got nothing."

He just nodded at that. "It's been so long since I lived here, I swear, it's like I almost forgot I'm an Ojibwa. But being here, I don't know, it makes me remember that I've got roots here, going back a thousand years. Like I'm just a little twig on this one big tree."

"Okay . . ."

"So I guess I've just been sitting here trying to feel where my son is. Or if he's still even on this earth and part of the same tree."

"Are you having any luck?"

"I'm pretty sure he's alive. That's all I can say."

"That's good to hear."

"You don't totally believe me," he said, getting up slowly, "but that's all right."

"Maybe I do. I've lived around Vinnie and his people for a while now. I've even done a few sweats."

"In that sweat lodge at Buck's place? Did you have any visions?"

I wasn't sure what to say to that. There had been a time, shortly after Natalie . . .

"It's a personal thing," he said, before I could even start answering. "I'm glad you did the sweats. It makes you a better man."

He took a minute to shake out the kinks. I had no idea how long he'd been here, but the rock didn't look too comfortable.

"Come on," he said. "Now that we know he's alive, let's go find him."

We started out with breakfast at the Glasgow. We might have been telling ourselves that we were being smart and fueling up before starting a tough day, but the truth was that we had no idea what to do or where to go. We had hit a brick wall.

When we were done eating, I gave Janet Long a call. It was something I should have done the night before, I realized, and besides, I probably needed at least one person to give me a hard time before I could call it a good day. But she didn't pick up her cell phone, so I just left a message.

"That's my friend at the FBI," I said to Lou as I hung up. "I was just hoping she might have some new information."

"Would she actually tell you?"

"No, actually she probably wouldn't. She'd probably just read me the riot act and tell me to stay the hell away from everything. But I honestly don't know what else to do at this point."

"Maybe we should go back down to the Kaisers' house," Lou said, "see if we missed something."

"Like what?"

"I don't know. Anything that might point us in the right direction, to wherever they went. Just some little thing we might have missed."

"You sound like Leon now."

"Who's Leon?"

"He's a local private-eye wannabe," Jackie said, wiping down the bar, "but he's twice as smart as Alex."

"Not today, Jackie."

"No, wait, *I'm* twice as smart. Leon is three times as smart. I get that mixed up sometimes."

"I said not today," I told him. "Leave us alone, please."

Jackie walked away, mumbling.

"No, seriously," Lou said. "The Leon guy. Do you think he can help us?"

"He's on vacation," I said. "Camping with his family."

"Damn."

"But we can think like him," I said. "Hold on. What would he say if he was here right now? He'd say we should go over everything we did, step by step, and figure out the one small thing we're missing."

"What *we* did? Or what we think Vinnie and Buck did?"

I looked at him.

"I'm just wondering," he said, "if we try to follow their footsteps instead of ours, it might get us closer to what we're looking for."

"Okay, so I'm Buck," I said. "These people from downstate come up here. I know these people, a little bit. Or if I don't, at least my dealer in the Soo does. He can vouch for them. Anyway, they want me to help them do this thing over at the airport. Maybe I know the whole story, maybe I don't. But they come pick me up."

"Your truck is still at your house," he said. "So yeah, they had to come pick you up."

"Well, plus I'm the driver."

"Or at least the navigator."

"Or the navigator. Either way, they need me in the vehicle if we're going to take the back roads. So that's the plan. We go to the airport, we're expecting the plane to land. Then unexpected company arrives, and all of a sudden I'm in a bad situation I didn't ask for. Things get out of hand fast, somebody takes out a gun, and now everybody's shooting."

"You take one in the armpit."

"I do. I'm bleeding, probably in mild shock, even if the wound isn't that bad. Just the whole situation has me freaked out of my head. I have to get out of there."

"Why not take their vehicle?"

"Because it's theirs. Because this is a multiple-murder crime scene and I don't want to drive away with their vehicle, their keys, their license plate . . ."

"Either that," he said, "or you just ran away. Then you called later."

"That could be," I said. "I'm bleeding and I'm walking down the side of the road. I don't want to hitchhike and have somebody ask me what happened. Somebody who will read the paper and make the connection later."

"Okay, so your good friend and second cousin or whatever the hell he is comes and picks you up. I'm Vinnie now. That's something I'd actually do, right? Phone call in the middle of the night? I'd come pick you up?"

"That's something you'd do, yes. You might give me hell about it, but you'd do it in a second."

He nodded at that, thinking about his son. Thinking about what kind of man he was, this man he hadn't seen in thirty years.

"So I'm still Buck and I've got this cousin down by the Saginaw rez," I said. "He's a vet, but I know he can patch me up. It's three hours away, too. Just far enough for us to lie low for a couple of days."

"I drive you all the way down there."

"Three hours, like I said. That's nothing. You drive me down there and the good doctor fixes me. By then I'm already starting to wonder what we should do next."

"I'm telling you we should go to the cops, tell them everything that happened."

"That's probably what you're saying, right. I'm a little more worried about it. I saw those men trying to hijack the operation. I saw the shootout. I was the only man to walk away from it. I'm thinking I'm in a world of trouble if the wrong people find out about that."

"But how would they? Everybody who was there is dead."

"They'd find out. It might take a while, but they would. Especially if I go talking to the cops about it. If I tell them I was there, put it down on the record, hell, I might as well go rent out a billboard."

"Okay," he said, "so I leave a message with the Bay Mills police, just to let everybody know we're okay. How come I don't call anybody else?"

"Because you don't want to deal with the questions," I said, starting to get worked up about it again. The man was helping Buck deal with a serious situation and he didn't call me, I thought. I'm going to kick his ass all up and down this bar when I get him back here.

"Then you make a call yourself," he said. "To your friends the Kaisers. The people who got you in this mess in the first place. They're the people who sent the two men to the airport. It was their idea for you to be there, too."

"Right. It's all on them. I call them, and I tell them they have to help me. They say, don't worry, everything's gonna be cool. We're gonna take care of everything."

"So that's two days ago," he said. "We spend one more night down there and then you make one more call to the Kaisers. That's yesterday morning. Then we're off."

"We're off in a hurry."

He thought about that one. "We're in a hurry because . . ."

"Because the Kaisers aren't stupid. They know they're in as much danger as we are. Maybe even more."

"Okay, so we drive to their house, right?"

"Yes."

We both stopped there.

"Vinnie and Buck left in a hurry," I said, abandoning the role-playing game, "and they drove to the Kaisers' farmhouse in Cadillac."

"Meaning that the Kaisers must have been waiting there."

"So they could all leave together."

"Right."

"They're convinced that they've got cold-blooded killers bearing down on them," I said, "and yet they wait for Vinnie and Buck to get there before leaving?"

"It doesn't make sense," he said. "They would have gotten the hell out of there in two seconds. Told them to meet them somewhere. Or something."

"It makes no sense at all."

"And yet they *were* in a hurry to leave," he said. "Vinnie and Buck were, I mean. I don't imagine it's because they wanted to make teatime at the Kaisers' house."

"Jackie, where's the phone?" I said.

He looked up from the other end of the bar, where he was cleaning some glasses.

"I thought you told me to go away."

"Just give me the phone."

He came down the bar, grabbed the phone from underneath, and put it on the bar top.

"You know where the phone is," he said. "You could have gotten it yourself."

I dialed Information and asked for Dr. Carrick's number in Mount Pleasant. When it connected, it was answered on the second ring by one of the assistants.

"I need to speak to Dr. Carrick right away," I said. "Tell him it's Alex McKnight, the man he talked to yesterday."

"I'll see if he's free."

I waited a couple of minutes, tapping my fingers on the bar top. Lou got up and stretched, walking to the window and then back when he heard me start speaking again.

"Dr. Carrick, I'm sorry to bother you," I said when I finally got him on the line. "I just wanted to ask you one more question. Actually, before I do that, is there anything else in general you might have remembered about Vinnie and Buck being down there, anything else they might have said or done that you didn't tell us yesterday."

"No, Mr. McKnight, I think I told you everything I could recall."

"Okay, then if you can just think back to yesterday morning. They're about to leave and they say they're in a hurry, right?"

"Yes . . ."

"Try to remember everything as it happened. They're packing up the truck . . ."

"Well, there was nothing to pack, remember. It's not like they had luggage or anything. They just got in and left. They were still wearing the same clothes."

"Okay, good. These are all good details. They get in the truck, and you said you wanted them to stay and have lunch at least?"

"Yeah, but they said they had to get there by a certain time."

"Wait," I said. "See, this is new. There's a difference between being in a hurry just because you want to get somewhere as fast as possible, or because you have to be at a specific place at a specific time."

"Oh, okay. Yeah. But I thought I told you that yesterday."

"No, but that's okay. That's why the police will interview

somebody a couple times, because you'll often remember something different every time you tell the story."

I flashed back to Detroit, and one particular witness who was trying to describe an armed robbery at a bar. There were two men, and one of them held a shotgun while the other one cleaned out the register. I kept asking the witness if the second man was armed and the witness kept saying no. It wasn't adding up, because we found a second gun on the scene. A revolver which apparently didn't belong to anybody. Finally, my partner asked him the same question and the witness said no, he wasn't armed because "armed" means you're carrying a gun and this man had the revolver tucked in his belt.

We joked about that one for a few days, but it was a good lesson. My partner was in the ground now and I was years away from being a cop, but that same lesson was about to get learned, one more time.

"They had to be there by a certain time," the doctor said. "That's all I remember. I didn't ask about it, but I guess I was just assuming it was because they had to make a certain ferry. So they just got in the truck and—"

"Wait, stop," I said. "What ferry?"

"The ferry that they had to take to get to the island. I thought I told you that yesterday."

"No, you didn't. Which island?"

"I don't know. They didn't say. I was assuming Mackinac."

Lou leaned in closer, hanging on every word now. At least my side of the conversation.

"When they left your office," I said, "they drove to Cadillac. That's where we found Vinnie's truck."

"Cadillac? Are you sure?"

"Yeah, I said that when we were . . . Wait."

I closed my eyes and flashed back to one more interview, this one just the day before, in the doctor's office. I tried to reconstruct the whole conversation, word for word. Something I'm usually pretty good at doing.

He's telling us about them leaving. I say they went to Cadillac . . .

No, I was about to say it. That's when Lou jumped in and asked the guy why he let them leave if he knew they were in some kind of trouble. We would have gotten there if Lou could have just kept his cool.

"I think we got a little derailed yesterday," I said, giving Lou the eye. "So I guess this part of the story is new to both of us. You say they were going to an island, but they didn't say which?"

"Let me think . . . No. Like I said, I was assuming Mackinac, because, well, it's summertime in Michigan. What other island do you go to?"

"There's Drummond Island," I said. "Right down the road here."

"Ah, okay. So they could have been going there, but I'm pretty sure they didn't say. They just said they were going to the island, and yeah, that's what Buck said. He's standing there by the truck. I can see him in my mind. They were going to the island and they had to make the ferry. I was assuming that these people they were going to meet, that they were going to meet them there."

"But they didn't actually say that?"

He thought about it. "No, they didn't. I was just assuming. But you said Vinnie's truck was in Cadillac."

"That's right."

"So maybe they went there first. And then they went to the island."

"Which would explain everything," I said. "It all adds up."

"I guess it does, yes."

"Doctor, I can't thank you enough."

"It's my pleasure to help, Mr. McKnight."

I hung up the phone and asked Jackie for the Michigan map. When he brought it over, I spread it out on the bar. I grabbed a pen and made a big star over Mount Pleasant. Jackie complained that I was ruining his map but I ignored him. I made a second star over Cadillac.

"They were all on their way to an island," I said. "They were in a hurry to catch a ferry."

"Maybe they've got a summer house on Mackinac," Lou said, looking over the map. "We know they've got some money."

"Good point."

I put a question mark next to Mackinac Island.

"It would be a hell of a place to hide out, too," I said. "A million people in the summer. No cars. Just horses and bikes. If you were in one of those houses up on the hill, how's anybody going to find you?"

"So there or Drummond Island. Lots of summer places there."

"Right," I said, marking Drummond Island with another question mark. "That's one more island and one more ferry."

"How about Beaver Island? You ever been there?"

"No, I don't believe I ever have. It's a lot less developed, right?"

"Yeah, but there is a ferry, so . . ."

"You're right," I said, sliding over to that side of the map and putting a third question mark next to the big island in Lake Michigan.

"There's a ferry at Sleeping Bear Dunes," he said, moving down the Lake Michigan shoreline. "It goes out to the Manitou Islands."

"But those aren't even inhabited. Unless they're hiding out in a tent."

"Yeah, I think we're talking about one of the big three," he said. "Let's just go to all of them. If we start now, maybe we'll find them by Christmas."

"If we have to pick one," I said, "it's gotta be Mackinac, right? It's got the most people by far. So just from a probability standpoint . . ."

"I don't mean to interrupt," Jackie said, "but why would you have to hurry to catch a ferry to Mackinac Island?"

We both just looked at him without saying a word.

"The ferry leaves every half hour. If you miss one, no big deal."

"It's the same story with Drummond Island," Lou said. "It's such a quick ferry ride, those guys are running it back and forth every few minutes."

"That leaves one island," I said. I didn't have to point. All six eyes were already drawn to it. Beaver Island, with the long ferry ride across Lake Michigan. Even in the height of the season, that ferry might go across two or three times a day. Maybe four times on a Saturday.

"Yesterday was what," I said, "Thursday?"

"They've got two ferries on Thursday," Jackie said. "Mondays and Thursdays, those are the slow days. I had a guy in here once asking about it."

"Do you remember what times?"

"I think the last one went out at like three or something. Maybe two thirty, I don't know. I remember thinking you better like being on Beaver Island because it sure sounds easy to get stuck there."

"That's a ferry you'd really have to hurry to get to," Lou said.

He didn't have to say anything else.

CHAPTER FOURTEEN

We took Lou's rental car again. The ultimate act of optimism, taking the vehicle with room for four people, in the hope that we'd need that many seats on our way home. Lou pulled out his cell phone and called ahead while I drove. He reached somebody at the ferry office and there was indeed a two-thirty ferry, so that's the one we were shooting for. Because it was Friday, there was actually a later ferry, at five thirty, but we wanted to get out to the island as soon as possible.

He called Information next and asked for any listing under Kaiser on Beaver Island. He came up empty, but then that would have been asking way too much out of the day.

He put his cell phone away and picked up mine from the front-seat console between us. "I thought *mine* was old," he said. "I'm surprised you don't have to wind this one up."

I kept driving. He tapped his fingers on his lap like a drummer keeping time. Then he'd stop for a while. Then he'd start tapping again.

"Do you think they know?" he finally said.

"Know what?"

"How much trouble they're in. How serious this Corvo guy who's supposedly looking for them is."

"I don't know who's worse at this point," I said, shaking my head. "Corvo or the Kaisers. I mean, Corvo's obviously a psychotic killer. We saw that ourselves."

"So how could the Kaisers be worse?"

"At least you know that the psychotic killer is bad. The Kaisers you might actually mistake for friends. People on the same side as you, anyway."

"Do you think they're telling Corvo the same lie they told Perry?"

"If they have any kind of communication," I said. "No doubt about it. I haven't even met them yet, but I'm sure they'd sell out Vinnie and Buck in two seconds."

We made good time through Petoskey, which is always a crapshoot in the summer, when half the remaining rich people in Detroit are in town. Little Traverse Bay was on our right, sparkling in the sunlight, and it was hard to blame all of those people for being there. Hard but not impossible. As much as Lou had on his mind, he couldn't help but look out his window with obvious wonder as we passed through Bay Harbor, with the golf courses and the yacht club and the equestrian club high on the hill.

"I know it's been a long time since I've been here," he said, "but damn."

"They call it Michigan's Gold Coast now."

"You're kidding, right?"

"I am not kidding."

We kept following the shoreline until we got to Charlevoix. That's where you can find the *other* half of the rich people from Detroit during the summertime. There's a drawbridge that separates Lake Michigan from the little Round Lake, which leads into Lake Charlevoix, one of the biggest inland lakes in the state. On a day like this you could sit on the shore and watch so many powerboats and sailboats and jet skis you'd probably lose count. The ferry to Beaver Island comes in and out of Round Lake when the drawbridge is raised. I'd never been on the boat before, but I knew it was big enough for a good three hundred people and a couple dozen vehicles in the hold.

"It's gonna take you forever to park," Lou said. "Just let me out here and I'll get the tickets."

I let him out when I stopped at the light, then I kept crawling along with the other traffic. There's one main street running through town, and it gets backed up all to hell even when the drawbridge isn't up. If you live in the UP, like I do, all you have to do is drive a couple of hours down to Petoskey and Charlevoix and you'll feel like you're in the middle of Times Square.

There's a little ticket booth on the promenade overlooking Round Lake. A bandstand, a few dozen little boutiques up and down the street, a good hundred boats parked down in the marina. The sun beating down on everything, never too hot with the breeze coming off Lake Michigan. It's one version of perfect, I grant you that. An overcrowded version, though, and definitely not for me.

I circled the block and came back to find Lou waiting at the same traffic light. He got into the car and told me to keep going.

"Wait," I said, "aren't we parking?"

"No, we're going to the airport."

"What are you talking about?"

"You know how long the ferry ride is?"

"It's like an hour, right?"

"Try two hours," he said. "If we go to the airport, we can catch a little plane and be over there in twenty minutes. The next flight leaves at two. We'll just make it."

He didn't have to do any more convincing. A two-o'clock flight would get us to the island before the ferry was even pushing off from the dock, and right now a two-hour head start sounded like twenty-four-karat gold.

Assuming that they were actually out there on that island. I kept coming back to our plan and telling myself it was the craziest long shot of all time. But at this point we didn't have anything else.

The Charlevoix airport was on the south side of town, just past all of the midday summer madness. I parked in the lot and we went inside. The whole airport was a one-room affair, with separate check-in desks for the two airlines that flew to Beaver Island. We went to the desk that had the two-o'clock flight, and that's when Lou stopped dead.

"What's the matter?" I said.

"Metal detector," he said, pointing to the door that led outside to the airstrip. "I wasn't thinking they'd have one here."

I put my hand on the small of his back and felt the gun. How the hell he'd gotten it out of the glove compartment, I had no idea. No doubt it was loaded.

"Go put it back," I said. "Hurry up."

He hesitated. "What if we need it?"

"Then we use a big stick instead. I'm pretty sure they have big sticks on the island."

"I'm serious. This is no time to be unarmed."

"You don't have a choice, so just go back and—"

"You get on the plane," he said. "I'll take the ferry."

"What?"

"You go and check things out. I'll take the ferry and meet up with you. That way, we'll have some heat and we'll have wheels, too."

The woman behind the desk told us we'd have to get on the plane if we were going. In the end, it was the car business that tipped the scales for me. It was a big enough island, after all, and it wasn't like Mackinac. You could actually take your car over and drive there. You didn't have to rely on horses or bikes.

"All right," I said. "I'll go start looking around. Or asking around. Or whatever the hell it is we're gonna do there. You bring the car over and I'll meet you at the ferry dock. If I'm not there, give me a call on my cell phone. Do you have my number?"

We took another minute to get that straightened out. Then I bought my ticket and hurried through the metal detector and the door and then I was outside, back in the bright sunlight, looking at a little six-seat Piper Aztec with a prop on each wing. I couldn't help thinking it was just like the plane I'd seen at the Newberry airport, back when this whole thing started. Only this plane wouldn't be stuffed to the rafters with marijuana, and when I got on the ground I could only hope there wouldn't be men with guns drawn, waiting for me.

It was a quick flight. I was one of three passengers. I sat directly behind the pilot, and as the little plane rattled down the runway I couldn't help remembering how much I disliked flying in these things. You feel like every gust of wind is going to turn you right over. It was still a crystal-clear day so at least I got a good look at the lake and then at Beaver Island as we got closer to it. It was the largest island in Lake Michigan by a long shot, that much I remembered. It was flat and sandy, sort of oval-shaped, and it kind of looked a little out of place, like it should have been out in the ocean instead. There were trees as you got in close to the middle of the island, and there were even two fairly substantial interior lakes. Lakes within an island within a lake.

The island had some unusual history, what with this man named James Strang bringing over a group of Mormons in the nineteenth century and declaring himself king. He ended up getting killed by some of his subjects, but the one main town on the island is still called Saint James. There's a lot more to the story, I'm sure, but that's all I know about the place. As the plane coasted in, I thought about the smugglers' plane again, and how the pilot was able to turn on the airfield lights automatically, even though it was the middle of the night and the place was deserted. I was about to ask the pilot just how that worked, but he was getting ready to actually land our plane, so I left him alone. He brought it in right on the grass, completely avoiding the paved runway for whatever reason. We bumped along on the grass for a few hundred feet, then he turned and brought it around to the airport, which wasn't even half the size of the airport we'd taken off from.

I got out with the other two passengers and stood blinking in the sunlight. The airfield was surrounded by trees and I couldn't have told you how close it was to the town of Saint James. The other passengers had cars waiting for them. I was about to ask one of them for a ride when the woman inside the terminal came out and told me she was going into town. I thanked her and got into her car.

"What brings you out here?" she said to me as she drove. She was young and attractive, and I couldn't help wondering how she'd ended up here on this island, working in this tiny little airport.

"Just paying someone a visit," I said. "They were supposed to pick me up, but I guess they must have lost track of time. I bet you even know them. You probably know everybody on this whole island."

"I probably do." She was driving maybe a little too fast on the narrow road, but I figured she knew this place so well, she could probably do it with her eyes closed. "I grew up here, after all. I tried moving to the mainland, but it just didn't work. I had to come back. The pilot who flew you in is my husband."

She was talking fast. I was waiting for my opportunity, and when she finally paused to take a breath I asked her the big question of the day.

"It's the Kaisers," I said. "The people who were going to pick me up. Do you know them?"

She frowned as she thought about it. "Are they summer people?"

"I believe so, yes."

"Oh, well, if they're summer people I might not know them. I've probably seen them at the airport, but I don't recognize the name."

"Harry and Josephine Kaiser," I said. "They look like a couple of old hippies."

"Okay, that sounds familiar. Yeah, I'm pretty sure I've seen them."

I didn't know if she was just being agreeable, or hell, how many couples look like old hippies, anyway? I had no way of knowing if these were the actual Kaisers she was talking about. The possibility that this was all just a wasted trip was still very much on the table.

"Where are you going, anyway? Main Street okay?"

"Yeah, that's perfect. I really appreciate it."

"No problem at all. I was heading to the grocery store, anyway. Are you wondering which one?"

I looked over at her, not sure what she meant.

"That was a joke," she said. "We have one grocery store on the whole island."

I couldn't help wondering if everybody on the island was like her. Friendly and outgoing and just a little bit batty. Either way, she was taking me a good five miles north of the airport, running along the east side of the island until we got to the town. There was a natural inlet there, protected from the lake, and that's where the ferry dock was, along with the grocery store, the post office, a couple of bars and restaurants, and pretty much everything else you'd ever need if you were lucky enough to live here.

She parked by the grocery store. I got out and thanked her again. Then I walked across the street to the dock. I looked at my watch. It was almost three o'clock. That meant the ferry was probably clear of the drawbridge, but still a good hour and a half away.

I sat down on a bench for a while, just getting the hang of the place. This was the main street in town on a perfect summer day, and there were people walking up and down the street, but it wasn't anything like Mackinac Island, where there'd be ten times as many people. Not to mention a hundred horses, two hundred piles of horseshit, and five hundred bikes. There were cars on this island, and I sat there and watched a dozen different people park on the street and then go do whatever it was they were going to do, not bothering to lock their car doors. It kinda figured, because who's gonna steal your car when there's no place to go?

I watched the woman who had given me a ride come out of the grocery store, get into her car, and take off. She waved to me as she passed. I waved back and smiled.

That's right, I told myself. Keep smiling. Try to look like you belong here, like you're just another one of these people enjoying the beautiful summer day on the island. You're not gonna get anywhere if you start grabbing people and interrogating them, asking them if they know where the Kaisers' house is. Or the house they're renting for the summer.

Damn, this is not gonna be easy, I thought. Once again, you fail to think things through before you act. Story of your life.

I got up and walked into the first restaurant on the street. I ordered a Coke and stood there watching the people sitting at the tables. Some of them were reading the paper. Most of them were talking. Every time someone new came in the door, there'd be someone else there to welcome him or her by name. Usually two or three people. That would get a new conversation started, and it didn't take me long to realize that most everybody on this island seemed to know everybody, and that once again I was an outsider.

I kept the little smile on my face. I made myself walk slowly. I listened carefully to every conversation I could hear, waiting for a name to drop. I saw Harry today. I ran into Jo. That's all I needed. Just one mention of one name. But I was coming up empty.

I spent about a half hour doing that. Just walking around, listening, acting like I was out for a stroll. Looking at my watch like a good friend would be meeting me for coffee any minute now. While actually I was counting down the minutes until the ferry got there, when Lou would get out with the car and we'd be able to cover more ground. Drive around and look at mailboxes, look for Kaiser or, hell, maybe they've got some cute pothead nickname for their cottage. Purple Haze or High Times or whatever the hell else.

And then what? Knock on the door? Ask if Vinnie and Buck are inside, hiding from killers?

One step at a time, Alex. Just figure out if they're really here. Then you can decide what to do about it.

Another half hour passed. I noticed a lot of people were going into the post office. They'd leave with handfuls of mail and smiles on their faces. Even bigger smiles than when they went in, I mean.

That gave me an idea.

I went into the grocery store and picked out a big fruit basket, one of those things with the shrink wrap and ribbon wrapped all around it. Ten dollars' worth of fruit and a ten-dollar basket, so of course the thing cost seventy bucks. But it was exactly what I needed. I went to the cashier and put the thing down on the counter.

"Somebody's getting a nice present," the woman said.

"Yeah, the Kaisers," I said. "I'm on my way over there now."

She smiled and nodded.

"You know, the Kaisers' house. Over by the . . ."

I let that one drift off. I waited for her to pick it up, but she just looked at me and blinked a few times.

"Thanks," I said, leaving with my big basket of fruit.

I walked down to the post office and maneuvered my way through the door, almost knocking a few people over with the basket. When I got inside, the operation was even smaller than I had imagined. One counter with a roll-up gate, a number of post office boxes taking up two of the other walls. One little desk for people to put packages on while they taped them closed and stuck on their stamps.

"Who's the lucky duck?" the postmaster said. She was one of those old yet ageless ladies, with the perpetual twinkle in her eye.

"I'm a little lost," I said, putting on my best slightly daft, totally innocent, completely trustworthy face. Looking like a true Michigander, in other words.

"You can't get too lost around here," she said. "You just keep walking until you hit water. Then you know to stop."

I gave her a good laugh on that one.

"I'm meeting my friend on the ferry," I said. "And then we're going out to some people's house. These two people he knows. But he won't be here for a while and I was just hoping I could—"

"What's the name, hon?"

"Kaiser."

"No, don't know them. And believe me, I know everybody on this whole island. Are you sure you've got that right?"

"They might just be renting the house for the summer," I said. "Harry and Josephine Kaiser."

She looked up in the air, shaking her head. "Nope. Sorry, hon."

I felt the whole thing falling apart then. I still had a half hour to wait. Then I'd tell Lou this whole thing was a bust and we'd have to go back and start from scratch. Our only consolation would be a basket of fruit to eat on the way back to Paradise.

"Wait a minute, you don't mean Harry and Jo Kennedy, do you?"

"I don't know. I don't think so. I mean, who are we talking about?"

"You know, Harry and Jo," she said. "With the hair? And the clothes? Like they went to Woodstock and never made it back?"

She started laughing again and I tried to laugh with her. It was hard to do while my mind was racing ahead. A different place, a different last name. Same first names. A classic soft alias for people doing something criminal and making a token effort to cover their tracks.

"She was just here," the woman said. "Ten minutes ago. You just missed her."

"Oh, that's too bad." I tried to replay the tape in my head, me standing outside on the street, watching the people walk by. I'd probably looked right at her.

"They're renting the Hoffmans' place," she said. "You know where that is, right?"

"I think so. It's right up over by the . . ."

I let it trail off and this time it worked. She filled in the gaps and led me right to the house, over on the western side of the island. She even drew me a map. I thanked her a dozen times on my way out the door. As soon as the door closed, the happy little fake smile on my face was long gone.

I spent the next few minutes back over by the ferry dock. I was looking at my watch. I was counting down the minutes until that impossibly slow boat decided to finally turn the corner on that inlet. Even when I saw it, I knew it would be another several minutes before it docked, and then even more minutes until the cars were driven out of the hold. I couldn't stop thinking about all those cars on the street behind me, all those unlocked cars left there by happy carefree islanders, some of them with the keys still dangling from the ignition.

Thirty more minutes, I told myself. Thirty minutes and you'll have backup.

I was still holding the fruit basket. It was getting heavy. I was just about to put it down. That's when I felt something jab into my ribs.

"Don't turn around."

A woman's voice. She was right behind me. Just inches away. I felt her breath on my neck.

"Nobody can see this gun," she said. "But if I have to I'll shoot you right through the gut. Do you believe me?"

I nodded.

"I don't care how much of a scene it would make. I'll shoot you dead and then I'll just start screaming and I'll pretend the gun is yours. That you tried to abduct me and somehow it went off. Are we clear?"

I nodded again.

"Good thing I happened to stop back in the post office, huh? Flo told me you were looking for me."

I felt her free hand slip around my waist. She was giving me a quick, expert pat down.

"Silly me," she said. "You've got your gun in the fruit basket, right? I'd like you to drop it now. Do not bend down, do you understand me? Just let it drop."

I did as I was told. The basket hit the pavement and half the fruit started rolling away. Oranges. Apples. Grapefruit. All ruined.

"That's a shame," she said. "But we'll get over it."

I still hadn't seen her face. I stood there looking out at the water. In the distance, I could finally see the ferry. It was still a good mile away. Maybe two.

"Okay," she said. "Whoever you are. It's time for us to take a little ride."

CHAPTER FIFTEEN

"This is how it's gonna work." She had stepped away from me. Now she was four feet behind me. Maybe five.

"You're making a mistake," I said.

"Shut up," she said. "Not another word, do you understand? I'll drop you right here and nobody will have any idea what happened. I've got the gun inside a plastic grocery bag right now. Don't turn around, just take my word for it. It's inside this bag and if I need to shoot you I will. Everybody will start screaming. Nobody will know what the hell is going on. Nobody will see the gun. I'll just drop the bag and run away, like everybody else. You get what I'm saying? Just nod your head if you do."

I nodded.

"All right, then. There's a parking lot next to the post office. Across the street. You're going to turn around and you're going to walk to it. You're not going to make a sound. You're not going to look at anybody. You're going to look straight at the ground. If you so much as take one step in another direction, or if you so much as raise one hand . . . If you do anything that isn't one hundred-percent perfect and cooperative . . . I will shoot you without even blinking. Again, are we clear?"

I nodded.

"There's a black Jeep Cherokee on the left side of the lot. When you get to it, I want you to open the driver's-side door and get in. Sit with your hands in your lap and don't do anything else. Last time, are we clear?"

She's talking a good game, I thought. But I can't imagine she really wants to shoot me. Not unless she's a psychopath or something. Problem is, her finger's no doubt on the trigger. She probably has the damned thing half-squeezed already. If I do something stupid, she might react without even thinking about it.

As I turned slowly, I got a quick look at her. She was a little older than me, one of those women who say the hell with it and let their hair grow down over the shoulders, no matter how gray it is. Green tie-dyed summer dress with a black belt. Her eyes were sharp and quick and she had probably been attractive in some other decade, but even I could have told her that green was the worst possible color on her. It made her pale skin look purple and the ugly sandals didn't help one bit. Not that she would have cared one little bit what I thought of her appearance. I or anyone else. No makeovers for this woman. She had the hard-set mouth of someone who stands around sucking every last ounce of poison out of a cigarette and complaining about life.

"Nice and easy," she said as she moved around behind me. "You're doing just fine. I'm glad you're not as dumb as you look."

I crossed the street and headed for the parking lot next to the post office. Give her a minute or two, I thought. Until we're in the vehicle and she gets a little more comfortable. Maybe even relaxes the grip on her gun. Then try to talk to her.

"All right, everything nice and slow now," she said as we got closer to the black Jeep Cherokee. "Remember, open the door and get in. Do it in slow motion. Then just sit there and keep your hands in your lap."

I did as I was told. I sat down in the driver's seat and put my hands in my lap. I took one quick peek back across the street. The boat was still a few minutes from docking. There's no way I'd be able to stall her, and even if I did, Lou would have to hit shore and somehow notice me sitting over here. And then actually do something about it.

I was expecting her to come around and sit beside me, but instead she opened the door right behind me and sat in the backseat.

"This gun is six inches away from the back of your head," she said. "Do one thing wrong and I will literally paint that windshield with your brains. Are you with me? Are we still on the same page?"

I nodded. Then I heard a collection of keys hitting the seat beside me.

"Take the key that says 'Jeep' on it and put it in the ignition."

Under different circumstances, I would have had a quick comeback to that. Like thanks, I would have tried this house key instead. But this obviously wasn't the time for wisecracks, so I did as I was told. I put the right key in and turned it. The engine came to life.

This is the vehicle that was missing from the farmhouse, I thought. This is the vehicle that brought Vinnie and Buck to this place.

"Now you're gonna back out and then go to the street, at which point you will take a smooth left turn. You need to keep believing me when I tell you that I'll kill you in a second if you give me any reason. At this point, I will happily tell the police that you tried to kidnap me, and then I grabbed your gun and shot you with it. The gun is not registered to me, and I am a very good liar. So I'm quite sure I'd get away with it."

I'm quite sure that would make me the most inept kidnapper in history, I thought. But if the paper on that gun was really that clean, I had no doubt she'd be able to sell the story. Or at least that she *believed* she'd be able to sell it, which was all that mattered.

I put the vehicle in Reverse and backed it up using only the mirrors. Something told me she wouldn't have appreciated me turning around. I put it back in Drive and went to the street. I waited for a few cars to go by. Then I took the left.

"Now you're going to keep going straight and you're gonna keep the speed at exactly twenty miles an hour. You got that? If you hit twenty-one, well, you know what happens."

There was a strange spin on everything she was saying now. When she had first stuck that gun in my ribs, back on the dock, I could hear the fear in her voice and I could practically feel her hands shaking. Now, she had clearly gotten her nerve back. If I didn't know better, I would have sworn she was almost enjoying this.

How ironic it was, having had two different men point a gun at me that week, first Dukes with his already-cocked revolver stuck stupidly down his pants, then Perry with the empty shotgun. Both bumbling and useless in their own way, and now here was this woman a few years older than me, and she was clearly starting to get the hang of this.

"May I say something now?" I said.

I felt the sharp jab of the gun barrel against the back of my head.

"You'll speak when I ask you a question," she said. "For now, just keep driving. When this road comes to a T, you need to make a right."

I wasn't about to tell her that I knew that. I still had the map from the postmaster, after all. We were cutting through the interior of the island, and then we'd have to head north along the western shore.

"Okay, so here's your chance to talk," she finally said. "How stupid does Corvo think we are?"

"What are you talking about?" I expected the gun barrel to jab me in the back of the head again, but it didn't.

"I thought we were square," she said. "After today we're all back in business, and everybody knows we're gonna play nice from now on. That was the deal."

"You've got the wrong idea, ma'am. That's not why I'm here."

I heard a sharp intake of breath. I waited for what was going to happen next.

"I should kill you right now," she said.

I struggled to keep my foot light on the gas pedal. One good push and I could send her backward in her seat. Then slam on the brakes and with any luck she'd be dumped right in my lap.

Just thinking about it, I was already starting to creep up above her twenty-miles-an-hour speed limit.

"You're going too fast," she said. "Slow down right now."

I eased up on the pedal. It would be a high-risk move and she was agitated now, making it even more likely she'd pull that trigger. Maybe the first shot would go through the roof, but I didn't like my odds on the second.

That's when my cell phone rang. It was in my right pocket.

"Who's calling you?" she said. "Is that Corvo?"

"No, it's not."

"Toss your phone back here. Without answering it."

I leaned over so I could reach into my pocket. I had to struggle to keep the vehicle going straight while getting the stupid phone out, while at the same time not doing something that might be construed as offensive. When I finally got the phone out, it had rung a few more times. I tossed it into the backseat. I heard her fumble to pick it up off the floor and for one split second I thought I had a chance to do something.

"Don't even think about it," she said, a genuine mind reader on top of all of her other charms.

She flipped open my phone and apparently looked at the display.

"There's no name," she said. "Big surprise. But the number has a 702 area code. That must be one of those other Chicago area codes, right?"

"That's Las Vegas," I said, picturing Lou still on the boat, close enough to the island now to be in range. Calling to check in, to see if I'd made any progress.

"Las Vegas, what the hell? Are you kidding me?"

She snapped the phone shut.

"You know, they make real cell phones now," she said. "This thing belongs in a museum."

"That was Vinnie's father on the phone," I said. "He's looking for his son. Vinnie and Buck, both of them. That's why I'm here. I've got nothing to do with Corvo."

"You don't say," she said. "Just looking for the Indians. Wouldn't *that* be interesting."

"It's the truth. I need to know if they're alive."

"You need to shut your mouth is what you need to do. Make this right turn, then I'll tell you when we get there."

"You're not going to shoot me. We both know that."

Say it like you believe it, I thought. Like it's a calmly observed statement of undeniable truth. If she had any doubt, she'll start to believe it. At least that's the general idea. Whether it really works or not, I guess we're gonna find out.

"The day is young," she said. "I got a feeling a lot of different things are gonna happen before the sun goes down."

The phone rang again. She didn't answer. She didn't even look at it. I tried to guess how much time had passed, tried to imagine where Lou was at that moment. Maybe off the boat by now. Standing on the dock, looking around and swearing at his phone. Maybe his car was off by now, maybe not. Either way, it was hard to put together any series of events that would lead him my way.

Unless . . .

"We're close now," she said. "Slow down."

Unless he follows the same general plan that I did. Take a look around at the main street, register the fact that everybody seems to know everybody else. Then start fishing. All you have to do is walk into that post office and you'll be one big step closer.

"I said slow down!"

I hit the brakes, not quite hard enough to send her flying but I heard her give out a little yelp of surprise.

"You want to die right now?" she said. "Turn into this driveway."

I made the turn. There was an empty driveway leading to a nice little summer house. The trees were thick on either side of the house, but I could see the lake through the branches. I could gun it right now, I thought. Make it through that one gap in the trees and I'd be in the lake before she could even think twice. She'd shoot me for sure, but at least she'd probably drown a few minutes later.

"Right here is fine," she said. "In case you're wondering, the houses on either side of us are empty right now. I could shoot this thing as many times as I want and nobody would notice."

Not exactly true, I thought. If you shoot outside, they'll hear it halfway around the island. If you shoot it inside, you'll still get people all up and down the street looking up from their papers and wondering what the hell just happened. Of course, maybe she knows that and she's just saying it for my benefit. Somehow, I didn't think it would be worth calling her bluff.

"Take the key out of the ignition and toss it back to me," she said when we were stopped.

"I assume you want me to put it in Park first."

"Watch the mouth," she said. "Yes, put it in Park."

I took it out of gear, turned the vehicle off, and tossed her the key.

"Now open your door, but stay seated."

I opened the door. She got out behind me and came up next to the side mirror. My door wasn't all the way open, so for one instant I thought about kicking it right into her, but she took a step backward before I could even try it. She kept taking quick looks behind her, as if expecting someone to come out of the house.

"Get out and put your hands on your head," she said. "You leave them there until I say otherwise. You got that?"

I didn't bother answering. I got out of the car and stood in the sunlight, with my hands on my head like some kind of prisoner of war. In a way, maybe that's exactly what I was.

"Turn and walk to the house. Nice and easy. You keep cooperating, you stay alive."

The first positive thing she'd said, I thought. The first ray of hope.

"Harry!" she yelled. "Where the hell are you?"

There was no answer from the house.

"God damn him. Just keep walking. Go all the way onto the back porch."

There were stairs leading up to the side door, and that same landing wrapped around to the rest of the porch. I went up the stairs, looking for some advantage, something I could use to knock the gun from her hand, or at least to use as a shield. But she was being way too careful.

As we turned the corner, I saw two men sitting there on the porch. They were both in their twenties, one of them long and lean, the other shorter and heavier. They were both wearing long shorts and elaborate tennis shoes and nothing else. The shirtless look did a lot more for the lean guy than the heavy guy, but either way it was like a visual battle of the tattoos. Between the two of them, they must have been carrying around ten square feet of ink.

"Sugarpie and Dumpling," the woman said. "Get the hell up and take care of this fool for me."

It took a few seconds for the two men to process what they were seeing. The joint they were sharing probably didn't help any. When it finally broke through that a stranger was standing on the deck and that Jo was pointing a gun at his back, they jumped up out of the chairs and grabbed me by each arm. The joint got put down in the ashtray and there it lay, still smoking, filling the porch with a dull haze.

"I didn't say pull him apart," she said. "Just sit him down there."

They did as they were told, planting me in the chair and standing over me like they both expected me to try something. Even though one had a few inches on me and the other about eighty pounds.

"Who is he?" the tall guy said, looking down at me with his hands clenched. "What the hell's he doing here?"

"We're still trying to figure that out," she said. "Where the hell is Harry, anyway?"

"He's not back yet."

"Not back from where?"

They both sneaked a look at her and then at each other.

"Wait a minute," she said. "Are you seriously telling me that Harry went out there by himself?"

"He had a lot of money with him," the heavy one said. "I guess he doesn't trust us."

"What were you gonna do, Dumpling?" she said, going over to the heavy man and squeezing his cheek. She literally squeezed his cheek like he was five years old, and at the same time she solved

forever the mystery of who was Sugarpie and who was Dumpling.
"Did he think you were gonna run off with the money or something?"

"Apparently that was the general suspicion, yes."

"God damn," she said, turning to the other one. Sugarpie, apparently. "And you just let him go on with this foolishness? You let him
go all the way out there by himself? What, like ten miles of open
water?"

"What was I supposed to do?" the tall one said. "He had his mind
made up. You know how he is."

"He's an idiot is how he is. God damn both of you. You should
have tied him up right here on this porch, like this guy. Which by
the way I notice you haven't done yet."

"I'll go get the zip ties," Dumpling said. He bounded off the
deck and down the stairs. That left me with just Sugarpie hovering
over me, balancing on the balls of his feet and extending his hands
out in front of him like we were about to wrestle.

The woman went to the railing of the deck and looked out onto
the lake. She still had the gun, and she was still too far away for
me to make a move for it. Especially with Sugarpie watching me.

I turned my head to look out at the lake. It was a beautiful view,
I'll say that much. There was a path leading down from the house,
through the wildflowers surrounding the trees. Out on the water,
the sunlight was dancing in every ripple. The shoreline itself was
rough and unforgiving, but for me that would have made this place
even better. No docks, no boats, no noise beyond the light breeze
tickling the wind chimes hanging in the corner. On any other day,
this would have been the best place in the world to be.

Today, well, maybe it was just the perfect place to spend my last
hours on earth.

"Eyes straight ahead," she said without looking at me. "Sugarpie, keep a lid on our guest, will you?"

He went to grab my hair, but I dodged my head out of the way.
He responded to that by smacking me across the face.

"You don't have to beat him to death," she said. "Just keep a lid on
him."

He folded his arms and stared down at me with a sick little smile.

"It's not like he could have gotten lost," she said, turning back to the water. "It's impossible, right? Even for him."

"That's right, Jo. I'm sure he's okay."

"Yeah, I'm sure he's okay," she said, speaking more to herself now than to anyone else. "There's no way anything could have gone wrong."

We spent another couple of minutes this way, as she stood there watching the lake, rocking back and forth in her sandals. Finally, the sound of a motor began to cut through the breeze. It was coming from the lake. A boat.

No, not a boat. As it got closer, I could hear that the motor was in a higher register. It was a small craft, probably a jet ski. Which made sense because you sure as hell weren't about to dock a boat down on that rocky shoreline.

In my peripheral vision, I saw her whole body language change as she watched someone dock whatever it was he was driving or riding, and then she followed his progress up the trail to the house. I was interpreting everything through her face, because it was all happening behind me, but she was obviously relieved and for one quick moment I could almost even see her smiling.

"What the hell were you thinking?" she screamed at him as soon as he was close enough to hear her. So much for smiling.

"That was the worst ride of my life," the voice said from behind me. "I'd like to see you go try it."

"You had me worried half to death, you idiot."

"Hey, I got back here as fast as I could! The currents were a lot stronger than I thought, so just get off my back, okay?"

I heard steps on the stairs and then the man himself, Harry, came around the corner, onto the back deck. He was dressed in a wet suit, and his hair was slicked back against his head. He was bald on top, but he was one of those guys who tries to make up for it by growing it as long as possible on the sides. Whether he tried to comb it over or not, I couldn't say, because now he just looked like a half-drowned rat.

He might have been older, but he processed the situation a lot quicker than Sugarpie and Dumpling had.

"Who the hell is this?" he said, nodding at me. "What's going on?"

"He's been looking for us," she said calmly. "He was asking about us, all over town."

"What are you talking about? How was he looking for us? How did he end up here? How did he . . ."

His brain overloaded about then and he couldn't speak any more. He just kept looking at his wife, then me, then Sugarpie, then back at his wife. All the while he continued to drip water onto the nice wooden deck.

"I thought he must be working for Corvo," she said. "I thought maybe we were getting double-crossed or something."

"What, you mean sending one of his men out here? Are you serious?"

He came closer to me, bending down a bit to look closer at me like I was some kind of exotic animal.

"Is that what this is?" he said to me. "Is this the old double-cross, Corvo-style?"

He straightened up and looked at his wife before I could answer. Then he bent down again. He was dripping water on my shoes now.

"I did everything he told us to do," the man said. "The Indians are out in the boat, along with the money."

That got me to the edge of my chair. Sugarpie knocked me back with one long arm and then he put his hands on my shoulders. If the railing hadn't been behind me, he would have turned the chair over with me in it.

"Stay right there," Jo said, pointing the gun at my head. "You try that again and I'll kill you."

"Are you talking about Vinnie and Buck?" I said. "God damn it, where are they?"

"He doesn't work for Corvo," she said to her husband. "There's no way."

"I don't know," Harry said. "Why else would he be here?"

"Look at him. He's too old, for one thing. And he's not all pumped up on steroids."

"I don't care who sent him," Harry said. "He's still trouble. He could have messed up everything."

"Relax," she said. "We'll be out of here on the next ferry, remember? We'll be long gone by tonight."

"What, you mean just leave the boat out there?"

"It's a piece of crap," she said. "And it's not even ours."

"Vinnie LeBlanc and Buck Carrick," I said, my head still pushed back onto the rough wood of the railing. "They came to the island with you, right?"

She looked at me, deep in thought.

"Who are you, really?" she said. "Tell me the truth."

"My name is Alex. I'm a friend of Vinnie's. I came here looking for Vinnie and his cousin. I swear to God, if you've done anything to them . . ."

She didn't bother to laugh at that. She gave Sugarpie a little nod and he pulled the chair back up. He kept one hand on my shoulder, just in case.

"Did you come alone?" she said. "No, wait, that person who called you . . ."

I hesitated over that one, trying to decide which was better, the truth or a lie. I settled on a little of both.

"I'm not alone," I said. "I've got five other people on the island with me. You'll never get away, believe me."

"Where were all of your friends when I found you at the dock?"

"They were on the ferry. I flew over separately and I was waiting for them. By now, they're all over the island. Five men, all looking for me. And for you. They know everything about you."

"That's a lie."

"All we want is Vinnie and Buck," I said. "You give them to us and you walk away."

"Yeah, I'm sorry to tell you," Harry said, "but you're a little too late for that."

"Harry, shut up," the woman said.

"I'm not shutting up, Jo. Don't tell me to shut up."

"Just be quiet for one second so we can think this through."

"There's nothing to think about. We made our deal and now we can get the hell out of here."

A phone rang. They looked at each other until finally she remembered my cell phone in her pocket. She took it out and opened it.

"This time it's a 313 number," she said. "That's Detroit."

It took me a second to figure it out. Then it came to me. It was Janet Long, returning my call from this morning. An actual FBI agent on the phone, but a hell of a lot of good it would do me now.

"Now I *know* he doesn't work for Corvo," Harry said, taking the cell phone from her. "I mean, look at this thing."

He tossed it to Sugarpie, who looked at it with wonder, like an archaeologist examining a dinosaur bone. When he was done, he dropped it onto the table, next to the ashtray.

"That's one more of my friends," I said, trying to put a little edge into it now, like this was just an inconvenience to me, something that happened all the time. "They must be all over the place by now. Maybe even right outside. I tell you, all you gotta do is give us Vinnie and Buck. We have no interest in you at all."

"And I told you it's too late," Harry said.

His wife reached over and gave him a little cuff on the cheek. Not quite a slap, but a hell of a lot stronger than a love tap.

"Ow," he said. "What the hell's the matter with you?"

"Take off those wet clothes," she said. "Then get your ass into the house. We have to talk about this."

"What about him?" the man said, nodding at me.

"Dumpling's getting the zip ties. They're out in the car, right?"

"No, they're in the house."

"Well, go get one, genius. And take off those clothes before you ruin the deck."

She watched him walk into the house, leaving a wet trail behind him. He was clearly doing things in the wrong order and she looked at me, shaking her head, like I was supposed to be on her side all of a sudden.

"You need to tell me what happened to Vinnie and Buck," I said to her. "Are they alive or not?"

"You need to stay quiet and relax," she said, as if that were possible. "But yes, they're alive. Maybe you'll even get to see them."

She gave me a grim smile and now I had no idea what to think. Then Harry came back through the door with a plastic zip tie about a foot long.

"He's going to put this on your wrists," she said to me. "It's for everybody's benefit. Then we'll take you to see your friends."

Harry stopped dead and looked at her like she was crazy. She raised one eyebrow at him and gestured to me, like, get on with it already.

"Hands together," he said to me. "Don't try anything funny."

I put my hands in front of me. In one smooth expert motion he lassoed my wrists and pulled the zip tie tight.

"Do the ankles, too," she said. "Just for now."

"You said get one zip tie. I only brought one."

"So go get another. But first take off your—"

He let out a breath and went back into the house before she could finish. On his way back out with the second zip tie she smacked him in the back of the head. He stopped and looked at her and I thought for a second they were gonna start swinging, but then he got down on one knee in front of me.

"Feet together," he said. "Slightly off the floor."

The second zip tie was a little bigger. He was able to slip it around my feet and pull it tight. This was not the first time he had done this. Probably not even the first time today. Wherever Vinnie and Buck were, I was pretty sure they were wearing the exact same things.

"Okay, now what?" he said.

She just looked at him until the light bulb finally went on. He stripped out of his wet suit right there on the deck, down to a tight little Speedo swimsuit. He was in decent shape for his age, but it still didn't exactly flatter him. There was a key on a plastic lanyard wrapped around his wrist. He took that off and tossed it on top of the wet suit.

"All right, I'm gonna go have a quick chat with Mr. Olympia here," the woman said. "Sugarpie's gonna keep you company."

The tie around my ankles was even tighter than the one around my wrists. I couldn't have gotten up out of the chair even if the house had been on fire. But Sugarpie pulled up the other chair right in front of me and sat down. He folded his arms and watched me. All I could do was sit there and look at his tattoos. A dragon and some barbwire around the biceps, all brilliantly original work. Some birds and some Chinese characters, and for some reason a clock on his chest with the hands at twelve and three.

I got tired of looking at his ugly skin and his ugly face. So I put my head down for a while and just hoped to God that Vinnie and Buck were still alive.

Dumpling came back up the steps and onto the deck.

"I couldn't find the zip ties," he said. "We're gonna have to—"

He stopped dead when he saw me trussed up like a turkey.

"Your turn to watch him," Sugarpie said. "I need a little smoke."

Dumpling took his place in the chair, giving me a whole new set of tattoos to study if I wanted to. This guy had more space to work with, but he obviously hadn't spent the money. Half of his ink was cheap stuff that looked like it had been drawn by a kindergartner.

The sliding door opened again. Harry and Jo came back out.

"Okay, Alex," she said, her voice different now. Like I was their houseguest and she had kept me waiting way too long. "Here's what we've decided. It's good news."

She paused and looked to her husband for confirmation. He just stood there. His hair was still wet.

"Harry's gonna go put on some clothes," she said. "Then we're going to go for a drive. Have you ever been to Beaver Island before?"

"Where are Vinnie and Buck?" I said.

"I'll take that as a no. In which case, we really need to take you on the tour. Doesn't that sound like fun?"

She looked at me with her eyebrows raised, like she actually expected an answer.

"Harry, go get dressed," she said to him, "and boys, put your shirts on. You look like a couple of monkeys."

"Where are they?" I said. "God damn all of you."

Dumpling looked up at her to see if she was offended, but she just smiled at him and gestured for him to get up and put his shirt on. He shrugged and then hauled himself to his feet. Sugarpie had picked up the joint and was busy smoking it down to nothing. Dumpling gave him a look and grabbed his shirt off the railing.

When Harry finally came back out, his hair was dry and it was sticking out in both directions. He had glasses on now, and the overall effect was that of an eccentric English professor. The kind who sells marijuana by the planeload and who knows how to zip tie your hands and feet.

"Okay, it's time to go," Jo said. She still had the gun, of course. Something told me she wouldn't have trusted her husband with it. Not for a second.

Harry cut the zip tie from my ankles. He left the tie around my wrists. They led me off the deck, all four of them, to the driveway. I looked around for some way to distract them. Some way to escape. I didn't see any opportunity. None at all.

Harry opened the back door and motioned for me to get in. Sugarpie got in behind me, and then Dumpling squeezed himself in on the other side. Then Harry got behind the wheel and Jo sat beside him. She didn't bother pointing the gun at me, and I didn't blame her. What the hell was I gonna do?

"Time to go set you free," she said in a voice as cheerful as an icicle. "Just like a little bird."

Then we were off. It was a beautiful, picture-perfect day on the island, and I was being driven to my own execution.

CHAPTER SIXTEEN

They drove back into town first, right back to the dock. I looked out the window, trying desperately to catch sight of Lou. But he was off the ferry and it was getting ready to head back to Charlevoix now. Lou might have been a block away, walking around, looking for me, but there was no way for me to know. Even if I'd seen him, what could I have done? With these men on either side of me, how could I have drawn his attention?

Harry stopped at the edge of the dock entrance. He and Jo got out. All of a sudden both of the back doors were open and I could see daylight on either side. Freedom just a few feet away. But then Sugarpie closed his door and stood there talking to Harry. Jo still had the other door open and she gave Dumpling a kiss right on the mouth that lasted at least three seconds. Something a little strange going on there, if I had bothered to think about it. She gave him the gun and he weighed it in his hand for a moment before pointing it right at my gut. He was smiling and wearing just a touch of Jo's lipstick.

Jo came around to the other side of the vehicle as Sugarpie took

Harry's place behind the wheel. She leaned and gave Sugarpie another three-second kiss on the mouth.

"Remember," she said, "if you're not back here in time to catch the ferry, just take the next one. We'll take your car from Charlevoix and go on ahead. We'll be waiting for you."

"Why can't you just wait for us?" Sugarpie said. "We can all go on the last ferry together."

"You'll be okay. You're big boys."

"I don't think you should go to the house alone. What if Corvo shows up?"

"He's got no reason to do that, Sugarpie. We're all square now."

Not that it's any consolation to me, I thought, but those two are in for a real surprise today. Corvo already did show up, and he's got quite a flair for redecorating.

"I don't like it," Sugarpie said. "I think you should wait for us."

"You just hush your mouth," she said, patting him on the cheek. "You got money for something to eat?"

"Yeah, I got money."

"Okay, then we'll see you on the other side." She gave him another kiss and then she closed the door. As Sugarpie drove off, I caught one more glimpse of the two of them. Harry waving, Jo blowing more kisses in the air. Then we were on the road out of town, riding south.

I kept looking for Lou. Here now at least I'd have the chance to catch his attention. Bang my head against the glass, let him see me. Whatever it took. But I never saw him.

As they drove me down the coast, eventually turning into the interior of the island, I started to wonder if I had made a big mistake. Maybe I should have made my stand there at the house, told them I knew they weren't going to shoot me. Not right there on the porch. Not in cold blood. Maybe they would have balked if I had done that.

Or maybe they wouldn't have. These were some seriously deranged people, that much was clear now. Maybe Harry would have taken the gun and shot me, just to prove something to Josephine. Or maybe she would have done it herself. Hell, every time I looked her in the eye, I felt like I was seeing something fundamentally defective, like somebody had forgotten to install all the circuit boards in the factory. I had a sick feeling that she could have shot me without thinking twice about it. Then gone inside and taken a nice afternoon nap.

I turned and looked at Dumpling.

"That's right, old man," he said. "It's showtime now."

"Where are they right now?" I said. "In a boat? Is that what I heard?"

"Who said that?"

"Harry said that. He said they were in a boat."

"So yeah, they are. They're in a boat. With the money."

"Why do they need to be in the boat?" Even as I said it, I already knew the answer.

"That's part of the deal. Two Indians. One million dollars cash."

"For Corvo," I said. "That's who we're talking about."

"We don't need to talk about him."

"Why not? Are you afraid of him?"

"Shut the hell up," he said. "Just keep quiet."

"Or what, are you gonna shoot me?"

He jabbed the gun barrel into my ribs. Hard. I spent the next two minutes trying to breathe again.

"What you're telling me," I finally said, "is that they sold out Vinnie and Buck to save their own skin. That's what you're telling me."

"Nobody will miss them."

"I happen to know they sold out a dealer in Sault Ste. Marie, too. You know what happened to him?"

"I have a feeling you're gonna tell me," he said, "whether I care or not."

"Corvo tortured him. He cut him up and let him bleed to death. At least, that's what it looked like."

"You saw it?"

"After the fact, yeah."

"Okay, then," Dumpling said. "So now we know. Thanks for the information."

"You guys don't get it."

"What?"

"They'll do anything to save themselves. *Anything.*"

"What are you saying?"

I tensed up, waiting for another jab in the ribs.

"Don't you think it's funny? Having you drop them off at the dock? You think they're really gonna wait for you?"

"All right," Sugarpie said from the front seat. "Everybody shut the hell up right now."

"You both know I'm right," I said. "You both know you're next."

Dumpling jabbed me again and everything flashed white.

"He said shut up. So just shut up."

My whole side was in spasm now. I tried to relax my muscles. Breathe. Relax. Breathe.

"You're making this easy," he said. "I'll give you that much."

I didn't know where we were. We'd left the shoreline and now it was just trees on either side of us. Now and then the trees would break and I'd see wetland. Yes, plenty of swamps around here, I thought. That's where we're going. Far away from anyone else. My body won't be found for days. Or weeks. Or maybe never.

These guys weren't going to give me anything close to a fair shot at getting away, that much I knew for sure. Certainly not with my wrists still zip-tied together. But I had to try something. Even if it was a long shot. At some point, I had to roll the dice.

I looked around the backseat. There was nothing to grab on to. I looked above me, below me, to both sides. Then I looked out the windshield. Still nothing but trees. Then I looked at the rearview mirror.

A car behind us.

A white car.

I tried not to show any reaction. I let out a breath, closed my eyes, dipped my head down. Counted to ten. Then I opened my eyes and looked around again, just happening to glance at the rearview mirror.

I couldn't quite make out what kind of car it was. I definitely couldn't see the driver's face. But the driver sat tall enough, I thought for sure it was a man, and I couldn't make out anybody in the passenger's seat.

One man driving a white car, just like the car Lou had rented. Who even buys white cars anymore? They all go to rental companies, right?

We made a right turn. There was an interior lake on our left. I took another quick look at the mirror. The white car could have turned the other way, but it hadn't. It was still about forty or fifty yards behind us.

"Is that car following us?" Sugarpie said.

"You're being paranoid," Dumpling said, without even looking out the back window. "There's like five roads on the whole island, remember? There's always *somebody* behind you."

"Yeah, but this guy said he had a bunch of friends with him."

"And you believed that? Come on."

We went down the road about another mile. Sugarpie slowed down as we came to another intersection. He was peering into the rearview mirror. He could have gone straight and stayed on the same road. He could have taken a right and gone back north on another road. He chose option C—take a left and drive down a trail that wasn't a road at all.

"The car went straight," he said as he started rumbling down the trail. We were in a Jeep Cherokee, after all, so it wasn't entirely crazy.

"Told you," Dumpling said. "Now slow down so you don't get us all killed."

"If I slow down, we sink in the soft ground. Speed is life. That's what the pilots say."

"Yeah, well, we're not in a plane."

"Just relax. We're almost there."

The car didn't follow us, I thought. That could mean one of two things. Either it was Lou and he made a quick decision not to take the car down this rough trail. Or it wasn't Lou. And really, why should it have been? Why should I be so lucky as to have him show up when I really needed him?

No, stay positive, I thought. You're gonna find a way out of this. Even if you have to do something stupid, all by yourself. You're certainly good at being stupid.

There was another trail branching off to the right. It was even rougher and narrower, if that was even possible. Sugarpie took the turn and kept going, the branches slapping at both sides of the car.

"What the hell is wrong with you?" Dumpling said. "We'll never get out of here."

"I know what I'm doing. I've been down this trail before."

"What, do you have a meth lab out here or something?"

They both laughed at that. A little too hard. They were whooping it up and in another minute they'd be shooting me and watching my body disappear into the swamp.

The ground rose slightly and Sugarpie gunned the engine. The tires spun for a moment and I thought the vehicle would be stuck for sure, but then it found purchase and we rocketed up to the top of the mound. He left the engine running, opening the driver's door and getting out. Then he opened my door and pulled me out. I was just about to take my shot at him, but then I realized that would never work. I had to get Dumpling first, as long as he had the gun.

As I stood there waiting for him to come around from the other side of the vehicle, the mosquitoes were already buzzing around my head and landing on my neck. Officially not my biggest problem at the moment, but it was annoying as hell not to be able to slap them away.

"God damn," Sugarpie said. "Where's the bug spray?"

"Never mind that," Dumpling said. "Let's take care of this so we can get the hell out of here."

Sugarpie grabbed my arm and pulled me over toward the front of the vehicle. The edge of the swamp was about ten feet away.

"Start walking," he said. "Straight ahead."

"So you can shoot me in the back?" I said. "I thought you guys had some guts."

He grabbed me again and spun me around so that I was facing the swamp.

"Walk," he said. "Right now."

I turned around so that I was facing them again.

"I'm not making it easy," I said. "If you're gonna kill me, you'll have to look me in the eye when you do it."

"I'm pretty sure I can manage," Dumpling said from behind him. "Especially now that you're being such a pain in the ass."

"Come do it then. Come shoot me like a man."

"Let me do it," Sugarpie said. He tried to take the gun from the other man, but Dumpling slapped his hand away.

This is good, I thought. I want the slower man. Now I have a two percent chance of making this work, instead of one percent.

"Right here," I said. "Step up and do it."

Another mosquito landed on my neck. I could feel its needle breaking through my skin.

"Don't get any closer," Sugarpie said. "Come on, man, give me the gun. You've never done this before."

"Get away from me," he said. "I'm not afraid of him."

As Dumpling came closer, Sugarpie tried to pull him away. He shook him off and came even closer to me, as if to make a point.

That's it, I thought. That's exactly what you want to do. I'm not even going to move. Just come right up to me and prove what a big badass you are.

He took a step closer. He was holding the gun in both hands now. He was looking me in the eye.

"Shoot you like a man?" he said. "I'm gonna show my friend here how a real man does it."

"Will you just shut up and do it?" Sugarpie said, slapping at his arm. "I'm getting eaten alive here."

He was four feet away. I wished it were two. Hell, would have settled for three. I stood there and I watched him raise the gun slowly. I felt another mosquito on my neck. I looked at him and I saw him sweating and I thought, come on mosquitoes, why are you bothering with me? Somebody go take some blood from that big boy.

Everything was coming into sharp relief. I saw every detail, every pore in his skin, every color and contour of every visible tattoo. The face on the Jack of Hearts, watching me with its one eye from his right shoulder. I smelled the fetid half-decomposed smells from the swamp. I heard the insects buzzing and crawling and mating and dying.

And eating.

Right there, on his neck. Go for it, mosquito. Do your thing.

He flinched and tried to rub it away by shrugging his shoulder. That was my chance. That was my last chance to stay alive on this horrible blue earth. I threw my body back like I was doing the limbo, brought my right foot up toward the gun. There was a deafening blast as it went off. I didn't even know if the bullet had hit me. I was still frozen in time, everything moving in slow motion. My foot coming up, my leg extended as far as I could make it go. I'd never played much football, being a baseball man. I'd never played soccer at all. So I never really had to kick anything. Never in life until this very moment. My desperate last-chance gamble as I felt my center of gravity going back farther and farther and I am absolutely going to fall flat on my back but if I can just manage to kick that goddamned gun out of his goddamned hand.

Impact.

First my foot.

Then my head hitting the ground. My back immediately after, knocking the wind right out of me.

I saw the gun flying in the air. Into the woods.

Dumpling was already stumbling after it. I swept at his leg and felt him falling.

The other man was coming to jump on top of me now. I rolled over just in time and I was halfway up as he climbed onto my back. I went all the way down to my knees and let his momentum take him right over me. My hands were still tied together, so I couldn't punch him in the face. But I could take both hands together and make one big fist and try to drive his head right into the ground. I felt the bones snap as I hit him square in the nose.

Then I was back on my feet. The big man was already crashing into the brush, a good ten feet away. He was looking for the gun and I had to make a choice right then. The key's still in the ignition, I thought. The engine's still running. I climbed into the driver's seat, not bothering to close the door. With both hands tied together it was a clumsy effort to shift the vehicle into Reverse, but I managed it. Through the windshield, I saw Sugarpie up on one knee now. He was doubled over and there was blood running from his nose. Dumpling was still in the brush, looking for the gun.

I stepped on the gas and felt the wheels spinning under me. Then all of a sudden I was moving backward. Too fast. I tried to steer but it was hard to do with both hands so close together. It was impossible to look behind me at the same time. The door was catching all of the branches and I heard a metallic screech in the hinges as it hit the trunk of a tree.

I was backing down the trail, doing everything I could to keep it straight. Not far to go, that much I remembered. He made this final right turn so all I have to do is back it right up and get it pointed in the right direction.

More branches scraped at the open door as the tires were throwing mud, and every other yard they were just spinning and spinning and me not going anywhere at all and then finding hard ground again and almost driving right off into the trees.

I hit the main trail and I tried to whip it around in a two-point turn but I couldn't turn the wheel fast enough and both right tires went off the edge of the road. I gunned it and the tires were spinning again and that's when I heard the gun go off again and this time the back window exploded.

I snapped back into real time. Everything speeding up from the slow-motion fog I was in. I looked out the open door and saw Dumpling coming down the trail, the gun raised. I reached to close the door and realized that wasn't going to work. It would have taken several days in the body shop just to get the damned thing to close again. I gunned the engine one more time and that's when I felt the shot ripping right through the fabric above my head. I rolled over to the other side of the front seat and opened up the far door. I dived out onto the ground.

Except there was no ground.

It was swamp. It was quicksand. I don't know what the hell it was, but it swallowed me up and held fast as I tried to get to my feet. I tried grabbing on to the side of the car but there was nothing to hold on to. With both my hands together I could barely push myself up. I kicked at the muck and tried to roll myself out and I was counting down the precious seconds because I knew Dumpling was coming up fast on the other side of the car. When I finally managed to push myself forward, I was on both knees, then one knee, and that's when I finally looked up and saw his shoes and tattoos on his legs. He was standing at the back of the vehicle. The gun was pointed at my head. This time, there would be no chance to knock the gun free. This time, he had me dead.

"You broke his nose," he said.

I didn't say anything. I was just trying to breathe.

"Get over here," he said to Sugarpie. "Come watch this man die."

Sugarpie was coming down the trail, holding his nose. There was enough blood to paint his shirt half red. He seemed to be wincing with every step. The blood was still running through his fingers.

Then *blam!* the air was torn apart by another gun blast. They both jumped at the noise.

Nobody moved for a long moment. Then Sugarpie went down. There was a hole in the side of his neck, just under his jawline. He took his hands away from his ruined nose and grasped at his throat. He tried to speak but the only sound that came out was a bloody gurgle.

"What the . . ." Dumpling said, looking down at him.

He looked back at me, like I had done this somehow. Like I had some sort of magic secret gun I could fire from any direction. Then he brought up his own gun again but this time he didn't even get to aim. The next shot caught him just above the left eye. He went down, dead on the spot, his hand still holding the gun.

Lou came running down the path, holding that gun we'd taken from Andy Dukes, the gun we had stashed in the glove compartment. The gun that had forced Lou to take the ferry instead of the plane. He had the gun trained on Sugarpie, who was still alive.

"Don't shoot him," I said. I bent down and looked at him closely. "Can you talk?"

He was still clutching at his throat. He was still making the gurgling noises.

"You have to tell us where they are," I said. "Where are Vinnie and Buck?"

He spit blood at me. I felt its spray, all over my face. Whether it was intentional or just a last gasp of air, that's something I'd never be able to find out for sure. Two seconds later, the lights in his eyes went out for good.

"Alex," Lou said, pulling me to my feet and looking me over. "Are you shot? Are you all right?"

"How did you find me?"

Lou bent over, trying to catch his breath. After a minute of wheezing, he straightened up and took a folding knife out of his pocket and cut the zip tie. I stood there rubbing my wrists.

"I went to the post office and asked the lady at the counter," he said. "She told me you had already been there, looking for the same house. She said there must be quite a party going on."

"Yeah, we had a party, all right."

I wiped the blood from my face. From the chest down, I was still covered in the thick muck.

"Just as I got there," he said, "I saw the vehicle leaving. So I followed you."

"Well, I'll thank you for saving my life later," I said. "Right now we have to find Vinnie and Buck. They're out in a boat somewhere."

"What? Are you serious?"

I had to bend over myself for a moment. Not so much to breathe but to fight down the bile rising in my throat. All the stress and adrenaline pulsing through my body.

"I'll explain on the way," I said. "Come on, we've got to find a boat of our own. We might not have much time."

"Alex, what are you talking about? Where are they?"

"I don't know," I said. "But we have to find them before Corvo does."

CHAPTER SEVENTEEN

"Come on, help me," Lou said. He took hold of Sugarpie by the arms and started dragging him toward the swamp.

"What are you doing?"

"We can't leave them here. Somebody will find them. Maybe today."

"Lou, we don't have time for this."

"It'll go a lot faster if you help me, God damn it! I'm not leaving dead bodies on the ground and walking away!"

The day was already turned inside out. I had come two inches from being in the swamp myself, so what the hell. I grabbed Sugarpie's legs and helped Lou heave him into the swamp. Then we went back and gave ourselves hernias doing the same for Dumpling. The green slime on the water parted for both bodies, then closed back up as if it had been undisturbed for the past hundred years.

"Someone will find their vehicle," I said. "It's stuck, so we can't move it."

"Let them find it. By the time they figure out these boys are in the swamp, we'll be long gone."

Lou's face was flushed and he looked like he was going to pass out, but it was all I could do to keep up with him as we ran back up the trail to the rental car. We got in and I promptly destroyed the front seat with all of the mud I was wearing. I had to move a bottle of wine to sit down.

"Throw that out the window," Lou said. "It was just a prop."

"Let me guess, you took it with you to the post office and told the lady you were looking for the party at Harry and Jo's house."

"Of course I did." He kept talking while he put the car in gear and hit the road. "Who else is gonna know where everybody lives? Even the renters?"

"So it took you two minutes, is what you're saying. It took me almost two hours."

"Whatever," he said, gritting his teeth as he made a hard turn. "I'm just a better con man, I guess."

"You think that ferry's left yet?" I said, wiping mud off my watch. I wanted to go straight to the dock and grab Harry and Jo, or hell, maybe even try Jo's own little trick. Stick the gun in her ribs and tell her to start talking. Make them tell us exactly where Vinnie and Buck were so we could go out and get them. Maybe even take Harry and Jo out there and leave them in their place. I couldn't remember ever wishing harm on a woman, but today Jo was begging to be an exception.

"I'm sure it's gone by now," Lou said.

"I can't get over how sick it is, the way Jo got those guys to do anything she wanted. She even made sure she and Harry were off the island when they took me out here. They were obviously just giving themselves alibis, and yet . . . ."

I ran out of words. I just shook my head.

"Who were those guys, anyway?" Lou said.

"A couple of losers? No family life? That's my guess. She had them wrapped around her little finger."

"Yeah, it sounds kinda sick to me, too."

I looked over at him as he drove. He'd just killed two men. No matter how justified it may have been, he'd done it and now he was back on the trail. His jaw was clenched tight but otherwise he looked perfectly composed.

We made our way back out to the shore, then north until he pulled into the empty driveway. I got out and went up the steps to the back porch. The breeze had swept away the last trace of marijuana smoke. Down on the water, I saw the jet ski Harry had been riding. Drifting with the current, it was pulling the anchor rope tight.

"What's the plan?" Lou said as he came up behind me. "Where are they?"

"They're out there." I pointed toward the water.

"Out there where?"

"I don't know exactly. I'm trying to remember everything Harry said. He came in on the jet ski and he said it was a rough trip. I think he said it was ten miles. Whether that's true or not . . ."

"He may have been exaggerating, you mean."

"We need a map." I slid open the glass door and stepped inside, something I hadn't had the chance to do on my first visit. It was a beautiful house inside, I suppose, simple and elegant, but I didn't have the time to appreciate it. I went over to the far wall where there were stacks of paper on the shelves. I was looking for a map.

"Right here," Lou said. He was standing by the coffee table I had walked by on my way in. There was an ashtray on the table, along with a lighter and some magazines, but then as I got closer I saw what he was talking about. I swept everything onto the floor and there, under the glass surface of the table, was a detailed nautical map of Beaver Island and the surrounding islands, complete with water depths.

"Okay, so we're about here," I said, pointing to the shoreline on the northwest corner of the island. There were seven smaller islands arranged to the north and the west.

"The scale's down there in the corner. How far is ten miles?"

It looked like the length of my hand corresponded to around ten miles, so I put my hand on the map, with the base of my palm at our starting point, then turned it in a half-circle to approximate the ten-mile arc.

"Which way did he come in?" Lou said.

"I couldn't see him at that point. But I don't think it would have mattered. You'd be coming in pretty straight no matter what, just to avoid the rocks out there. That water goes out pretty shallow for a while."

He stood there watching me, waiting for me to think it through. The seconds ticked by.

"I'm trying to remember," I said, playing it all back through my head. "He's standing there and he's telling Jo what a rough trip it was, and yeah, he's pointing right out that way. To that big island right there."

We could see it through the window, dominating the horizon. I looked back at the map.

"High Island," I said. "It's five miles away."

"As big as it is, I still don't see any roads on the map. I bet the far side of that thing is totally deserted."

I stood up and went out onto the deck.

"Yes, it's right there," I said. "That's the direction he was pointing in. It's right there."

I spotted my cell phone on the table. I picked it up and opened it. The signal was weak.

"Alex, they're right out there. *Right there. Right now.* We have to go get them."

"We don't have a boat, Lou."

Then I stopped. One more detail, coming back to me. Harry stripping off his wet suit, then tossing the plastic lanyard from his wrist. The wet clothing was still there, piled in a heap. I went over and picked up the lanyard. I was expecting a key, but instead it was a little black U-shaped tab.

"No boat, but we do have this," I said. "Let's go."

I found a half-full gas can near the foot of the stairs. When we reached the edge of the water, I looked up and down the shoreline. I couldn't see one dock. Either there was some kind of rule on the island, or else it really was impossible to bring in a boat on this side.

I didn't know how much gas the jet ski had in it. Even if I had known, I wouldn't have been able to translate that into miles. My feelings on jet skis are about the same as my feelings on snowmobiles, so I wouldn't own one even if you gave it to me. I had never ridden on one, that much I knew for sure. But that was about to change.

I waded out to the jet ski, stumbling on the rocky bottom. When I got to it, I opened up the gas cap and poured what was left in the can into the tank. Then I screwed the cap back on. I put one wet shoe on the deck and swung my other leg over. The jet ski dipped under my weight and then quickly reestablished its buoyancy. It was a big Yamaha WaveRunner, with plenty of room for both of us. And plenty of horsepower, I was sure. Which made sense. A little underpowered toy jet ski might be fine on an inland lake, but you'd be a fool to ride one on Lake Michigan.

"Do you know how to drive one of these?" Lou said. "I've been living in the desert for the past thirty years. I hardly ever *see* a lake."

"It can't be too hard. Get on."

He waded out and climbed onto the back, fighting for balance and finally grabbing hold of the rear handles. I pulled up the anchor and stored it in the forward compartment. Then I took a few seconds to look the machine over, finally figured out that I had to use that little black tab on the lanyard to pinch the kill switch. I put the lanyard itself around my wrist, thinking, okay, if you fall off, you take the tab with you and the kill switch shuts off the engine. Not that I had any plans to fall off.

I pushed the Start button and the engine came to life. Then I squeezed the throttle and just about put us both in the water. I'd had no idea this thing would have such power.

"Take it easy," Lou said from behind me. "Don't get us killed yet, okay?"

I eased into it this time and we were on our way. As I got the hang of it, I started pushing it and soon we were slicing through the water at forty miles per hour. Then we hit a few rougher waves and the spray came right over the top of the craft, drenching my face. I didn't care how warm the water was supposed to be that summer, you take it in the face like that at full speed and it's like somebody turning an ice-cold hose on you.

But then of course that wasn't even full speed at all. I squeezed the throttle all the way and watched the speedometer keep climbing until it topped out around sixty-five. The surface of the water was racing past us and I started to understand how somebody might consider this fun. A different kind of somebody, who doesn't mind making a lot of noise. On a different kind of day.

The water started getting rougher as we got farther from the shore. I felt the machine starting to fight against the current. I knew we'd be getting out into some dangerous waters soon. There was a good reason why more people died on Lake Michigan every year than all of the other Great Lakes put together.

I kept pushing it through the rough water, taking the full spray in the face every minute or so. My clothes were soaked against my body. I was starting to feel numb.

High Island was ahead of us, getting bigger with every passing minute. I gritted my teeth against the wind and the spray and tried to keep my eyes open. I pictured Vinnie and Buck in a boat, just on the other side of the island. I pictured another boat on its way, getting closer by the second. I squeezed the throttle all the way down again and punished myself even more.

It was a blur of noise and vibration and cold water. I started to veer south as the island came even closer. I saw a sandy beach on the eastern side of the island and a green hill rising in the center.

As I finally started to come around to the western side, I felt the current grow even stronger. Lou was searching the shoreline. There was nothing to see but rocks and sand and trees.

"Keep going!" he said to me over the din of the motor. "They have to be here!"

There was another long beach on the western side of the island, and here the sand rose high onto the hillsides. It was like something off a postcard, and yet there was not one person in sight. Not one boat. If Harry wanted to leave them in an abandoned spot, this would have been perfect. How could he possibly take them anywhere else?

I throttled down for a moment as a terrible thought hit me. Maybe he *did* leave them here. Maybe Corvo came and found them, and then he took the boat with him. Maybe both boats are on their way south now. It was three hundred miles from here to Chicago.

"They're not here," Lou said. "We have to try that other island."

I nodded. I knew he was right. Or at least I knew it was our only shot left. To our west was the farthest island in the chain. Gull Island. The map showed a national wildlife preserve on the land itself, meaning it was a federal crime to set foot on it. Meaning it was as deserted an island as you could possibly find in the Great Lakes.

Meaning it was the perfect drop-off spot.

So Harry wasn't exaggerating, I thought. It was a true ten-mile trip, and it was hard as hell, even wearing a wet suit.

I checked the gas level. We had about half a tank left. The engine had been working hard, fighting against the waves and the current. We'd have enough to get out to Gull Island, but a return trip? That I wasn't so sure about.

Of course, Harry didn't have to make a round trip. He probably towed the jet ski behind the boat and rode it back. He didn't have to make the commitment to a blind one-way trip out into the lake, with no way to get back.

"Come on," Lou said. "Let's get going."

I couldn't feel my hands anymore. I couldn't feel my face. I turned the jet ski due west and opened up the throttle.

It was another five miles across open water. We were heading into the teeth of the current now. We were heading into those infamous straits that bend around the islands as the unimaginable weight of that water makes the turn toward Mackinac.

Gull Island is a lot smaller than High Island, so it looked like nothing but a smudge on the horizon. We rode and the engine fought and yard by yard we kept going until we started to make out the trees on the island. The current was pushing us north so I went with it, figuring I'd circle in that direction. The gas gauge showed just under a quarter tank now.

I felt Lou practically leaning off the jet ski as I started the big turn around the island. On the shore I saw a sign warning away trespassers. That was the only indication that a human being had ever been anywhere near this place. I kept going around the arc, fighting harder now as we hit the current on the far side of the island. There was a natural inlet there, a long strip of sand curling out into the water.

"There!" Lou said. "I see a boat!"

I kept going around the inlet. The boat was anchored in the protected backwater. It was a fishing boat, like any of a thousand you'd see on this lake every day, with a white canopy protecting the two captain's chairs from the sun. A small cabin with maybe a table and a marine toilet and not much else. The kind of boat you'd expect to see with a half-dozen fishing rods sticking out in every direction, but there were none. I also didn't see any sign of a living person onboard.

I brought the jet ski into the backwater and we pulled up alongside the boat. I still couldn't see anybody.

"Vinnie!" Lou yelled. "Are you onboard?"

He reached for the gunwale and fell into the water. It wasn't deep, and we were already soaked anyway. I helped pull him up onto the back deck of the jet ski, and from there he was able to climb over the gunwale and into the boat. I pulled the anchor out of the compartment and tossed it into the water. Then I followed him into the boat.

He was already on his knees, looking into the cabin. As I bent down next to him, I saw big Buck Carrick, sitting on the floor of the cabin. His hands were zip-tied together and tied to the table post. His legs were zip-tied, too. He was crying without making a sound, his mouth open. He was looking up at us like he couldn't believe what he was seeing.

Vinnie was lying next to him, his eyes closed.

"Vinnie," Lou said, putting his hand on the man's shoulder. "Are you alive? Please tell me you're alive, God damn it. Open your eyes."

"Help him," Buck said, the sound finally coming back to him. His voice was hoarse. "You have to help him, please."

"What happened?" I said. "Is he breathing? Can you feel his pulse?"

Lou was hunched over him now. It was hard to do in such close quarters.

"He's alive," Lou said. "He's unconscious."

"They hit him in the head," Buck said. He was shaking. He took a long breath and tried to keep talking, but he could barely form a sentence. "He got knocked out . . . They hit him . . . He came to, but then . . . he was out again. He has a . . . He's . . . a concussion. He needs to . . . we need to . . . get him . . ."

"Okay, take it easy," Lou said. "We're here now. We're gonna take you both back. Everything's gonna be all right now."

"Who are you?" Buck said to him. "How did you . . ."

Lou took out his folding knife and cut the zip ties from Buck's hands and ankles. Then he got to work on the rope, which would obviously take a lot longer. He kept looking down at Vinnie's face as he sawed at the rope. Vinnie was still unconscious.

"While you're doing that," I said, "I'm gonna see if we can get this boat started."

I started to stand up. That was the exact moment when I heard the last thing in the world I wanted to hear.

The sound of a motor.

It was the high-pitched whine of something built for speed. It didn't sound close yet, but I knew we'd probably see him before the next minute ended.

Corvo had arrived.

CHAPTER EIGHTEEN

"What's that sound?" Lou said, still sawing at the rope.

I didn't answer him. The key had been dangling from the ignition, and I was too busy trying to start the engine. When it finally caught, I revved it and heard the pistons knocking and felt the whole motor shaking like it would fall right off into the water.

"We've got to get out of here," Lou said. "We're sitting ducks."

"We've got no chance," I said. "I don't care how big a head start we have. That boat will run us down."

"I can't hear it," he said, as he stood and cocked his head toward the sound of the approaching boat. "How close are they?"

An idea came to me. Desperate and probably doomed to failure, but it was probably our only shot left.

"Where's the money?" I said.

There was a duffel bag sitting just below the other captain's chair. I hadn't even noticed it until that very second. I picked up the bag and opened it. I saw the bundles of hundred-dollar bills inside.

"What are we gonna do with that?" Lou said. "Come on, we've got to make a run for it. We've gotta try, at least."

"It's ten miles back to Beaver Island, Lou. You take the boat and go around to the other side of this island. I'll stay here and see if I can talk to this guy."

"What, are you crazy? He'll kill you in a second."

"Maybe, maybe not. I know he's expecting a bag full of money plus two Indians. We'll have to see what happens if he only gets the money."

"I'm not leaving you here, Alex. No way."

"We're wasting time," I said as I pulled up the anchor. Then I reached over the gunwale and pulled the jet ski close. "They won't hear you as long as they've got their own engine running. So get over to the other side and then cut your engine. Have that gun ready, just in case. If they come around, try to surprise him with it. You'll probably only get one shot."

Assuming the gun's even dry enough to fire, I thought. Yet one more thing stacked against us.

"You take the boat," he said. "I'll stay here."

"Bad idea. They're looking for Indians, remember?"

"This is madness," he said, but he didn't stop me as I took the bag and climbed off the boat and onto the jet ski.

"Get going! Now!"

He pushed the throttle forward and cranked the steering wheel. The boat made a tight circle around me, churning up sand in the shallow water. He left the inlet and went around the northern end of the island. I could hear the other boat's engine now. It was much closer.

This island's about a mile long, I thought. We're on the northwest corner. If this Corvo guy is coming from Chicago, he'll approach from the southwest. If our boat's on the eastern side, he shouldn't see it. Unless he circles around, just to make sure the coast is clear. Which is exactly what I would do if I were in his place. Making this now officially the dumbest idea I've ever had.

The motor was getting louder. I knew it was just a matter of seconds now. I looked back and saw that Lou was almost out of sight. I willed that old fishing boat to go faster, to get around that bend before it was too late.

That's when Corvo's boat came into view. He'd come up from the south and hugged the shoreline, so when he cleared the bend in the island he was suddenly *right there*, right on top of me. I didn't dare look back to make sure Lou was clear now. I just stood up on the jet ski, straddling the seat. I held the bag of money in the air and put my other hand in the air, as well. I said a silent prayer and tried to stop my knees from shaking.

It was one of those cigarette boats, long and sleek and ridiculous. Twin engines churning up the water. I'm sure the thing could hit one hundred miles per hour without breaking a sweat. There were two men in the boat, one behind the wheel, one standing and holding a rifle. There was a scope on the rifle. Both men were wearing sunglasses. The driver throttled down and sent his wake ahead of him. It rocked the jet ski and I had to reach down to grab one handle. That caused the standing man to aim the rifle right at me. I'm sure my face was clear in his crosshairs.

I fought to keep my balance as I raised both hands again. I held that bag as high as I could. The boat swung away and made a loop in the open water. Then it came back into the inlet dead slow, its engines purring.

The man kept the rifle trained on my face. Yet one more gun pointed at me in these last few days when it had seemed almost constant. If you think you ever get used to it, you don't. That's what I was learning.

The man at the wheel stood up and looked around. He was especially interested in the island itself. He was scanning the shoreline like he expected something or someone to surprise him, but there was nothing there but sand and trees and what looked like a healthy crop of poison ivy.

The man with the rifle was wearing a bright Hawaiian shirt. I finally noticed that detail. The man at the wheel was wearing a nice light panel shirt, perfect for a day out in the summer sun. Not quite as casual as a Hawaiian shirt. It seemed odd to me that they'd be dressed that way. But then maybe they were trying to blend in with the other boaters on the lake. Of course, if they put the rifle away, they'd have a better shot at it.

Neither of them seemed in any hurry to talk to me. I was holding up that bag and my arm was starting to shake. I didn't want to move.

"What's the gag?" the man behind the wheel said. The boat was ten feet away now and drifting closer.

"No gag," I said. "I have your money."

He narrowed his eyes for a moment. Then he took another look around, like he was trying to spot the hidden camera.

"You'll excuse my political incorrectness," he finally said, "but you're not an Indian. And there's only one of you."

"Right on both counts. There's been a change in plans."

"A change in what?" There was a look of pure amazement on his face. "Did you actually just say that?"

"I did."

I kept breathing. I kept my legs locked straight.

"Throw me the bag," he said. "Understand that if you do anything else, Mr. White here will shoot your head clean off your body."

I tossed the bag to him. I kept my hands up afterward. I waited and watched while he opened the bag and took a quick scan through the stacks of hundreds.

"Okay," he said, "so explain to me why I'm finding you here on a jet ski instead of two Indians on a boat, like I was expecting."

"I told you, there's been a change in plans. I came out here to personally deliver the money to you, and to explain the situation."

He looked amazed again. I figured I should probably change my approach a bit.

"I'm not trying to dictate anything," I said. "I just ask that you listen to me. I assume you're Corvo, by the way."

"Wow," he said. "Okay, then. This should be interesting. Get in the boat."

I hesitated.

"If you want to talk, talk," he said. "But you'll do it here in my boat."

Mr. White lowered his rifle. He handed it to Corvo, who simply held it by the barrel as Mr. White extended one hand to me. Either it was a gesture of extreme trust or they knew that nobody would be so stupid as to try something.

"I'm not that old," I said, brushing aside the man's hand and climbing over the rail of their boat. I lost my balance for one instant and the man grabbed me. There was a pure animal strength in his grip as he straightened me up and gave me a quick once-over. My wallet came out of my back pocket. My cell phone out of my front pocket. These items were placed on one of the seat cushions. He patted down the rest of me, from shoulders to ankles.

Mr. White took back the rifle. With his hands free now, Corvo opened up my wallet and looked through its contents. I knew all he'd find would be my driver's license, a few credit cards, and maybe a hundred dollars in very wet bills.

"Alex McKnight," he said, reading from my license. "What do you do for a living?"

"I rent out cabins."

He pushed down his sunglasses for a moment and looked at me.

"Something tells me that's not all you do. But let's go somewhere where we can be a little more comfortable. Have a seat."

He straightened his sunglasses, sat down behind the wheel, and pushed the throttle forward. Any questions about actually sitting down became moot as I was thrown back onto the seat cushions.

Mr. White tucked the rifle behind him. Now that he knew I wasn't carrying, he clearly couldn't imagine me being any kind of threat. I couldn't imagine it, either. I sat there and felt the wind against my wet clothes as Corvo took the boat straight out into the open water of Lake Michigan. He took a quick glance back over his shoulder to make sure I was appreciating the ride. I gave him a nod. Yes, I get it. You've got the fastest boat in the Great Lakes.

When he had taken us about ten minutes away, he throttled it back. I turned and looked at Gull Island. It was a small thing on the far side of the world now. Lou and Vinnie and Buck were somewhere on the other side of it, safe for the moment. Corvo swiveled in his chair and faced me, not bothering to look where he was drifting. We were miles away from anything.

He picked up my cell phone and looked at it. For once, I didn't get a wisecrack about how old it was. Then he picked up my wallet. This time when he opened it, he took out the license and examined it closely.

"Paradise, Michigan," he said. "That's in the UP, right? Near Sault Ste. Marie?"

"Yes."

"How far is it from the Newberry airport?"

"Forty miles, maybe."

"Yes, you see? Now it's coming together. Forty miles away. I'm going to ask you some questions now, and I'd like you to give me some totally straight answers. Are we okay with that?"

He took his sunglasses off. He had dark eyes. I couldn't tell if maybe he had some Latin blood in him. Maybe even Indian. There was definitely a mix of races going on, along with something else. Robot or space alien or something. He looked me dead in the eye and he didn't waver for one second.

"I'll be straight with you," I said.

"Good. Okay. So first question. Were you at the airport that night?"

"No, I wasn't."

"The two Indians. They were there."

"One of them was. The other came to pick him up when he called. You have to understand something."

He looked taken aback again. But this time he was smiling.

"I have to understand something?" he said. "Really? Okay, then. Enlighten me."

"I don't know what the Kaisers told you, but I'm sure it's all bullshit. Those two men had nothing to do with what happened at the airport."

He was nodding his head. He was still smiling.

"The two men we're talking about," he said. "Buck Carrick, and the other one. Vincent LeBlanc. Right? Those are the two men?"

"Buck went along for the ride. That's all. When things went wrong, he just wanted to get away. So he called Vinnie. End of story. What the Kaisers told you—"

"Was bullshit. Yeah, no kidding. You don't think I know that?"

He just sat there, shaking his head, still smiling, still drilling two holes through me with those eyes.

"Alex, how well do you know the Kaisers?"

"I just met them today for the first time. It wasn't a good experience."

He laughed a little at that one.

"I don't imagine it was," he said. "But even if you just met them today, can we agree that they would sell out their own grandchildren to protect themselves?"

"Yes," I said, recoiling at the very idea of Kaiser grandchildren. Maybe coming to visit them at their rented summer house on the island.

"Here's the situation. You see, we had a business arrangement as of last month, and I thought everybody was getting along just fine."

"After you muscled in on their operation, you mean."

I wasn't sure why I said it. It just came out and it hung there in the air for a moment. Then, before I could even see how he did it, a knife appeared in Corvo's right hand. He twirled it between his fingers.

"After we agreed on the new arrangement, is how I prefer to put it. If you don't mind." His voice didn't change at all, but the blade was more than enough. He was an absolute master at twirling it, I had to give him that much.

I nodded for him to go ahead. I tried to look him in the eye and not watch the knife.

"I know the Kaisers have the place on Beaver Island," he said. "They think they can hunker down there and send me out a bag of money and a couple of Indians to take the blame for them. If it seems like I'm playing along, believe me, it's only because I know I'll catch up to them eventually."

"They're on the ferry back to the mainland right now."

"Let them run. It doesn't matter. I'll find them."

"I don't think they're running. In fact, I'm pretty sure they're going back to their house."

"Do tell," he said, looking a little surprised.

"I think they're under the impression that you're all square now," I said, nodding toward the bag of money.

He shook his head slowly. Almost sadly. Like the very idea of this was just too much to bear. We were facing directly west now, the sun bright in my eyes.

"So where are they?" he finally said.

"I just told you. They're on the ferry. They're going back home."

He smiled again. He stopped twirling the knife.

"The Indians," he said. "Carrick and LeBlanc."

"I thought we agreed they had no part in this."

"We agreed that the Kaisers' story was a lie, and that the Indians almost certainly had nothing to do with the planning of the new drop site. Or even the execution, for that matter. But when they were offered up as part of this deal today, I agreed to take them. Do you want to know why?"

I didn't answer. I sat there and waited.

"Those two men who were left on the ground up there . . . Those two men who were betrayed and gunned down . . ."

You mean the two hijackers who somehow found out about the new location, I thought. Who went up there armed to the teeth, no doubt to kill someone and make a point.

"One was my brother," he said. "The other was just as close as a brother to me. Do you understand what I'm saying?"

"Yes, but—"

The blade came so fast it was invisible. It was just a sound in the air. I felt the steel against the skin of my cheek. He was already sitting back in his chair when I felt the first drop of blood hit my arm.

"But what, Alex? But what? What were you going to say?"

I didn't reach up to hold my cheek. I let it bleed.

"They called me from the airport," he said. "Eldon did. My brother. He was still alive. He said O'Neil was alive, too. They were both sitting on the ground, bleeding."

He leaned forward and cupped a hand under my cheek. When he drew it back there was a great drop of blood in his palm. He looked at it for a moment, then he showed it to me, like he was sharing a secret.

"They were dying on the ground, on some godforsaken little airstrip in the middle of the woods. Eldon was talking to me and he was saying, you gotta send help, you gotta get up here, and I'm doing the math, Chicago to the UP, it's at least six hours away. Then I hear him yelling at somebody, he's saying, 'Hey, over here, you gotta help us. Get over here. Hey, where you going?' And it turns out it's this Indian guy. Eldon even said that to me, over the phone, he said there's an Indian guy here, he's gotta help us. You gotta call him and tell him, like he expects me to know this man's name and his number so I can call him up and tell him to go save the two men who are dying. He was getting delirious at that point. He started saying all these strange, random things and then he'd come back into focus and he'd call to the Indian again, saying, 'Come on, don't leave, you gotta help us.'"

He weighed the knife in his hand again. I wondered which part of me would feel the blade next.

"So I found out," he said. "The Kaisers were saying it was the Indian Carrick who was there at the airport, and the Indian LeBlanc who drove him away. I asked them who else was involved and they gave me the name of a two-bit dealer in Sault Ste. Marie. They said he helped put it all together, which once again I knew was a total fabrication. But at the same time I wondered if perhaps ten percent of it was true, like most lies. I had to find out, so I went up there and I talked to the dealer up there to get his side of the story."

Yeah, you talked to him, I thought. Him and his neighbor both. You talked to them with that knife in your right hand.

"The dealer had his own take on the situation," he said, "as you can imagine. But he was solid on Buck Carrick. He confirmed that connection. So now I knew that yes, it was Carrick at the airport. When Harry and Jo offered me both of them, well, let's just say that it'll help me keep a promise I made. To myself. To my father. To O'Neil's father. This is beyond business now, you realize that. So I'll ask you one more time. Where are they?"

I wasn't sure what to say. I didn't think anything would satisfy him, short of telling him that they were currently back in that boat, waiting on the other side of Gull Island. So I stayed silent. I began wondering how many times he would cut me, out here in the middle of the lake. How many times would he swing that blade before my life bled away and he dumped my body into the water?

He raised the knife until it was inches from my face.

"What am I supposed to do, Alex? Give me an idea, because right now I don't have what I want. All I have is you."

I looked him in the eye. I waited.

"Make him take us to them," Mr. White said. It was the first time he had spoken, and his voice was surprisingly soft. "He must know where they are."

Corvo didn't look away from me. "Mr. White makes a good point," he said. "Where are they?"

I shook my head. I didn't say a word.

He brought the knife to my face. He touched my other cheek, the one that wasn't already bleeding. I felt the point of the blade breaking my skin.

"Where are they?" he said.

I didn't move. I didn't close my eyes.

"Make him find them," Mr. White said. "Make him find them and bring them to you."

Corvo raised one eyebrow. He kept the knife pressed against my cheek.

"Now that's an interesting idea," he said, "but what guarantee do I have that he would deliver?"

"He looks pretty smart to me," Mr. White said. "He knows that the two Indians are walking dead men. Nothing he can do will change that. If he doesn't bring them to you, he'll get exactly the same thing."

"But if he does bring them to me," Corvo said, "then he walks away. That's what you're saying. His payment for performing this service would be his life."

"That's right."

"And what if he calls the police?"

"He won't do that."

"Why not?" Corvo said. "Why wouldn't he do that?"

"Because he knows you'd smell a setup a mile away. Then it wouldn't just be him and the Indians dying. It would be every family member of every man involved. It would be a river of blood."

"What do you think?" Corvo said to me. "Are you really smart enough to understand what Mr. White is saying?"

It sounded like a conversation they'd already had, in the past, more than once, and it took me right back to what Janet Long had told me. These guys weren't from the cartels, but they'd been shown the light. This is how you do your business now. No rules, no restraint. Everyone is fair game.

"Yes," I said, figuring it was time to finally open my mouth. "I'm smart enough to understand what he's saying."

He kept the blade against my skin for another few seconds. Then he pulled it away. He folded the knife and put it into his pocket. He turned his chair around and looked at his compass. Then he opened up the throttle and turned the boat in a tight arc. We went racing back toward Gull Island, skimming across the waves like a smooth stone. I watched ahead, my eyes watering in the wind, wondering if the boat was still on the other side of the island. I hadn't heard a motor, but maybe we'd been far enough away. Would they have taken the chance to escape?

A few minutes later, Corvo pulled up short of the inlet and drifted in, just as he had the first time. The side of his boat knocked against the jet ski and sent it drifting toward shore.

Corvo killed the engine. Then he reached into a side compartment and brought up a first-aid box. He opened it and took out a large, sterile pad. He opened the paper wrapping and gave it to me, careful not to touch the pad itself.

"Here," he said. "Put this on your face. You need to take care of that."

I didn't move. I felt the blood all down the left side of my face now.

"We've already established you're not a fool," he said. "Don't act like one."

I took the pad from him. I pressed it to my face.

"I'm giving you this." He took out his wallet and extracted a business card. Then he picked up my wallet and put the card inside. "You call that number and let me know when I should expect you. I'm giving you exactly forty-eight hours. You bring them both down and you turn them over to me. Then you drive away. You'll never see me again."

I took the wallet from him.

"I've been a little out of my head the past few days," he said. "You should be glad that Mr. White came up with such a sensible plan. But please, Mr. McKnight, remember everything he said. The Indians are already dead. There's nothing else you can do. So please don't disappoint me. Don't make me come find all of you."

I kept sitting there, thinking it through. If I play along, I buy us some time, at least. Enough time to do what? I don't even know yet. But at least we have a chance to think of something.

"We'd like to get back before it's dark," he said. "So I'll say good-bye now. I'll talk to you in forty-eight hours. Please don't make it forty-nine."

I got up, still holding the pad against my cheek. I jumped over the rail, right into the water. It was up to my waist. I went to the jet ski, cursing myself that I hadn't kept the gun. I could have hidden it in the front compartment, taken it out right now, and shot both of them.

But no. Even as I thought that, I heard Corvo starting his motor and then pulling away. As I turned, I saw them leaving the inlet, then gunning as they hit the open water. It seemed like Mr. White was looking back at me, but it was hard to tell with the sunglasses. He certainly didn't wave.

I climbed onto the jet ski and started it. If Corvo circles the island now, I thought, then this will all be a moot point. White would gun them all down and then they'd come back and finish me off, too. I went out into the open water and turned around the north end of the island, wondering exactly what I'd see.

One boat. Not two.

I pulled up alongside the boat and grabbed on to the gunwale. As I pulled myself up onto the deck, I saw Buck on the bench in the galley, holding his head in his hands. Vinnie was still lying on the floor. The zip ties had been cut from his hands and ankles. He was untied from the table post. But his eyes weren't open. At that moment, he honestly looked more dead than alive. Lou was sitting on the other bench, watching his son.

"We have to get him somewhere for help," he said. "As soon as possible."

Then he looked at my face.

"What happened?" he said. "You're bleeding bad."

I ignored him, trying the key in the ignition. The engine sputtered once and then came to life. I pulled up the anchor and turned us out of the inlet. The jet ski would have to stay right where it was.

When we were in the open water, I pushed the throttle all the way forward. It wasn't a cigarette boat, but it would have to do.

"Just stay alive," Lou said, holding Vinnie's hand. "We finally found you, but you have to stay alive."

CHAPTER NINETEEN

A wind had picked up, out of the southwest. The waves were getting higher. I drove that fishing boat back toward Beaver Island, pushing it hard through the waves. Buck stumbled up from the cabin and sat in the seat next to me. Lou remained down below with Vinnie.

"What happened to your face?" he said to me. Then he answered his own question. "You got cut."

"I'll be all right."

"Do you want me to drive? You should be keeping pressure on it."

"Just sit there." I could already feel the emotions rising. A mixture of relief that we had gotten away alive and worry about Vinnie's condition, wound through with a bright thread of anger at the man sitting to my left. The time would come when we would have it out, but I knew it was best to wait.

"I'm so sorry, Alex. This is all my fault."

"It sure as hell is. If he dies, it's all on you."

So much for waiting.

"I just went for a ride with them. One ride to the airport. They paid me a thousand dollars to sit in the backseat and tell them where the trails were."

I took a breath and counted to three. I didn't get the chance to see how well that worked, because that's when Vinnie started to come to. He pushed Lou away from him, throwing a weak punch like his muscles were still trying to fight off the men who were putting him on this boat.

"It's all right," Lou said, wrapping up his arms, his whole upper body. "You're okay now, Vinnie. Take it easy."

Vinnie shook his head and opened his eyes. His father would be the first person he'd see, and I couldn't even imagine how disorienting that would be. Waking up and seeing a face you hadn't seen in thirty years.

"Lou, come here," I said.

He looked up at me.

"Just take the wheel," I said. "For one minute."

He looked back down at his son, then he stood and came to the captain's chair. I got up and he took my place. Buck had his eyes down. He was rubbing at the red marks on his wrists, and I'd never seen him look so small.

I found a half-full plastic bottle of water in one of the rear compartments, God knows how old and normally the last thing in the world you'd want to drink. But I opened it and I gave it to Vinnie as I bent down next to him.

"What the hell happened?" he said.

"You got knocked out. Do you remember?"

"Not really, no. I was at the house with Buck. Then we were about to go outside and . . ."

He shook his head like his eyes were going out of focus.

"Sit still a minute," I said. "Let me see your eyes."

I held his chin and looked at each pupil. They were dilated, but they weren't unequal. One of the more serious concussion signs I'd been trained to look for, long ago.

"What happened to your face?" he said.

"A little disagreement. Nothing to worry about right now."

"I'm still not seeing right," he said, blinking his eyes. "It's like tunnel vision."

"It's okay. We're gonna take you somewhere. Right now."

"Where's Buck?"

"He's right there. In the chair. He's okay."

"Who's that man driving the boat?"

I looked back up at Lou. I met his eyes and he nodded.

"That's your father," I said. "That's Louis LeBlanc."

He squinted and tried to focus. "That's impossible."

"It's him, Vinnie. It's your father. He came out here to help find you."

Vinnie blew out a breath and started to sway a little bit.

"This light is killing me," he said, holding up a hand to shield his eyes.

"Get in here," I said, helping him to back up a few more feet, until he was fully inside the cabin. He half lay down on the cushion, still shaking his head and blinking.

"How did you find us?" he said.

"We got lucky. I'll tell you about it later."

"Alex, I want to know. Tell me how you found us. Those people brought us to the island. Those people who Buck thought were going to help us. They put us on the boat and they . . . They took us. I should have called you when I had the chance. God, my head hurts."

"Stop talking," I said. "Just shut up and close your eyes."

Lou called to me. I left Vinnie lying there and went up to the wheel.

"We're getting close," he said. "I don't see any docks anywhere."

"Take us north. We should probably go right to the main dock. If there's a medical center on the island, I'm sure it's close to that."

"They're going to ask questions," Buck said.

"Sorry, I didn't hear what you said," I said low into Buck's ear. "Would you like to repeat it?"

"No. Never mind."

I stared him down for a few seconds. Then I took the wheel again while Lou went down to watch Vinnie.

I circled the island on the north end. The shoreline stayed rough and rocky all the way around. The sun was finally starting to go down on this, officially one of the longest days of my life. I felt my own vision start to waver a little bit, just a product of sheer exhaustion. That and the aftereffects of the adrenaline, now that that hard part was over. We just had to get Vinnie to a doctor. Then I could collapse completely.

I held the boat steady as we made our way around that last bend and into the main harbor. There were half-a-dozen places I could have gone, but I chose the marina right next to the ferry dock. I figured that was closest to the main street and probably whatever medical facilities they had around here. I pulled into a slip and bumped the dock a little bit too hard. Some guy in white shorts and deck shoes came running down the dock, waving at us. He had sunglasses tucked into the neck of his alligator shirt. He took one look at the blood on my face and turned from an annoyance into an actual helpful human being, tying up the boat and helping Buck onto the deck.

"You need a doctor," he said to me.

"My friend needs one first," I said. Lou and I helped Vinnie out of the cabin. He tried to stand on rubber legs and he kept blinking in the light. The three of us half pulled, half lifted him onto the dock. Then the man helped us down to the street and walked with us right to the door of the medical center. I thanked the man, thinking this was the Michigan version of a yuppie boat snob. They dress the part but they just can't manage the attitude.

There was a physician's assistant on duty. She was just about to close for the day, but one look at us and she was on the phone to the two resident doctors. A few minutes later, Vinnie was in one room, getting the vision test and mental-acuity test and whatever the hell else they do to you when it's obvious you have some grade of concussion. I was having my own fun in the next room over, receiving a tetanus shot and seventeen stitches in my face.

The doctor asked me what had happened to us. I told him it was a boating accident. I knew we'd be talking to the police eventually, but I thought we'd probably rather go home first and talk to the officers who knew us personally, for better or worse.

They weren't about to let Vinnie go anywhere for a while. He ended up going home with one of the doctors, so he could be woken up every couple of hours for observation. That's still the protocol for concussion. Lots of rest but not too much sleep at one time. I walked out of there with fresh white bandages taped all over my face. The PA took Lou over to the Kaisers' rental house to pick up his car. She even found us a two-bedroom suite at a little place called the Emerald Isle Hotel.

It was turning into a five-star vacation. Aside from being taken down to the swamp to be killed, then riding a hard ten miles out onto the lake to rescue our friends, followed by a sit-down with a psychotic Chicago gangster and a knife wound to the face. After all that, the place was finally being redeemed by some grade-A island residents.

We ate a late dinner at one of the restaurants on the main street. Just me, Lou, and Buck, sitting there at the window table as the sun set. It felt wrong not to have Vinnie with us, but we knew he was being taken good care of at the doctor's house.

Lou didn't say much. He kept looking at me and then out at the water a block away from us. Buck ate like he hadn't seen food in a couple of days. Which maybe he hadn't.

When he was done, he slumped back in his chair. There were still red rings around his wrists. I wondered if he'd have them forever. Maybe he should, I thought, as a constant reminder of the choices he'd made that week.

"Everybody started shooting each other," he said. "I panicked and ran away. When I was down the road, I called Vinnie. I didn't know what else to do. I didn't even realize I'd been shot until I got in his truck and he noticed the blood on my shirt."

"There was somebody still alive," I said. "He was calling out to you. You left him there."

"How do you know that?"

"Let's just say I have it on good authority. Whether it's justified or not, there are certain people who aren't going to let you off the hook on this."

"That's why we were left out in the boat?"

"Well, the Kaisers were trying to blame you for everything. The new drop route, and probably the Kennedy assassinations, too. The man who was going to pick you up was more interested in the simple fact that you were the only man who lived through what happened at the airport. You would have done everybody a big favor by just getting shot there and dying with everybody else."

He looked back and forth between Lou and me, waiting for one of us to let him off the hook. But all he saw were two weary faces. It was the wrong day to expect me to pull any punches.

"I did all of this," he said. "I know that. When I talked to Harry and Jo, I mean, I thought they were going to help us. I thought everything would be okay. But it just got worse."

"Everybody's worried about you," Lou said. "Both of you. They've got every Ojibwa in the state keeping an eye out for you."

"Are you really Vinnie's father? Did I hear that right?"

"You heard right."

"I thought you were dead."

"Apparently I'm not."

"I'll start thanking both of you right now," he said, "and I'll keep doing it. I'm not sure what else I can do."

"Just do me one favor," Lou said. "The next time you get yourself in a jam like this, don't call Vinnie, okay?"

"Okay," Buck said, giving that one a little smile. "I promise. I'll call Alex instead."

I just looked at him.

"It was a joke," he said.

"Yeah, I know. You should call your family now. Tell them you're all right. Vinnie's family, too."

"If you don't mind," he said, "I'd like to do that tomorrow morning. As soon as word gets around, all hell is gonna break loose."

"You're probably right about that," I said. "You're gonna be a very popular guy once you get back home. I think Chief Benally gets the first dance."

As tired as I was, I couldn't sleep. My face was throbbing now. I took some aspirin and sat out on the couch. Buck was snoring away in one bedroom. Lou was in the other. I sat there and looked out the window at the darkened library behind the hotel. After a while, Lou came out and sat down in the chair across from me.

"Tell me what happened," he said. "I want to know what that man said to you. Every word."

"I didn't want to bring it up yet. I figured those guys should both recover a little bit first."

"I understand. But it's just you and me here."

My face was killing me. It hurt to talk. But I thought back carefully over every word Corvo had said to me. I told Lou everything I could remember. After everything we had been through that day, I owed him the full story.

I ran through everything, including the last instructions Corvo had given me. Bring the two Indians down to Chicago. You have exactly forty-eight hours.

"And if you don't do that?" Lou said.

"Then it's pretty clear what will happen. Corvo will come looking for us. Me included. If I call the cops, it gets even worse."

"So what do we do?"

"It's too bad he didn't want just Buck. I would have turned him over on the spot."

"Seriously, Alex."

"Seriously, I don't know. But we've got about a day and a half left to figure it out."

We picked up Vinnie from the doctor's house the next morning. He was looking more like himself, but we got some pretty detailed instructions on taking him to a doctor back home, and watching for symptoms of post-concussion syndrome. Severe headaches, dizziness, sudden changes in mood. Basically anything out of the ordinary. While I was there, the doctor took the opportunity to change the bandages on my face. It still hurt.

We settled the bill and the insurance and everything else. Then we thanked him a few times, because he had obviously gone out of his way for us. There was room for only one more car on the ferry, so we took it. We got onboard and we stood on the deck, watching the boat push off from the dock. I saw the fishing boat from the day before, still sitting in its slip. I figured someone would take care of it eventually, take it back to wherever it belonged.

The ferry was slow. Two hours to go thirty-two miles. We had plenty of time to sit there in the indoor lounge, feeling the gentle rhythm of the boat, seeing the water just outside the window as it moved past, inch by inch.

Buck hadn't said a word yet that whole morning. Neither had Vinnie, but for Buck it was out of character. I figured he must have been thinking about the day ahead, and how it would be one of the longest of his life.

"So what's our story?" he finally said.

Vinnie just raised an eyebrow at him.

"I mean, what are we going to tell everybody when we get back? We should get on the same page here."

"Why don't you just tell the truth?" I said.

"Well, think about it. Everybody who was at the airport is dead now. There's nobody who can even put me there."

"I picked you up," Vinnie said. "I can put you there."

"But if you didn't pick me up *there*? That's what I'm saying."

"If I didn't pick you up there, how would you explain the gunshot wound?"

"What gunshot wound?" Buck said, raising both arms and waving them around. "I sure don't see any gunshot wounds, do you?"

"Your cousin treated you," Vinnie said. "We drove you all the way down to Mount Pleasant to have him patch you up."

"We did go down there, yeah," Buck said, frowning. "We can't ask him to lie about that. That's why I'm saying we should work this out now."

"Just tell the truth," I said again. "You never have to be on the same page if you do that. Makes life kinda simple."

"Okay, okay, I get it," he said. "I was at the airport. Vinnie picked me up. Ron fixed me. Everybody's got the same story there. But as far as me being at the airport in the first place . . . That's just my story, right? You see what I'm saying? Nobody else needs to corroborate it. Is that the right word? *Corroborate*?"

"Cut to the chase," Lou said. "What are you going to tell them?"

"I don't know exactly. I'm just saying. If those guys came to my house to pick me up, and up until then it was just an abstract idea . . . Then here they are and all of a sudden I'm having second thoughts. . . . I mean, I'm actually being honest about that. I did have some second thoughts. But they didn't seem too interested in giving me a choice at that point, you know what I'm saying? In hindsight, it kinda feels like I was being forced to go along with them."

Lou was nodding at every word. A fresh reminder that this was a man who had spent some long years in prison. It was only natural he'd be looking for the angle here. It was practically hardwired into his brain now.

"You were on the scene when five men were murdered," he said to Buck. "But if you were there against your will . . ."

"Just tell the truth," I said one more time, even though I might as well have opened the window and told it to the squawking seagulls.

"Come on," Lou said to me. "Give the man a break. He's just trying to be prepared for what's coming today. You never give these guys the rope if you don't have to. That's what any good lawyer would tell you."

"Okay, so you were kidnapped," I said. "You were taken to the airport and everybody got killed. Now you're free. You should have called the police right then."

"I panicked," he said. "It was a natural reaction."

"So you had Vinnie drive you all the way down to Mount Pleasant. Then, the next day, you willingly went to the Kaisers' house. These same people who were supposedly behind your 'abduction' the day before. Hell, you even came out to the island with them. I assume that was voluntary, too. Unless they put you in the trunk."

"They totally fooled me," Buck said. "Vinnie, too. They're like the world's best con men, and you have to admit, once they got us out here, everything got turned upside down pretty quick. You think we wanted to be tied up in that boat and left out there?"

"No," I said, raising both hands. "I'm sure you didn't. See how convincing you sound? Because you're telling the truth now. Just do that from the beginning."

"I'm getting a headache," Vinnie said. "There's too much noise out here."

He tried to stand up, but then he had to hold on tight to the back of the chair. Lou and I got up to help him and he waved us away. When he got his bearings, he left us and went down the hallway to the "quiet room," where people could read or just close their eyes for a while. Lou followed him. I wasn't sure if that was such a great idea, but what the hell. He and Vinnie hadn't talked to each other yet. At some point, they'd have to get into the father-son business, no matter how strange that would be.

"Vinnie's truck is still at the Kaisers' house," Buck said. "We should go get it while we're down here."

"Actually, it's at an auto-glass shop in Cadillac," I said. "But it's still an hour and a half out of our way."

"We'd have to come down again and get it anyway. That's three hours down, three hours back. This way we take care of it today."

"You're stalling, Buck. You don't want to face this stuff. I get it. I wouldn't, either."

He stopped talking and looked out the window. I got up and was just about to walk down the hall to see how Lou and Vinnie were doing. Then I thought, no, better to just go up and get some air on the deck. Let them work out whatever it was they had to work out. It was something only the two of them could do.

We ended up going to Cadillac after all. Vinnie wanted his truck, although there was no way we were going to let him drive it. Not until we knew he was a hundred percent better. We got the rental car off the ferry and we all piled in and drove down to Cadillac. I was driving. Buck was in the front seat with me. Lou and Vinnie sat in the back. Neither of them said anything. I had no idea what they may have said to each other back in that quiet room on the ferry. Maybe they hadn't said anything at all. It was the quiet room, after all.

The ride seemed longer because of the silence, but an hour and a half later, we were close to Cadillac and I realized that we were about to drive right by the Kaisers' house. I knew that Corvo would have had plenty of time by now to get the boat back to Chicago and then drive up here. Or hell, even just take the boat right to Charlevoix. He could have practically met them as they were getting off the ferry.

So I wasn't sure what to expect as were rolling down that same road. Police cars? A burned-out, still-smoking building? But as I came up to the driveway, everything looked calm and quiet.

"This is their house," Buck said.

"Yeah, I know. I told you we were here before. That's how we got Vinnie's truck over to the shop."

"So why are we stopping here? If his truck is in Cadillac . . ."

"Yeah, this might not be a great idea," Lou said.

Vinnie had his head back against the seat. His eyes were closed.

"I can't just drive by," I said. "I have to see."

I pulled into the driveway. As we broke into the clearing, we saw the house. The same vehicles were parked inside, plus one more. A beat-up old clunker that looked like something Buck would drive. This must have belonged to Sugarpie and Dumpling. I remembered Jo Kaiser telling them she would pick up their car in Charlevoix. Now it was here, parked in front of their house, and I wondered if maybe I should turn the car right around and get the hell out of here.

But Lou was already out his door. He had the gun ready. I put the car in Park and followed behind him. He went to the front door of the house. It was closed tight. I took a look through the window, into the kitchen. Some of the cupboard doors were still off the hinges, but most of the mess on the floor had been cleaned up.

I drew back and did a quick scan of everything I could see from where I was standing.

"They really came back," I said. "If they had any sense, they'd be five hundred miles away by now."

"If they came back," Lou said, "then where are they?"

We heard the noise from around the corner. Lou broke first, but I caught up to him and was the first man to find Buck standing at the door to the barn. I stood there looking at the same horrible sight, and a few seconds later Lou and Vinnie had the misfortune of showing up behind us. We'd all surely see it in our nightmares, for the rest of our lives. Harry and Josephine Kaiser, both strung up and hanging from the rafters of the barn, their feet just inches from the ground. The ropes around their chests, cinched under their armpits, holding them aloft without choking them. Giving Corvo the chance to take his time with them.

They'd been here for hours. The blood had stopped draining from their bodies. One of the chickens lay dead on the ground. I didn't see any of the others.

I pulled Buck away from the door. Vinnie followed us, but Lou stayed behind.

"Let's get the hell out of here!" I called to him. "Right now."

He stood there looking through the doorway for a few more seconds. Then he caught up to us as we all got back into the vehicle.

"This is who we're dealing with," he said as I whipped the car around and headed back down the driveway. "This is the kind of thing these guys do."

CHAPTER TWENTY

Nobody said anything for a while. I made myself stick to the speed limit. Buck was holding on to his knees, leaning forward like he was about to throw up.

"That would have been us," Vinnie said from the backseat. It was the first time he had spoken since we'd left Charlevoix. "Both of us."

"There's no such thing as 'would have,'" I said. "It didn't happen. That's all that matters. You're safe now. We're all safe."

Not quite true, I thought. But I still wasn't ready to drop that on him.

When we hit Cadillac, I found the same auto-glass shop again. Vinnie's truck was out in the parking lot, its windshield fully restored. Lou went in to talk to the man while I stayed outside with my cell phone. I called Janet Long and she answered on the first ring.

"Alex, I was trying to call you back yesterday. What happened?"

There was a joke there about being tied up, but I wasn't about to say it.

"I've got something to tell you," I said. "You have to listen very carefully. I'm going to give you an address just outside of Cadillac. There are two dead bodies in the barn. A man and a woman."

"Alex, stop right there. You need to go to the local police immediately."

"We're on our way back to the UP right now, and that's the first place we'll go, I promise. You just need to send somebody over there now."

"What the hell is going on up there? There were two dead men found in Sault Ste. Marie just a couple of days ago. Are we talking about the same perpetrator?"

"The same perp," I said, smiling grimly at the cop talk. "It's a man out of Chicago named Corvo, if you want to know the truth. Although I don't imagine you could tie it to him just yet."

"What was that name?"

"Corvo. You know who I'm talking about?"

There was a silence on the line.

"Alex, you have to go to the police right this second," she said. "The nearest station you can find. You may be in some serious danger."

You don't know the half of it, I thought, and then that's when I had to make my choice. I flashed back on what Mr. White had said to me. If you try to set up Corvo, he'll smell it from a mile away. Then every family member of every man involved, every single one of them, dies in a river of blood.

"You're the only person I can trust with this," I said. "So let me ask you a question. If you're putting together a case on Corvo—"

"I didn't say that. I just said you—"

"Needed to go to a station right away because I might be in big danger. I got that part, okay? I heard you. Obviously you wouldn't be saying that if you didn't know about this guy. And you wouldn't know about this guy unless he was on your radar. Look, I'm not asking you to tell me any secrets. Just give me a general idea here. Are you close to moving on him?"

Another silence.

"Janet, are you there?"

"I'm here."

"There's a good chance I'll be seeing him again. Soon. I need to know if there's any chance of you putting him away. Like maybe even with my help."

"This is insane," she said. "You cannot be involved in this."

"Too late. I'm already involved."

I heard her let out a long breath. "I need to go talk to somebody, Alex. I'll call you back as soon as I can, all right?"

"Okay. I'll be here. Thank you."

I ended the call, just in time to see Lou coming out of the glass shop. I figured that meant we were ready to go, but he stopped me and waved over Vinnie and Buck.

"I have something to ask," he said, "from all three of you. When we get back up north, I know the police are going to be asking a lot of questions. I know Alex said we should tell the truth. But in my case, I'm afraid that even the truth might get me into a lot of trouble."

"It was all justified," I said. "It was self-defense."

"Let me finish, Alex. If the police start asking me questions and they find out who I really am, I'm going to have a big problem. I'm a convicted felon, remember? I'm technically still on parole?"

"There's no 'technically' about it," I said. "You're either on parole or you're not."

"Okay, I'm on parole. If they find out back in Nevada that I'm mixed up in this? Never mind if anything I did was justified or not, it's gonna hang me up for a long time just trying to explain what happened. As you can imagine, I'm not accustomed to getting any breaks when it comes to the police."

Vinnie shook his head and for a second I thought he was going to turn and walk away. But he stayed put and kept staring at the ground.

"I hope Alex will agree I've been good to have around this week. If I get sent back to Nevada today, I lose any ability to keep helping you."

"I'm getting a headache again," Vinnie said. "Can we get going now?"

"I'll drive the rental car," Lou said. "You guys go with Alex in Vinnie's truck. All I'm asking is that you guys leave me out of the story. Okay? That's all I'm asking."

"Fine," Vinnie said. "You weren't here. I can live with that."

"He helped save our lives today," Buck said. "Come on, give the man a break."

"It's okay," Lou said to Buck. "We still need some time to sort things out."

Vinnie and Buck got into the truck. It was a tight fit sitting three across, but we'd been through a lot worse. I gave Lou a nod and told him I'd see him back in Paradise.

Vinnie sat in the middle. I could see him trying to focus, until he finally gave up and closed his eyes. I didn't want to disturb him. Let the man rest, I thought.

I looked at my watch. About twenty-four hours had passed since I'd been given my little assignment. We were halfway to the deadline and I still hadn't told them that Corvo considered them both walking dead men.

Buck didn't seem too happy about it, but I drove right to the Bay Mills Tribal Police Station. I figured we might as well get right into the fun part of the day. Chief Benally made us all wait in the lobby while he called in a detective from the Michigan State Police post in the Soo. Some of this reached beyond Chippewa County, after all. I recognized the man who showed up. I knew him well enough to nod hello to, anyway. Chief Benally and the detective took Buck into the interview room first. Then Vinnie. Then it was my turn.

I told them everything I knew from direct experience. I didn't speculate about anything else. Like how willingly or unwillingly Buck became involved in the first place. I gave short, direct answers and told them what had happened. Except for the parts involving Lou. I didn't say one word about being taken to the swamp, or what happened when we got there. My story was that the Kaisers left me alone in the house, taking their two lackeys with them, and then I went to find Vinnie and Buck in the boat.

I also left out my entire conversation with Corvo. I was still waiting to hear back from Janet. I knew she was my one last hope to get any real help.

Then it was Vinnie's turn again. Then Buck's again.

It wasn't clear for a while whether Buck or possibly even Vinnie would be taken into immediate custody. In the end, Vinnie was allowed to leave. The chief said we shouldn't bother waiting for Buck. Even if he was released that day, he lived just down the road, so he could walk home.

So I drove Vinnie back to Paradise. He put his head back, yet again, and closed his eyes.

"Your father saved my life yesterday," I said to him. "So really, he saved all of our lives."

"I know that."

"I'm not trying to tell you how you should feel about him. But you should try to talk to him."

He didn't answer.

"Let me ask you one thing," I said. "That night Buck called you, why did you go out to get him?"

"I had to. He's my cousin."

"The first night you ever got drunk, in your entire life, is the night you drove to Newberry. That's what you're telling me?"

He looked over at me.

"I'm just saying, if you had hit somebody, you would have gone away. Just like your father."

"So I'm no better? Is that your point?"

"No. My point is that you had a good reason, so yeah, maybe there was more to the story than just another drunk Indian. If you had a chance to explain yourself, maybe somebody else could understand it."

I let that one hang for a while. Finally, he opened the door, but then stopped before he got out.

"Tell me the truth," he said. "We're not done with this guy yet, are we?"

"Who, Corvo?"

He waited for me to keep talking. He wasn't going anywhere until I did.

"No, we're not done with him," I said. "You get some rest and I'll meet you down at the Glasgow for dinner, okay? We can talk about it then."

He didn't move.

"I promise. Get some rest and I'll see you down there."

He got out of the truck. Before I could back out, he came over to the driver's side. I rolled down my window.

"Thanks for everything," he said. "I'm not sure I even said that yet."

"It's okay. I figure we're about even now."

He put a hand on my arm for a second. Then he let me go.

It was a couple of hours later, after a shower, a change of clothes, some new bandages, and four aspirin. My landline-phone rang. It was Janet.

"Alex, are you there? I tried your cell earlier . . ."

"I live on the edge of the world, remember? Cell phones are always a crapshoot up here."

"You need to come down here and talk to us," she said. "Right away. Even if you get here late."

"What, in Detroit?"

"Yes. Do not initiate any further contact with Corvo. Just get down here and—"

"Janet, are you guys close to moving on Corvo, or not?"

"We'll talk about that down here."

"Tell me now. Do you have a case or do you not have a case?"

"We have pieces," she said. "Okay? We don't have enough to move on yet. In fact, if you really want to know the truth, we're not even close. If you have something to give us, it might help . . ."

"Yeah, it'll help all right. Look, I know how it works. It takes months to put together a RICO case. Sometimes years."

"Alex, what do you have for us? You have to tell me."

"I have talk," I said. I closed my eyes and rubbed my forehead, feeling suddenly very alone. "I have a bunch of words between three men sitting in a boat, in the middle of Lake Michigan. That's what I have."

"Okay, then. I can't wait to hear about it. You're coming down, right?"

There was a knock on the door.

"Yes," I said. "It'll be good to see you again. I should have come down by now, taken you to dinner like I promised."

"Alex—"

"I have to go. Somebody's at the door."

"Do not hang up, God damn it."

"I'll come down, Janet. Not tonight. But soon, okay? It's good talking to you."

I hung up the phone and unplugged it from the wall. Then I answered the door. It was Lou. He had obviously gone back to the other cabin for a shower and some clean clothes himself. Between the two of us, we looked almost like regular humans.

"Is Vinnie in his cabin?" he said.

"He is. He said he'd meet us down at the Glasgow a little later."

I could tell he was about to say something about how we were supposed to be watching him closely for any signs of PCS, but he let it go. If I knew Vinnie at all, I knew he'd want a few hours to himself.

"Alex, what's going on? Who were you talking to?"

"My friend in Detroit," I said. "I thought maybe she could help us."

"I thought you weren't supposed to contact anybody. Wasn't that one of the things they made very clear to you?"

"Look, I'm an ex-cop," I said. "I had it drilled into my head, all those years. Call for backup. Do things by the book. But you know what? I'm just realizing tonight . . . even if I still had a badge and a gun, I don't know if I'd even believe in the book anymore."

Lou stood there in my cabin, his wet hair slicked back, looking tough and old at the same time, like he'd seen everything there is to see in life, most of it bad. He listened carefully to every word.

"The rules are all gone now," I said. "They've been torn up. People do things that would have seemed unimaginable just a few years ago. I mean, when those guys told me that they'd kill everybody . . . not just us but every family member they could find . . . Meaning *your* family, Lou. All of them. When they said that, I believed them. I know they weren't just talking. I *know* it. I saw their eyes when they told me what would happen. You understand what I'm saying?"

He nodded slowly.

"But still, I figured I had to try, you know? Just take one chance to get somebody else on our side. "

"There's nobody," he said. "Not for something like this. I could have told you."

"We can't run, either. Not forever. So yeah, that leaves one choice. We go down there and we take it to 'em."

"I'm with you," he said. "But it's just you and me, right? We leave Vinnie out of this?"

"I think he has the right to know what's going on."

"No, Alex. We can tell him afterwards. I'd like to keep Buck out of it, too. Maybe for different reasons. I mean, we've already seen how he functions under pressure."

"I hear what you're saying, but come on, we don't have much time left. Tomorrow's the deadline."

"We'll have time. How 'bout we all have a meeting over breakfast? See who's really up for it?"

"I'm just thinking, if Vinnie's feeling better tonight . . ."

"You gotta promise me," Lou said. "He gets one more night to recover. No talking about this until tomorrow morning."

"Okay, I promise."

"Thank you," he said, grabbing my shoulder. "We've got a deal. But right now, I think I need a drink."

The sun had gone down on another tough day. At least I knew that Vinnie was in his cabin as I drove by. That was one thing that was right in the world. Lou and I drove down to the Glasgow in his rental car and sat at the bar. Jackie broke out the cold Molsons for both of us from my personal fridge. A Tigers game was on the television over the bar, the sound turned low. It was cold outside tonight. Legitimately cold. Logs burned and crackled in the fireplace.

"I can see why you like this place," Lou said to me. "I think I'd be here every night myself."

"For the love of God," Jackie said, bringing the beers over and looking at the bandages on my face, "what the hell happened to you?"

I didn't want to get into it. I just asked the man for a plate of his beef stew and hoped he'd let me be for the rest of the night.

Vinnie came in a little while later. He could have chosen to sit next to Lou or next to me. He chose the stool next to me.

"At least you did come down," Lou said. He was staring at the label on his beer bottle and he didn't so much as glance in Vinnie's direction. "Even if you're not going to talk to me."

Vinnie didn't respond. Jackie fixed him a plate of beef stew and slid over a 7UP. I was pretty sure I'd never see him drink another drop of alcohol.

"I did what you asked me to do," Vinnie finally said. "I covered for you at the station. I also realize that we all owe you some gratitude for what you did today. So you have that from me."

"Okay, then," Lou said. "I'm glad I was able to help."

"I'm afraid I can't give you much else. But that's the choice you made thirty years ago."

"Just tell me this much," Lou said, his eyes still fixed on the bottle. "I brought some things with me from Vegas to give to your sisters and their kids. How many are we talking about?"

Vinnie stopped eating.

"I just want to know how many grandchildren I have," Lou said. "Is that so much to ask?"

"My sisters have two kids each," Vinnie said. "But I wouldn't call them your grandchildren. Not if you don't even know how many there are."

"There we go," Lou said. "Now we're getting somewhere. You got anything else to say to me?"

"Yes. You shouldn't have come here."

"You just got done thanking me."

"I changed my mind," Vinnie said. "On second thought, I'd rather be back on that island than owe you anything."

"You're saying you'd rather be getting sliced up like those people at the farmhouse? Is that what you're saying? He'd probably be doing that to you right now, as we speak."

"Gentlemen," Jackie said, "I'm not sure this is appropriate dinner conversation."

I looked at him and shook my head. Jackie let out a huff and walked away.

"I'm your father," Lou said. "I made enough mistakes for ten men, and I paid for them, believe me. But I'm still your father."

"Fathers don't leave," Vinnie said. He was holding on to the rail of the bar and I could practically hear the fizzing sound as his extra long fuse burned away.

"Sometimes fathers *have* to leave. Sometimes they have no choice."

"You beat your wife," Vinnie said. "My mother. That makes you the lowest kind of man on earth."

Lou took a long breath, nodding his head. "I laid my hands on Nika in anger exactly one time. One time in my life and I had a reason."

"Don't say her name. I don't want to hear her name pass your lips."

"They made me leave, don't you understand? Everyone on the rez turned against me. I was driven out. They told me to never come back."

"A solid idea," Vinnie said. "I wholeheartedly agree with them. I should go find every person on the rez past a certain age and thank them."

"Which is it, Vinnie? You can't have it both ways. Am I supposed to stay away or am I supposed to try to come back? Tell me what I should have done."

"You should have come back for your son's funeral," Vinnie said. "That's what you should have done. Oh no, wait, you couldn't do that because you were in prison for murder."

Lou stood up from his bar stool. Vinnie stood up to face him.

"Vinnie, you're supposed to be taking it easy," I said to him, figuring it was finally time to step in. "I don't think this qualifies."

"Stay out of this, Alex."

"You're right," Lou said. "I couldn't come to Tom's funeral because I was in prison. Not that it would have mattered. I wouldn't have been welcome, anyway."

They stood there looking at each other. A log shifted in the fireplace and let out a loud pop.

"He wasn't my son," Lou said. "Nika was sleeping with Henry Carrick."

There's that moment. The fuse burns out. You don't hear the fizzing anymore. There's one second of silence, maybe two. You think the bomb might not go off.

"I know it's hard to keep a secret on the rez," Lou said, "so it's kind of ironic. The biggest secret of all, and only me, Nika, and Henry know about it."

"No," Vinnie said. "No."

"I shouldn't have hit her. I admit that. They made me leave and I accepted it. I kept the secret all of these years. But now you know the truth. It was your mother who destroyed our marriage."

Then it happens. The bomb goes off.

He was on him before I could get off my stool. Vinnie hit him once in the face and then drove him to the floor with his shoulder. He got a few more shots in and it looked like Lou wasn't even trying to defend himself. I tried to pull Vinnie off of him and we both went crashing against the bar rail. I got the worst of it, taking the rail right in the ribs, the same spot where I'd been jabbed twice with a gun barrel when I was being driven to the swamp. I had to hold on and wait for my breath to come back. Instead of launching at his father again, Vinnie walked out the door.

Lou took a while getting off the floor. Jackie stood there watching us and for once in his life he had the good sense not to say anything.

"It's okay," Lou said as he slid back onto the bar stool. "He needed that."

"What in God's name are you talking about?" I said. "What happened to taking care of him? Letting him recover from his goddamned concussion?"

"It was eating him up, Alex. I wanted him to get mad at me. He needed to get that out of his system."

"Oh, well then excuse me. I guess you played that just right."

"You don't understand," he said. "I had to do that while I had the chance. Who knows where we'll all be after tomorrow. . . ."

He picked up his bottle and drained it.

"Was all of that stuff true?" I said. "About his brother?"

"Ask Henry Carrick. Next time you see him."

"You're gonna have a hell of a black eye tomorrow," I said, looking at him. "He really caught you."

"Good. Like I said. It was a long time coming."

"You are absolutely insane," I said, picking up my beer. The muscles in my side were finally beginning to relax.

"I'm going to go. I'll see you in the morning."

He stood up before I could say another word. Then he was out the door, even quicker than Vinnie. I heard him start the motor of the rental car. I finished my beef stew, watching a little of the ball game and listening to Jackie complain about things. It almost felt like a normal night for a change. I should have known it wouldn't last.

I left around ten o'clock. An early night, but probably just what I needed. Until I realized that I had no way to drive home. So I started walking up the road. Good thing it was late summer, so it was only cold and not brutally cold.

As I walked up my road, I saw Vinnie's truck parked by his place. I considered stopping in and then thought better of it. Instead, I went up to the second cabin, figuring I'd see what Lou was doing. Smoking a joint, no doubt. But when I got there, I didn't see the car.

He might be on the rez, I thought. He might have dropped in on his daughters. Which would be quite a sight, especially with the newly added bruises on his face, courtesy of Vinnie.

I went back to my cabin, wishing that I could sleep for the next week straight. That brought me back to Corvo's deadline and guaranteed I'd be lying awake for at least a few hours, staring at the ceiling.

Around ten thirty, my cell phone rang. It took me a moment to find it in the filthy pants I had taken off and thrown on the floor of the bathroom. I finally wrestled it free and answered it.

"Janet, is that you?"

"No, it's Lou. I need some help."

"What are you talking about? Where are you?"

"I'm in Sault Ste. Marie. In the jail. You gotta come get me out."

CHAPTER TWENTY-ONE

The City-County Building in Sault Ste. Marie, perhaps the ugliest building in the entire Upper Peninsula, is where you find the county holding cells, along with the county sheriff's office and the Sault Ste. Marie Police Department. It's all in that one gray rectangle on Court Street. They talk about renovating the place, or moving out the city police, or a dozen other things, but they never talk about actually knocking it down with bulldozers, which is what they should have done a long time ago.

It was getting close to midnight when I walked through the door. In this city there are few people working at midnight, unless they happen to be serving alcohol on Portage Street. I walked over to the desk and rang the little bell. A county deputy came out and I asked him if I could see someone in the holding cell. He told me I should come back the following morning.

"I really need to see him," I said. "I'd appreciate it."

"And you really need to come back tomorrow morning," he said. "I know we've got a few gentlemen down there right now. They all need to settle down and dry out a little, if you know what I mean. We'll sort them out in the morning."

I wasn't sure what to try next, but that's when I saw Chief Roy Maven walking past the front door. He must have come out a side entrance, and he was probably on his way to his car now after a long night in the office. Something special must have kept him here. I didn't care what, I was just happy to see him.

An incredible statement to make, I realize. After a full week of dealing with law enforcement officials at every level, from that state trooper I talked to out at the airport, to my friend and maybe now former friend Janet Long, the FBI agent in Detroit, to Chief Benally of the Bay Mills Tribal Police, here at last was the man with whom I had the longest history. Chief Roy Maven of the Sault Ste. Marie Police Department, known affectionately around here as the Human Buzz Saw, known unaffectionately by a number of other words, some of which correspond to parts of the male anatomy. We'd taken an instant chemical dislike to each other, the very first time we met, and things had gone downhill fast from there.

Then, finally, we got to work on something together. Something terrible. It's funny how going through something like that with another person will make you see him differently. I wouldn't exactly call us best friends now. But we had made our peace.

"Chief!" I yelled as I went out the door. "Wait up a minute!"

He turned and looked around with all the good humor you'd expect from a man who'd just worked about eight hours of overtime. "McKnight? What the hell's going on?"

"I've got a friend in one of the holding cells. I need to get him out."

"I don't have anybody down there right now. I can't help you."

He shares the cells with the county. He pretty much shares *everything* with the county, and he usually doesn't get the best of any of it. His office, for instance, somehow doesn't have a window.

"It's not one of yours," I said. "It's county. Some guys got picked up at the Cozy. Out in Brimley."

"I know where the Cozy is, McKnight. I was drinking there

when you were still a beat cop in Detroit. And thank you for answering your own question. You have to talk to the county guys."

"They say I have to wait until morning. I was hoping you could just let me go see him, at least. Find out what happened. That's all I'm asking."

He was standing there with the door to his car open. Just a few minutes away from a late dinner and a bed. He looked up at the sky, shaking his head like somebody up there owed him an explanation.

"Why did you move up here?" he said to me. "Seriously, why?"

"Just a few minutes," I said. "I'd really appreciate it."

He owed me, that was the thing I wasn't saying. He owed me and he knew it, and I knew it, and that's why he finally slammed his door shut and led me back into the building. A few minutes later, the master door to the holding cells was opened and I was let inside.

"Five minutes," he said to me. "Knock on the door when you're done. The deputy will let you out. I'm going home now."

"Thanks, Chief."

His response to that was the dull clang of the jailhouse door closing. I walked down the line of cells and found the last two occupied.

There were five men in all, and whoever split them up obviously didn't understand the history. The three men in the one cell were all old-timers from the rez, more faces that I vaguely recognized, either from events at Vinnie's mother's house or from just seeing them walking down the road. If it was winter, they were sure to be so underdressed you'd wonder how they didn't freeze to death.

These were men who grew up on the rez, who remembered how it was before the casinos came. These were men who knew Lou LeBlanc from way back when. They all knew about Lou being banned from the rez forever. They were all there to answer the call when he came back, thirty years later.

In the second cell sat Lou and his old nemesis, Henry Carrick. Henry was sitting against the back wall. Lou was up front by the bars. They both had scraped-up faces that would look much worse by the next morning.

I stood in between the two cells, so I could see them all at once. "Aren't you guys a little old for this?"

The three men on my left started laughing. Henry and Lou just sat there like they were made of stone. I went down to the end of the cell closest to him and knelt down on the floor.

"Okay, so what happened?" I said. "Or is it already pretty obvious?"

"I stopped in at the Cozy," Lou said. "My old pal Henry over here, he was sitting at the bar. He told me I had to leave. I tried to point out to him that I wasn't actually on the reservation, but that didn't seem to matter. He made some calls and next thing you know he's got three of his buddies and they're all trying to start something with me. I figured I'd already given Vinnie enough free shots tonight. So yeah, this time I fought back. When the owner of the Cozy couldn't get us to take it outside, he called 911 and that's how we ended up here."

"Did the Bay Mills cops bring you?"

"No, there was a regular county car down the road. I tried to explain to them that I was just defending myself. I might have gotten a little belligerent at that point."

"Lou, did you hit a cop?"

"No, I didn't. I swear. I was just trying to make them understand. But they didn't want to hear it. They just called another car and they brought us all down here."

He dabbed at the corner of his eye and looked at the trace of blood on his fingers.

"So it sounds like you need to spend the night," I said. "That's pretty standard around here. They don't have enough manpower to do much else after hours unless they absolutely have to."

"I can't do that."

"I think you've done a lot worse," I said. "A night in the county jail, you can do that standing on your head."

"You don't understand. They took down our names before they

dumped us down here, but they didn't really *process* us. You know what I mean?"

"At this hour, I'm not surprised. Like I said . . ."

"Alex, do remember what I told you earlier today? About being on parole?"

"Yeah, but this is just a routine disturbance at a bar. They'll just kick you out in the morning."

"I didn't tell you everything today," he said. "I didn't tell you that I wasn't supposed to leave the state under any circumstances. Technically, I violated my parole as soon as I got on that airplane."

"Okay, is there anything else you want to tell me?"

He lowered his head and his long hair fell down to cover his face.

"I've done a lot of really bad stuff in my life," he said. "You don't even know the half of it. I've had this feeling that the next time I see a jail cell, it'll be the only thing I ever see for the rest of my life. Just being here right now . . . I can't take it, Alex."

"Just take it easy. I know I owe you one today. Let me figure this out."

I owed him one, all right. Never mind the rest of the week, I owed him a huge debt just from what he'd done in that swamp alone.

Speaking of debts . . .

"Just sit tight," I said, standing up. "I've got one card I can play."

I knew exactly where to go. I knew exactly how well I'd be received when I got there. But I went anyway.

Chief Maven's house was a raised ranch over on Summit Street. I parked on the street and walked up to his door. It was the ass end of midnight, but I rang the bell and waited for a minute. Then I rang it again.

The door opened and Maven looked out at me with something that I probably wouldn't call excitement or delight. He had obviously gone right to bed when he had gotten home. Now he was wrapped up in a bathrobe and blinking in the glare from the porch light.

"What in goddamned hell," he said slowly. "Do you have any idea what time it is?"

"I need one minute, Chief. Then I'll leave."

"You're seriously standing here right now. I'm not dreaming this."

"One minute," I said. "Please let me come in."

It was so outrageous, I think he was kind of stunned. He just stepped back and let me come through the door. Once I was in his front hallway, I just stood there and told him what I wanted.

"There's one man in the holding cells," I said. "His name is Louis LeBlanc. He needs to be released immediately."

"You have lost your mind, McKnight. I knew it would happen eventually."

"It was just a stupid bar fight. Four guys jumped him and he wouldn't take his beating like a good boy. That's it. He'll never be charged with anything. None of them will. They'll just get kicked out tomorrow morning."

"Then why—"

"Because I'm asking you. That's why."

"He's in county custody. You know I can't do anything."

"If you call the sheriff and ask him yourself, he'll do it. You know that."

"Are you kidding me? Call the sheriff in the middle of the night? Wake him up and ask him to go down to the office?"

"He doesn't have to go anywhere," I said. "He can call it in and go back to bed."

"I can't believe this," he said, turning from me and walking half-way down the hall. "Of all the bizarre, stupid things I've ever heard."

"He was helping me, Chief. He was helping me the same way I once helped you. So I owe him one. Just like you owe *me* one."

"Oh, here it is," he said, turning around to face me. "I was wondering when you'd pull that on me."

"I didn't think I ever would. But you know it's true. You owe me exactly one big favor, no questions asked. Just one. This is it."

He looked at the floor and shook his head.

"One phone call to your buddy the sheriff. Tell him it's important. Apologize for how late it is. Just tell him he has to call over and spring a man who shouldn't be there in the first place. Then you're done."

"Then we're square?" he said.

"Then we're square. Forever."

He let out a long breath and walked into the kitchen to get the phone.

"My wife's sister wanted us to move to Arizona," he said as he dialed. "I said I'd never live in a state that has rattlesnakes and scorpions. But you know what I didn't think of?"

I stood there watching him as he waited for the sheriff to pick up on the other end. I didn't figure I was supposed to answer his question.

"No Alex McKnight in Arizona," he said. "That should have sold me."

The sheriff picked up. Maven started talking. A few minutes later, I was in my truck, heading back to the City-County Building.

And Maven and I were square.

I was waiting by my truck when Lou walked out of the place. He got in and we took off, back toward Paradise.

"Stop at the Cozy," he said. "My car's still there."

"I think we made a mistake," I said as I drove. "We should have told those guys about Corvo's deadline today. Both of them. We had all day to make a plan together."

"I thought we were giving Vinnie one more night to rest."

"Says the man who goaded him into a fight . . ."

"No, it was the right call," he said, looking out the window. "Give it tonight. I think you'll have a clear answer in the morning. In fact, I'm sure of it. You'll wake up and it'll be right there in front of you."

"That didn't work the last time."

"Have faith," he said. "I believe you'll see it."

I didn't feel like arguing. We'd all talk about it tomorrow, no matter what. If the answer magically came to me in the middle of the night or not.

I pulled into the Cozy parking lot and let him out.

"I'm going to go drop off those things at my daughters' houses," he said. "Just leave them on the doorsteps, some of my old mementos from when I was growing up here. I still don't think I'm ready to face them yet. Vinnie's been tough enough."

"I thought you weren't supposed to be on the rez."

"Henry and his posse are still in jail tonight, remember? Now's my chance."

I had to smile at that one. I told him I'd see him in the morning. Then I left.

As I was driving through the rez, I saw the lights on at Buck's house. On an impulse, I pulled into his driveway. It was after one in the morning now, but I heard music playing. I knocked on the front door. When nobody answered, I ran through all of the horrible scenarios that this week had taught me to expect. But when I pushed open the door and called his name, he answered me from somewhere in the back of the house. I walked through and found him on the back deck. He was in the hot tub.

"Sorry to bother you," I said. "I saw the lights on and I wanted to check on you."

"It's all good," he said. It was just his head and shoulders above the swirling water. "Everybody's home safe. It's over now."

That's what you think, Buck. The thought burning in my head, along with Lou's doubts about this man. About having him involved in whatever we decided to do the next day.

"I've been pretty hard on you," I said. "I know you didn't want any of this to happen."

"You were on the money, Alex. I'm an idiot."

"How did the questioning go?"

"I'm sure I'm not done with it, but the tribe's already sent over a lawyer to help me. That state guy, he was a real piece of work, but I think Chief Benally's on my side."

"That's good to know."

"Yeah. He even told me today that there's no way the DA would want to prosecute me. Everybody else on the rez wants to beat my ass, but they're all glad I'm safe at least."

He's strong, I thought. He's built like a linebacker. And I know he'll come through if he has the right motivation. Like looking after Vinnie.

"Listen," I said, "I need you to come out and have breakfast with me and Vinnie and Lou tomorrow. We have to talk about something very important."

"What is it?"

"I'll tell you tomorrow. Just get some rest, okay?"

I said good night to him and left him there, soaking in the hot water. It was another cold summer night in the UP. As I went out to my truck, I looked up at the stars. The rest of the reservation was quiet. I didn't see anyone else around.

I drove back to Paradise.

Once again, I tried to sleep and failed. I was lying in my bed, staring at the ceiling. I was already imagining how the whirlwind would come. Maybe a car, as long and sleek as that cigarette boat, driving silently up my road. I wondered how we could ever be ready to face the men who would step out of that car.

Then I heard a soft knock on the door. Before I could say a word, Lou cracked the door open and stuck his head in.

"Alex? Are you up?"

"Come on in," I said. "What's going on?"

He came into the cabin. He was walking slowly, and his face was already starting to swell up from the two fights he'd been in.

"You need some ice," I said. "Let me get some."

"Only if it's in a glass. Whatever you have. Whiskey, gin, I don't care."

I'd taken my watch off and put it on the table. I picked it up now and looked at it. It was just after three in the morning.

"What's going on?" I said. "You look wrecked. You should be sleeping."

"I just had to talk to you. Sit down for one minute. After you get that drink for me, please."

I looked for the bottle of Jim Beam. Then I remembered it was empty. It was the bottle Vinnie and I had killed that night, not that long ago. The same night he got the call to come pick up Buck at the airport.

"I only have cheap stuff," I said. "I think somebody gave me this a long time ago. It's not even open."

"Sounds perfect."

He sat at the table, looking at nothing. I made the drink and put in a few ice cubes. I put it down in front of him and he took a long swallow. The room was dark except for the one light on over the sink. The way the light hit him, it picked up all of the old scars on his face, along with all of the new damage. He looked old and tired.

"It was the best of times," he said. "It was the worst of times."

"Lou, what are you talking about? What's wrong?"

He took another drink.

"When I was growing up here," he said, "there was this old Ojibwa story I heard, and there's a couple different variations to it, but the basic idea is this. A boy is living with his grandmother, who's very old. Before she dies, she says to him, 'You're going to be all alone now, but before long a stranger is going to come to you. I want you to do whatever he says.' Then she dies."

He tipped the glass again. Then he went on.

"A few days later, a stranger comes to the village. And he says, 'Who is the best man among you?' The elders gather to talk about it, then they send the boy to the stranger. The boy has a meal with the stranger, and finally the stranger tells him why he has come to the village. He tells him that he was sent there by the Creator to test him, to see if he and his people are worthy. The boy asks him what the test is and the stranger says they have to fight each other. If the boy wins, he lives. If he loses, he dies."

He stopped again. He didn't take another drink. He looked at the glass for a long moment before continuing.

"The boy agrees to the test. So he and the stranger go outside to a clearing in the forest and they begin to fight. All night long they fight, until they are both so tired they can't continue. They both sleep during the day, until it is time to get up and eat, and regain their strength. They have their meal together, then they go back to the clearing to fight again. A great battle, back and forth, neither one of them gaining the upper hand. Until once again they are too tired to continue. They sleep through the day, until it's time to get up and eat together. Then, once more, they fight."

I watched him as he told me the story. It felt like the whole world was slipping away and it was just Lou and me, here in my cabin, surrounded by nothing but darkness outside.

"This time, as they fight, the boy hits him with a club. The stranger finally goes down to his knees. The boy plunges a knife into the stranger's back. The stranger is dead. He has killed him. But he isn't happy about it. The stranger has fought so well, and the boy has spent all of this time with him and he has learned so much about himself. He weeps for the stranger and he carries him to the graveyard and buries him next to his grandmother. He visits the grave every day, looking after it the same way he looks after his grandmother's grave. Then one day, on the first day of spring, the boy finds a plant growing on the stranger's grave. He doesn't know what it is, but he tends to it all that spring and summer, until it is even taller than he is. In the fall, when he finally decides to open up the leaves on this plant, he finds yellow kernels. He tastes them and they are sweet. This is how the people were given corn. Through the death of this stranger."

He looked up at me, finally, his eyes wet. I wasn't sure what to say to him.

"You told me everything that happened on that boat with Corvo," he said. "Every detail, and I appreciate it. I know it was probably the scariest thing you ever lived through, but you trusted me enough to share it with me."

"Lou, wait, how do you go from that story to—"

"The funny thing is, Alex, when he wanted to know what your name was, he took out your driver's license and he looked at it. You remember telling me that?"

"Yes . . ."

My wallet was right there on the table, next to my watch. He picked it up now, exactly as Corvo had done. He opened it and looked at my driver's license.

"It makes sense, right? He's a smart guy. He knows your driver's license wouldn't lie."

"I'm afraid I'm not following any of this."

"Do you want to know what my driver's license says?"

I just looked at him. I didn't answer.

"It says the same thing yours does. My full name. Louis. Vincent. LeBlanc."

"I still don't follow you."

"My first name is Louis," he said. "But nobody ever calls me that. Ever. I go by my middle name instead. Everybody I know. Everybody. They all call me Vinnie."

I shook my head. I still wasn't getting it. I was inches away, but still not there yet.

He put my wallet back down. He had taken something from it. Not my driver's license. No, he had taken the card that Corvo had given to me. The card with the phone number.

"What are you doing with that?" I said. "Lou, come on."

Still calling him Lou. Because I knew that was his name. Even the old-timers here on the rez called him Lou. He'd been Lou all his life. This whole strange business about everybody calling him Vinnie . . .

"No," I said, feeling an icy wave wash over me. "You can't be serious."

"He's never met me, Alex. He'll never know the difference."

"This is crazy. You know what Corvo will do to you. He won't just kill you."

"I'm not afraid of him. Besides, I've done enough bad things in my life. I keep telling people I've repaid my debts, but I can't tell that same lie to you. I know I've caused a lot more pain than I've ever had to feel myself. A lot more by a long shot."

"No," I said. "Stop it. Just stop talking like this. Even if it wasn't the craziest thing I've ever heard, it still wouldn't even work anyway. That maniac won't be satisfied if it's just some guy named Vinnie who shows up. It was Buck who . . ."

I couldn't say one more word. I stood up.

"Alex, don't."

I pushed past him. I went outside and threw open the driver's-side door of his rental car.

"Where is he? Where's Buck?"

I threw open the backseat door. There was nobody inside. Lou came up behind me.

"He was a dead man anyway," Lou said. "I did him a big favor. Corvo won't be happy about it, but what's he gonna do to me that he wasn't gonna do already?"

I grabbed him by the shoulders.

"Where is he?" I said. "God damn you, where is Buck?"

He didn't fight back. He just looked at me with a cold and perfect serenity in his eyes.

I looked back at the car. My heart stopped as it hit me. I pushed him away. Then I went to the driver's seat and fumbled around for the trunk release, finally found the button, and pushed it. The trunk popped open and I went around to the back. Buck was inside. I couldn't process the fact that he was wearing a bathing suit. I couldn't process the fact that his body was wet. I put my fingers to his neck. Then something hit me in the back of the neck and I was down on the ground, looking at the undercarriage of the car.

"He drowned in his hot tub," Lou said, his voice close to my ear. "It was quick and it was painless. Now the two of us are going to Chicago and you're not going to try to stop us."

It felt like my whole body was paralyzed. I didn't know what he hit me with. To this day, I still don't know. Maybe just his hand. Maybe he was that good.

"You'll think about calling the police. Or coming after us. But then you'll realize. You can't save Buck. He's already gone. But you *can* save Vinnie. If this works, he's free. Forever."

Move your body, I said to myself. Get up and stop this madness.

"Just to be sure, you gotta watch over him, Alex? Okay? Do you hear me? Watch over Vinnie or I swear to God, I'll come back from the other side and haunt you."

I saw his shoes as he went around to the driver's seat and got in. The car started up, sending a sick plume of exhaust right into my face. I reached out to grab the bumper. To stop the car or to make him drag me all the way down the road. But the car pulled away from me and I could only watch the taillights disappear around the bend in the road. The car passed Vinnie's cabin, and then it was gone.

I stayed on the ground for a long time. If it had been winter, I surely would have frozen to death. Vinnie would have found my body the next morning.

But it was summer. The end of July. It was the middle of the night and it was cold, but not deadly cold. I felt the strength flowing back into my body. I pulled myself to my knees. Then finally to my feet. I stood there thinking about every word he had said. His prediction about what I would do now.

He was right.

God damn him, he was right.

CHAPTER TWENTY-TWO

Summer ended. The warm days disappeared and I saw the first flakes of snow carried by the wind on a cold afternoon in early September. A doctor in Sault Ste. Marie took the stitches out of my face, and he told me that unless I had some plastic surgery, I'd forever have a scar on my cheek. I told him I'd think about the surgery, but I knew I'd never do it. I guess in my heart I really wanted that scar. I wanted it to always remind me of what happened that summer. I wanted to see it every time I looked in the mirror, and feel it under my fingers every night when I washed my face before I went to bed.

That scar was a reminder of the secret I would keep for as long as I lived.

Chief Benally came to my cabin one more time. He had found out about Vinnie's father, long after he ever got the chance to meet him. He knew the general story, he knew that Lou had been arrested. He knew that I had gotten him out and that soon after that, he and Buck had both disappeared. I answered every question I could, until I got to what actually had happened that night. Then I had nothing more to say. I had no knowledge of where they might have gone, or if they had even left together.

It was a lie of omission, of course. I hated the lie and I hated that I was able to tell the lie. But no matter how many times he asked me the same question, he always got the same answer.

I told the same lie to Vinnie. He started making some plans about going down to Chicago to look for Buck, but I think he knew it was hopeless. I think he knew that Buck was dead, and maybe, just maybe, he was able to figure out what his father had done for him. If he did, then maybe he also knew that I knew the same thing, or at least suspected it. Either way, he hasn't pressed me on it.

Somehow, we're still good. We have breakfast together at the Glasgow and sometimes dinner if he doesn't have a shift at the casino. He is still my best friend and I would lay my life on the line again for him, no matter what. I know he'd do the same for me. It's the one thing that helps me to sleep at night.

And yes, he still lives in his cabin. He didn't move into his mother's house. He still goes to the reservation, whether it's to go to work or to see his sisters and nieces and nephews.

For me, it's a different story. When I have to go to Sault Ste. Marie now, it means going down to the highway and taking that flat monotonous stretch all the way across the hayfields. I don't take Lakeshore Drive anymore. It's the road that follows the shoreline of Whitefish Bay and it's my favorite road in the world, but to get to it you have to drive through the reservation. It has been made clear to me that if I am found on their land, certain members of the Bay Mills Indian Community will make me very sorry for this mistake.

It's not that Chief Benally would pull me over and give me a cheap speeding ticket. That's not the kind of game he would play.

No, I'm thinking more about Henry Carrick and what he said to me the night he came out to find me at the Glasgow Inn. He knew I had gotten Lou out of the holding cell that night. Hell, he was right there to see me do it. He didn't even bother asking me if Lou was involved in Buck's disappearance. So I didn't have to tell the lie again. He just made his promise to me about the consequences of setting foot on the rez, and then he left.

Someday I'll try him out. I think I'd actually like to see how much he means it. But for now, I can't afford the trouble. I can't afford to take my eyes off Vinnie LeBlanc for one minute. Not yet. Not until I'm sure that Corvo isn't on his way up from Chicago.

I have a gun now. I have a well-earned hatred of the things, and my last gun had ended up on the bottom of Lake Superior, but I went down to the gun shop and picked up a Glock G21. I'm a former cop and I still carry a PI license, even if I seldom use it. So I had no problem getting a carry permit. I wear it in a shoulder holster during the day, whether I'm tacking plastic onto the windows of the cabins, or splitting firewood, or sitting by the fireplace at the Glasgow.

At night I keep it close to my bed. I watch the road and I listen.

That's the part that Henry Carrick doesn't get. Henry Carrick and Mary LeBlanc and Regina LeBlanc and every other member of the tribe, they just don't understand that Vinnie doesn't live on their reservation anymore.

He lives on mine.

Don't miss the next book in
the Alex McKnight series by Steve Hamilton

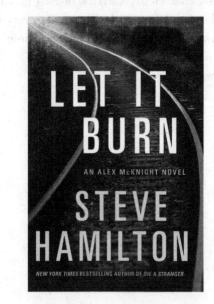

Available July 2013